GREED

&

JEALOUSY

TINA ELLERY

GREED & JEALOUSY

First Edition

Editors: EJ Runyon, Bethany Robinson, and R.A. Weston.
Proofreading: Sherri Hildebrandt
Formatter: The Write Assistants
Cover Design: Hang Le

ISBN: 978-1-945592-00-3

DEDICATION

This book was written for me.

CHAPTER 1

TOVA

I stood in the Department of Motor Vehicles, pen poised over the form in front of me.

A shadow fell over my papers as someone approached. *My savior.* "Do you know the date?" I asked.

His voice honey, the man across from me said, "It's Saturday."

Tilting my chin, I lifted my head and gazed into eyes a clear light blue. Stunning. They reminded me of chalcedony, one of my favorite stones, and warm winter sky. "I'm sorry, what?"

"It's Saturday." He half-grinned and held out his hand. "Can you pass a change-of-address form?" *That I could do.* And I should, instead of stare at the man.

"I meant the actual *date*, not the day," I clarified. His attention refocused on me. Mischief flickered across his face, like he'd been up to no good. Was he messing with me? No. Not possible. He smiled outright, and since I lack a filter, I blurted, "Are you being cheeky?" My grandmother, Lizzy, always used that rhetorical question when I'd get sassy with her. I'd picked up the habit.

He rubbed the back of his neck and put his hip against the counter separating us. "You're right. I was being…cheeky." He drew out the word, laced with innuendo. "No one's called me that since my grandma."

"Hmm. They do that." He was taller than most, handsome under a two-day scruff. Untamed curls. "So?" I asked. "The date?" Was his chestnut hair too long or just right?

His gaze dropped and came back up again as he told me, "Just checking to see if you were payin' attention."

The air conditioner hummed, a static electric noise mixing with the burr of his voice. I wished I could look at this man from across the room, take him in without him being aware of my perusal.

"Oh, I'm payin' attention." Seriously, who wouldn't? Our table-tennis exchange of words reminded me of a movie I didn't belong in. *Andrew used to flirt with me. Didn't he?*

He hesitated. A question arose in the form of a wrinkle on his brow. Life experience marked the space between his eyes with that charming line. "It's April eighth," he said, and then he winked.

My heart sped up and I found myself smiling. I hadn't smiled in days. I needed to stop this. But I couldn't. Attempting self-preservation, I pointed my grin down and and returned to putting pen to form. Otherwise, I would've kept staring. And that seemed pathetic, even for me.

Sun streamed through the DMV's floor-to-ceiling windows. I could feel its heat along with his. Unable to concentrate, filling out the rest of the forms became impossible. *I couldn't do anything today.* Why did I want to look at him again? Trying not to move my head, I shifted my eyes. Flat footed, I'm five-ten, so I didn't have to glance up that far.

Handsome stared, his eyes hot blue fire.

He'd started to bend over the counter's high partition. My breath caught. His gaze lowered, slid over paper and pen, and my heart plummeted. He was checking out my hand. Not just any hand, though—my left. The wedding ring hand.

The ring Andrew'd given me.

The ring I'd told myself I'd fight for. What was I doing?

Handsome refocused on my face. His eyes had lost their heat, gained a layer of disdain. Something in me cracked—a fissure spreading. Like a broken pane of glass, spider-webbed lines marring the surface, but I somehow stayed together and didn't crumble.

His mouth formed what seemed to be a disapproving line. Ignoring me, he said nothing more and returned to his paperwork.

I'd done the one thing I never thought I could. I'd turned into my father. I'd openly flirted while married.

I suppose that's what happens when your husband hasn't called you in days.

Over the loudspeaker, a monotone voice announced my call number. It took six steps to pass by him. Six steps to capture one last glance and snap a mental picture of the most handsome man I'd ever encountered. I wanted to forget it happened as much as I didn't.

Have things with Andrew gotten that bad? Yes.

The clerk pushed my new registration tabs forward with a single arthritic-twisted finger. "Is there anything else I can do for you?" Her voice cracked at the end, much like my pride.

"No, but thank you."

A man's voice rose over the din of the waiting room. I spun to see a guy in a dirty baseball hat shake spilled coffee off his hand.

"You should've stayed home!" a woman with short, pink hair screeched as she bent for the fallen paper cup.

Dirty Hat's head shot up. "What'd you just say?"

3

The woman stood as her face fell. I realized then I knew her. She'd modeled some of my jewelry in a fashion shoot. Her hair had been dark then. I couldn't remember her name, but I did recall how excited she'd been to be at the studio. And how cruelly another model, a friend of hers, had treated her. She'd said, "Good thing you've got that face." It reminded me of how my dad had talked to my mom—a verbal slap with a backhanded compliment.

Dirty Hat grabbed her arm, fingers biting into her flesh as he pulled her up. "Apologize for making a fool of yourself." My belly dropped as she let out a sharp cry.

The rest of the room stared, although some pretended not to. *Typical.*

She wobbled on heels and winced as Dirty Hat yanked her hard. "Sorry." *That was it.*

Seeing red, my feet moved. "Let her go," I demanded. Quiet knifed through the space.

Dirty Hat's vicious eyes landed on me. "Mind your own business."

"No."

A hand grabbed my forearm. "Let me handle it," Handsome whispered. Skin-to-skin, his palm slid down and captured my hand, halting my progress. I wished he hadn't touched me. I didn't need to know what that felt like.

I twisted and scanned his face. This time, his eyes held no disdain, only concern. He squeezed my hand. "Please."

"Good call, buddy. Tell your wife to back off."

"I'm not your buddy." Handsome tilted his head. "Guessing a few of the cops upstairs are making their way down here. Maybe you should head out."

Lena was her name. I remembered now. "Maybe you should go, Billy," she said.

"You know me, babe, I'm just trying to get through the day." Moving forward, he knocked her shoulder. She stumbled, her pink hair tumbling in her eyes.

Billy locked his sight on me. I felt caught in a trap, and I didn't like it. What did he plan to do? Handsome dropped my hand and gripped my hip, drawing me toward him.

Nerves made me shaky. Billy stopped in front of me, his eyes slivers of hate. Handsome tensed.

"You should be afraid of me," Billy growled.

I stood still even though I wanted to back up. He flicked his gaze from me to Handsome, then strode off with ease, as though he threatened people all the time. Shallow, adrenaline-soaked breaths came out of me.

Handsome gave me a light squeeze, stole a few strides, and grabbed Billy by the scruff of his neck and the back of his jeans. "You're not going anywhere now."

"Get your fucking hands off me." Sharp and sadistic, Billy threw his head back.

As though he knew the head butt was coming, Handsome leaned out of the way. "*Stop*," he growled.

"You're dead. Dead." Billy squirmed, kicked his feet, but Handsome had forty pounds of muscle and six inches on him. He wasn't going anywhere.

Billy yanked his head to look at me. "If you... I'll have to teach you a lesson. People don't interfere with my life and get away with it."

"Keep your trap shut, tough guy." Handsome shoved him forward.

Two cops rushed in. "Damn it," Lena mumbled behind me.

I reeled around. "Does he grab you like that all the time?"

Her fingertips worried the space below her hairline.

When she looked up, tears swam in her eyes. It struck me, then. Gorgeous face, high cheekbones, plump lips—she was as stunning as I remembered. The pink hair made her look young, but she was closer to my age. "Not usually." Resignation marked her tone.

Karma would get me for being a wiseass. I knew better than to point out the obvious. "You don't want to cry over him."

Her chin trembled. "He's all I have."

I reached into my bag and handed her some tissues. "That can't be true."

Lena shook her head and I cringed. With my own marriage a mess and coming from a long line of divorced women, obviously I couldn't offer much in the way of relationship advice. Yet I wanted her to realize she deserved more.

"Please tell me you're not gonna give him the chance to do that again. Life is short. You deserve the best." I flung my hand out. "Not that."

Again, she shook her head. I wanted to give her a hug and tell her how wrong she was, but before I could, she slunk away toward the police officers.

How come it's easier to call someone else on their shit than looking inward at your own?

Two additional cops strode into the central part of the DMV and led the couple out. Not knowing if they needed me to make a statement, I approached as one of the police officers stopped to speak to Handsome.

"Excuse me." I gestured to where the pair had stood. "I weighed in there. Do you need me to make a statement?" Handsome aimed his attention out the window.

"No, we have everything we need. You can head out," one of the cops responded.

Handsome didn't look at me. Thinking he'd at least

acknowledge me, I waited—until it got awkward.

"Thank you," I mumbled. On autopilot, I walked out.

Wind, turbulent and crazed, whipped my blonde hair around my face.

I'd been ignored by men before. Andrew, for instance. But the fact Handsome ignored me *again* made me feel unreasonably irate and foolish. It stung almost as much as I found my own behavior distasteful. I'd just witnessed a woman I knew being assaulted and my pride getting bitten was what I chose to dwell on?

I unlocked my Land Rover. Handsome had hugged me, possessively, to his side.

Andrew hadn't laid a loving hand on me in months. A harsh curse shot from my mouth, and I threw my purse across to the passenger's seat. In a flurry, papers, lip gloss, and wallet scattered.

What was this dormant need aching in my chest? I was a married woman who flirted. Blatantly. Why would he want to talk to me?

Protecting me meant nothing. Gallantry had made him step in. I was like a job that needed doing so he'd have a clear conscious.

My watered-down latte waited in the cup holder. I sucked on the green straw as though it held whiskey, like it could calm my anger.

Would he have gotten involved himself regardless of my actions? Or did he get involved for me?

I looked at the mess I'd made inside my car.

How egotistical. He'd gotten involved because of Lena.

I gathered my tools, slammed the door, and got to it.

An aggravated sun beat down on the asphalt. I knelt at my back bumper, placing the tip of the screwdriver in the clear acrylic license cover—but got nothing. I hated that stupid pretentious thing that Andrew had insisted on and now it wouldn't budge. *Perfect.*

A breeze sliced between my shirt and jeans, cooling me off.

"Doesn't your husband do that for you?" Handsome asked behind me.

"Not in this lifetime." I pulled my shirt down. I'm sure he'd gotten a glimpse of panties. At least they were my sexiest pair. Cranberry red lace.

Never in a million years would Andrew do anything that could get him dirty. Besides, he was never home, so how could he?

Handsome's running shoes stopped inches from me. I glanced at his long legs clad in cargo pants, shaded my eyes, and kept going to his face. "My husband's never even mowed the yard." I waved the tabs in my hand. "He isn't going to change out these stickers." How embarrassing. I sounded—and I'm sure looked—ridiculous.

Handsome hesitated, then knelt beside me. My emotions hovered on a teeter-totter. Back and forth they swung. He looked me in the eyes with such seriousness it hurt. "Let me." He reached for the screwdriver.

I wanted to cry and bit the inside of my lip. I let him pull the tool from my grasp. Why was he helping? I thought he didn't like me. Part of me wanted to tell him to get lost.

But I couldn't.

He smelled like ocean air and fresh laundry. Pushing his sleeves up, he exposed his forearms, capable and strong, with one vein raising the surface.

The utterly impractical plate cover, which Andrew thought looked classy, came off, so I handed Handsome the stickers without a word. He grinned, and I grinned back, happy to have his smile and not his indifference.

Andrew had grinned when I bought the Rover. He'd been so pleased I'd decided on a safe, family vehicle.

The wind blew through the parking lot. Handsome's chestnut curls caught the light. I'd give up coffee for the chance to run my hands through his hair. *Yeah, I want to save my marriage. I probably should stuff that thought way down deep.*

He finished. His hand enveloped mine, and he pulled us both to our feet. "I'm Neil."

"Tova."

He cocked his head. "Tova? Never heard that before."

Who has? "It's not common. My mom moved here from Sweden when she was a baby. She named me after her doll."

He leaned against the Rover. "What does it mean?"

"She said it meant beautiful. It also means good, pleasing, if you look it up online." Something tilted his grin, and I changed the subject. "Do you rescue all the women at the DMV?"

His right eyebrow shot up. "Do you?"

"I wasn't going to stand by and watch her get manhandled." And I would've helped her even if I didn't have a connection with her.

His comfortable posture disappeared. "You could've gotten hurt back there. Next time you need to look the other way."

"That's ridiculous. I'm more than capable of taking care of myself." I'd been doing it forever, after all.

"That guy might've looked harmless, but he's not." Neil gazed at the horizon, searching, before coming back to me.

"I'm fine, *right?*" Did I sound silly asking such a stupid, rhetorical question?

His focus dropped to my lips. "You know he could've had a gun."

"You can't have guns in the DMV." I hoped.

"Did you notice I have a gun?"

"You do?" Grateful for the excuse, I let my gaze meander unabashedly. "Where?"

He twisted, placed a hand under his shirt, and lifted. "Back here." My eyes settled on smooth olive skin *and* the deadly weapon tucked in his pants.

"Wow," I managed. His exposed flesh, his strong back, his incredible ass. *Wow*. Forget the hair, I wanted to run my hands from shoulder to derriere.

"You shouldn't jump into trouble." He turned and his words held a bite. "You never know when someone might have a gun and bad intentions."

I did always want to see the best in people. That part of me wasn't jaded.

What did this guy do for a living that he carried a gun in his pants? He couldn't be a criminal. Criminals didn't go around doing good deeds all day. Maybe he was a police officer. But then wouldn't he have just arrested Billy himself?

"I had to help her. I couldn't just stand there watching."

Our verbal tussle stiffened his spine. "No, you didn't."

"I can't just *not* do something. I'm not made that way." I might be spineless in regards to Andrew—a regular doormat—but I'd never ignore blatant abuse.

"You're not made that way?"

"No. I'm not."

"Your husband wouldn't like it."

I huffed. "He wouldn't care."

CHAPTER 2

TOVA

Neil's stubbled jaw ground back and forth. "Stubborn."

I shifted on my feet and looked at a pile of melting snow. "Me? No. Not at all."

When I met his gaze, his eyes narrowed. "Both of you would care when you found out he's a murder suspect." Automatically, I pulled back with the shock of his statement. "I'll finish the front."

My stomach revolted with the idea that I'd stood up to a possible killer, but I didn't want Neil to know. I followed him to the Rover's front end and squatted down to help. "Are you a cop?"

"No." He removed the second screw.

"Then why do you have a gun?"

"I need it for my business."

I held my hand out. "What kind of business?"

He glanced with shrewd eyes and dropped the screws and couplings into my palm. "The private kind." *What the hell did that mean?*

"Do you have a permit?"

Assured fingers plucked the stickers from my waiting grip. Neil gave me a subtle look of respect. "I do."

I bit my bottom lip so I wouldn't laugh at this cockiness, and then I got it. Private *investigator*. "Just checking. I don't want to fraternize with criminals."

And there I went flirting again. *No more*, I told myself.

He shook his head. "Are we fraternizing?" I didn't answer. Tightening the screws, he placed the cover back on. Neil needed a good flaw to curb this attraction. I couldn't find one, other than he'd ignored me after seeing my wedding ring. And when I thought about it, that didn't imply a flaw.

He helped me up.

"Are you always chivalrous?"

"Anytime I see a woman with a screwdriver, I feel the need to take over."

Smartass. "Oh, really?"

I couldn't help noticing no ring clicked against the screwdriver as he rolled it around between his fingers. "Really." I checked the mental box for chauvinistic. That counted as a flaw. The American flag rattled in the wind behind me. "Tova." Neil rubbed his lips together. His eyes lingered on mine. "Are you separated?"

He may as well have scissor-kicked me in the gut. I was one-hundred-percent married, but for a brief moment, I let my imagination run wild. If I said no, what would he do? Ask me on a date?

When Andrew had invited me out for coffee and then pleaded to see my studio, I'd figured we would be friends. After all, I'd gotten the friends vibe.

But if Neil asked me on a date, it would definitely lead to kissing.

I missed kissing.

No doubt he'd be great at it, which made me contemplate lying. I stuffed the deceptive thought back into the cabinet in my brain. I'd never be my dad.

"No, I'm not separated." This flirty talk tread a fine line, but I'd never cheat. I made that promise a long time ago, even before I took an oath to Andrew.

Neil gave me his best attempt at a smile. It failed. "Had to ask."

I watched him, wanting to see something, anything, in the way he looked at me. I wanted him to speak with his body if he couldn't with words. But I got nothing. I held out my hand for the screwdriver. "Thanks for your help—Neil. You're very kind."

"You're welcome." As I took the screwdriver, he reached into a pocket. "Here's my card."

I rubbed it between my fingers—thick card stock. *Hamilton & Waters,* it read. Neil Hamilton, an email address, and a cell number.

"Thanks." I slipped it in my back pocket. Why would I need his card? Would I ever *need* to call him? More likely I'd *want* to call him.

It didn't matter how much I might want something. Life didn't work like that.

"Bye, Tova."

"Bye, Neil."

I got into my Rover and laid my head on the steering wheel. I needed a minute.

———•———

NEIL

Married. She'd have to be married. "Should've asked for her last name, Neil," I told the windshield. For some fucking reason, it mattered. I wanted to know a hell of a lot more. I shifted into gear and pulled out onto York. Why'd she have to be so irritatingly gorgeous and unsuspectingly brave?

Damn if that didn't make me want to grab her chin and kiss her. Especially after the high of listening to her.

I turned onto Sixty-Sixth Street, my mind making an inventory: married, not happily; money—the car and jewelry proved that; sassy; and the husband's a dumbass. Doesn't mow the yard? Probably travels, and she's bitter about it.

One thing I'd sure as hell remember—those panties peeking from the top of her jeans.

"Tova." *Tov-ah*. It fit. Unusual and sexy. She flirted, then seemed shocked with the results.

She had nerve, yet no clue she'd stood up to a murder suspect. Jumped in and just stood with a backbone of steel. I liked that.

I don't want to fraternize with criminals. That was as good as her telling me I was cheeky. *Cheeky.* I rolled that around like a hard candy.

I could Google "*Tova in Minnesota*" but what would I do when I found her? Ask to be friends? Wasn't interested in a relationship, but I sure as hell didn't want to break one up.

"She's married for Christ's sake." I knocked my steering wheel lightly with my fist. Unhappily, but married.

She must be unhappy—the set of her mouth told me so.

Her hands, fingers rough with calluses, told a story. Probably played the guitar. She'd be good at it. But her arms, so soft, remembering didn't help my dick. Didn't help remembering her, tall and graceful next to me, with her provoking perfume.

Now Billy Culver, aka Billy the Carver, would be going on my radar. The punk. He wanted to get his hands on Tova. That's why I should've asked her last name. To let her know when he gets out.

I needed to find her.

She was untouchable. Why would I want a part of that? Seen too much of that crazy with work. Certainly couldn't trust a woman who fooled around on her spouse. If only she'd said she was separated.

At a light, I looked at the clock on my dash. My brother TJ was at the station. Needed to have him get me info on Billy. He could also have Tova's last name and address back to me in a minute. But that constituted cheating.

I didn't cheat.

—— · ——

TOVA

I sat in the parking lot, grabbed my phone, and looked at the screen. Still nothing from Andrew. Why did I keep hoping? I tossed the scattered contents of my purse back into my bag. Andrew would have a fit if he saw my mess. Once upon a time, I'd found his need for perfection endearing. When he arrived for class, he would lay out his materials and straighten them, aligning every pen, pencil, and notebook in right angles with the flair of someone who needed to relax.

I dialed Grace next. I needed to talk to my levelheaded friend.

"Tova, what's going on?"

"You got a minute?" I turned north on York. The limbs of trees hung over the road, bare and empty.

"Yeah, how are you?"

"Fine."

"You don't sound fine."

Unthawed Christmas decorations occupied large planters in front of the independent shops of Fiftieth Street. They needed to go yesterday. "Really, I am. You wanna get a drink with Cassie tonight?" People walking the cobblestone sidewalks wore smiles. I wondered if they were genuine, or false and then I thought of Mom and Dad. I craved a different kind of life than my parents. That's who those faces reminded me of—people hiding the truth.

My dad was on marriage four. I sure in the hell didn't want that. And I didn't want to be bitter and resentful like my mom had been. Always putting on a happy face for the eyes of others, never acknowledging her husband led another life without her until her life was almost over. I often wondered if she'd left him sooner, would she have found some happiness? Maybe gone to the doctor sooner?

Instead, she'd lived with pain.

By the time my beautiful mother couldn't bear it any longer, her colon cancer had been too far along.

"Are you sure you're okay?" Grace asked.

Not really. "I had a slight altercation at the DMV." I drove through the golf course district, with its looming homes of excess, and continued by Mirror Lake.

"Are you okay? What happened?"

"Yeah, I'm fine. I just need a night out and a stiff drink. I'll tell you about what happened tonight."

"Have you called Cassie?" Grace asked. "Because I need to call her about something else. How's Redstone at seven?"

"That's perfect." I made my final turn onto Cobblestone Lane. A century-old oak tree stood guard. I loved that tree, how protected I felt seeing it canopy over my house.

"I'll call if anything changes," she promised before disconnecting.

My rambler sat on nearly half an acre. I'd bought my house for the yard. But the mountain ash out front sold it. In late summer, the whole thing would be covered in delectable but deadly orange berries.

The garage door closed behind me, a *creak* and *thunk* that said home. Gathering my purse and ignoring the drink in the cup holder, I shoved my way into the mudroom. Rocco awaited, butt in motion, and a *wooof!* for me.

"Have you been good, Rocco?" His tail whacked the wall in joy. I leaned down and gave him some love.

Who else would I give my affection to?

———•———

The day dragged on. I distracted myself by working on some new designs and hammering metal.

The Band-Aid on my finger was not from daydreaming about a certain man. Not in the least.

The day ended, and I went out to my deck. My backyard stretched out toward the water. On bright days, Minnehaha Creek looked like glass, and then a fish would jump and stir up the perfection. The sun streaked across the lawn. I plopped down in one of the red Adirondack chairs facing my creek. Looking south, an expanse of bare, silver-colored limbs twisted and dropped into the water. Mile-high oak trees stood on the banks, and the hypnotic sound of birds telling stories could've lulled me into sleep. But my noggin wouldn't turn off.

The sweet chirps of chickadees peppering the air. They exchanged tales of adventures or maybe confided in one another like good friends and lovers. Stirring envy in my belly, I closed my eyes and listened to their chattering.

Lucky birds.

I couldn't make myself go inside to get ready to meet Grace and Cassie.

———•———

I finally left the deck. Remembering my grandmother Lizzy's motto of never leaving the house without mascara or lipstick, I stepped back into the bathroom and slapped some burnt red gloss on my naked lips. I needed the color or the girls would see I looked off.

The restaurant's two big stone fireplaces greeted me as I walked in.

I grabbed a booth near the bar, and halfway through my drink, Cassie came up behind me. She tugged my sleeve down, baring my shoulder and displaying my pink bra strap. *The goofball.* "The eighties called. They want their sweatshirt back."

I laughed.

She tilted her head. "Drinks, huh?" Her dark hair glowed in the amber light.

"Yeah, drinks." A familiar redhead swung the door open. Her heels clicked on the elegantly stained concrete floor. "Grace is here."

I stood and gave Cassie a hug, then whispered in Grace's ear. "Thanks again."

"Of course."

They each ordered wine. Cassie held up her glass, her voice overly bright. "Let's make a toast." She loved a good toast. "Here's to Tova's anniversary." As our glasses clinked, my shoulders sagged. Of course she'd remembered.

"Don't toast our anniversary," I stuttered. "*We* didn't even celebrate it."

Grace raised her arm higher, gold bangles falling from her wrist toward her elbow. "I'm stealing Tova's motto. Here's to an extraordinary life."

Their glasses rose again, but I couldn't lift mine. That glass with the fissure, the one inside me that I clearly recognized from the DMV, felt on the edge of crumbling.

Amplified, every noise in the restaurant barreled over me. I could hear the couple bickering two booths over, the gossip between the waitresses, and the rattle of dishes being jostled. Everything. I could hear everything. Even my own heart, pounding in my ears as my messy life flashed in my head.

I stared at the glossy surface of the table below my fingers and remembered how Andrew and I had walked out of the bank a week ago. A pseudo river of melting snow had divided the parking lot. I'd taken a careful step. For the first time since I'd picked him up at the airport that afternoon, a smile had tilted his usually surly mouth. Actually, the smile hadn't just been a smile but a greedy grin that said, *I got what I wanted.* He had, too. The papers he held. Knuckles turning white, he'd grasped the documents. In response, my fist had closed around my purse and I'd wondered if it was a mistake cosigning another loan.

He'd just flown home that afternoon. I'd missed his face and the smell of him in bed. Always so clean and yet so like a man.

Andrew had unlocked the car. "I'm going to drop you off and get us some champagne."

"That would be nice." I'd reached out, put my hand on his runner's thigh. Humans long for physical contact; my desire to touch him was normal. Back and forth, my thumb had stroked the hard muscle. Not having touched him in so long, I hadn't even hesitated, but I had held my breath.

His typical reaction—the one I'd been bracing for—came. He'd picked up my hand and set it on my lap.

He hadn't wanted me to touch him.

The memory stung. My head snapped up. "Do you want to know how we spent our anniversary?" Across from me, worry washed over Cassie's face. "I cosigned a loan for him, and then he went to play racquetball with his friend."

Grace leaned forward into my line of sight. Something about all that startling red hair pulled me from the haze I'd been in.

"He left. Like he always does." I downed half my wine.

"What's going on?" Cassie slid my glass away. I didn't miss that move.

They don't know any of this. "He hasn't called for a week. Refuses to go to counseling. And I don't know what to do."

"Did you know something was going on?" Cassie demanded from Grace, who pursed her lips and gave her head a quick shake.

"When he does come home, he's been ignoring me, and we haven't had sex in ten months."

"What!" Cassie's eyes grew to the size of butterscotch lollipops. "You seriously haven't? For *ten months*?"

"Can you keep your voice down?" Grace hissed at her.

"Nope," I answered. "No sex."

"I didn't think that was possible."

"Well…it is." I knew Cassie would concentrate on the no sex. She slid my drink back.

Grace signaled for another round. "Why didn't you tell us?"

Why hadn't I? My stupid, stubborn pride? "I kept thinking things would improve."

Grace twirled the stem of her glass. "You should've told us, hon."

"You guys don't need the burden of knowing all the crap going on in my life."

"Knock it off." Cassie gave me a rueful smile. "We love your crap."

"Not that again, Tova." Grace's voice turned stern. "If you aren't telling us, who are you telling?"

I frowned. She knew I wasn't telling anyone.

"What exactly happened last weekend?" Cassie wanted to know. "Is that why you canceled coming over?"

I nodded. "We signed the papers for the new loan, and

Andrew wanted to stay home. Sorry. And I made dinner while he stared at his phone. When I got up the next morning, he was gone. To work out, which ticked me off. When he finally showed, we fought and I told him we needed therapy."

Grace's hand clutched her napkin into a wad. "What'd he say?"

"He told me I could forget it. Doesn't that sound like a lovely weekend?"

"He's being an ass," Cassie stated. He was, but I didn't like hearing her say it.

"I should've put my foot down about him being gone all the time. I should've fought more." Maybe that's why I'd stood up for Lena today. If I couldn't stand up for myself and what I wanted, I could for her.

Grace's pat on my knee was almost as good as a refill. "You wanted to be supportive."

"I'm just as much to blame." If I'd told him no traveling, would we be in this spot? "I'm so bull-headed. I thought we could muscle our way through his constant traveling." I turned to Grace. "When you mentioned my toast to an extraordinary life, that had always been my plan." I wanted to be the one who'd break the divorce cycle in my family. I wanted a happy marriage, my business, travel, and kids playing in my yard. I wanted to live *that* life. It took a lot to admit it, but I did. "I want to make it work." *I needed to make it work.* "Even if he's not acting like the man I fell in love with. Remember how he use to send me pink roses every week and spend every minute with me? I just need to get us back to that."

The drinks arrived. "He'll come around," Grace promised. I didn't dare look at Cassie. I'm sure she thought otherwise. "Tell us what happened at the DMV. Some incident thing, when you called today?"

I filled them in on my attempt at valor with Lena and standing up to Billy. However, I did skip over my obnoxious flirting with Neil and how that made me feel dejected. How pathetic would that sound after I'd waxed on about saving my marriage?

After the alcohol wore off, we all walked out under a midnight sky. There weren't many cars out, and the quiet amplified the sound of tires on pavement. Cassie handed over her valet ticket, got in her car.

It was the two of us now. Grace and I stood beside each other, leaning against my Rover.

"No more secrets, Tova," she said, watching me over the corner of her thin shoulder. "No more."

I nodded, feeling better after telling them. Lighter. I didn't know why I hadn't told Grace and Cassie. Did I think divorce was that horrific? Or did I just not want to fail?

My mom had always said I was too self-contained. Maybe she was right.

"Do you need to talk some more?" Grace asked.

I kicked at a rock with my shoe. "I'm okay."

"When you need to, call me, any time of day. Okay?"

"I will." I hugged her and got in my car and cried all the way home.

When did I stop sharing my life, my secrets, my hopes and dreams with others? A long time ago, I figured. Was I sinking into a hole of artificial relationships? Where I'd slap on a happy face and pretend everything remained grand? Like my mother had?

I didn't want everyone to see a veneer, a coated, glossy version of my life because I'd lost the ability to expose the truth of it.

Can I see the truth of it?

When I got home, I poured another glass of wine and pulled out Neil's card.

I sat down at my computer. Rocco sighed and lay down and dozed at my feet. I Googled Hamilton & Waters as I finished my wine.

His website was nice, simple, and professional. They provided solutions for missing persons, witness locates, skip tracing, stalking problems, and personal protection.

Maybe he could investigate where the Andrew I once knew had gone.

I stashed Neil's card under a stack of files. Best to hide it.

CHAPTER 3

TOVA

Early morning light filtered through the four large windows, adding a dim, almost blue cast over my workspace. I sat in my desk chair and peered at my stack of files and tried not to think about what hid underneath. It had been a week since I met him, and I'd pulled that card out every day. The edges were now worn.

Like watching a movie I loved over and over again, I kept rewinding my encounter with Neil. I wanted to be sure I hadn't missed anything. A detail, perhaps, lost in the background.

I checked my email and did my best to ignore the urge to take out his card, but soon I relented and studied the card stock, as if making a wish would magically make him appear. That only happened in fairy tales.

I put the card down and got up. Rocco's bright green tennis ball lay plunked in my left Nike when I went to get the newspaper. The sucker I am, I showed pity on him. "Come on, Rocco." I tossed the ball down the hallway. It bounced off the mirror at the end of the hall. "Where's your ball?"

A loud thud sounded as Rocco hit the floor. He went from carpet to wood, his nails scraping on the floor like a cartoon character unable to find purchase. Eventually, he reached the ball and flailed his body down the hall. His big form nearly ran into me but stopped in time. I couldn't help but smile when he twisted this way and that way, his happy eyes silently begging me to get my shoes on faster.

"Hold your horses." I slipped them on and went to go open the front door. Rocco flew out, dropping the ball by the steps, only stopping when he hit the middle of the front yard and turned around, waiting for me to fling it into the yard.

My attention caught on a pickup truck and Yukon—both black and ominous—outside the house across the court. The new folks were moving in. Ann, my neighbor, had reminded me the day before. I'd made brownies with her girls as a welcome present, but still I'd forgotten, too lost in my head.

I tossed Rocco the ball a few times, then glimpsed someone walking down their driveway. The man appeared to be in his thirties, tall, with longish blonde hair.

I brought Rocco inside, checked my appearance in the hallway mirror, and concluded my hair looked beachy. That's what I called the wavy strands. My mother called them *a mess*.

With my killer chocolate pecan brownies, oozing caramel from the middle, I crossed the cul-de-sac. I was well known for these babies.

The new guy stood at his truck. He lifted his head at the slap of my shoes on asphalt.

"Hi, I'm Tova." I smiled and held out my hand.

His smile reminded me of a clever boy, one who had a secret. "I'm Charlie." Blond and tan. The ladies on the street would think he'd walked off a California movie set.

"I made you these as a welcome-to-the-neighborhood present."

"Thanks, but I'm not your new neighbor. I'm just here carrying heavy things."

Funny. "Aren't you lucky?"

"If you say so." He turned and motioned for me to follow him up the inclined driveway. "Come on, I'll introduce you."

The screen door cracked then banged. Startled by the noise, I looked up and stopped dead, as though soldered to the walkway.

Over Charlie's shoulder, I could see Neil, *my Neil*, take two steps.

Gobsmacked, my heart stuttered. He looked as handsome as I remembered—better, actually—dressed all in black with a happy expression on his face.

Charlie threw a hand back in my direction. "Neil, your new neighbor brought you brownies." I wet my lips.

Neil's eyes widened when they stopped on me. No doubt he wondered why I stood in front of him, my stomach clenched with his shock. He looked at Charlie, then me again.

"Tova?"

"Do you two know each other?" Charlie asked. Had he noticed Neil scanning my face?

"Yeah," we answered in unison, staring at each other like two awkward statues under the morning sun.

"Brought me brownies?" Neil asked. So simple. How could he do that?

"Yeah, the brownies have nuts. Hopefully, you aren't allergic." I shrugged. "The girls and I stuffed them with caramel, too." I needed to stop yapping. "Hopefully, you like caramel."

"Girls? Your daughters?"

"Ah, no, I don't…um, we don't have kids. The neighbor girls helped me make them. I'll introduce you next time we're all outside." I pointed down the street, mouth still rushing on ahead. "They live in that brick house."

He took a step toward me, his eyes on my body. "Which

house is yours?"

I could hardly believe he was here. Then it hit me right in the gut. Neil lived a hundred feet from me. I pointed to the other side of the court, three houses down from where we stood. "That light gray one." My brain couldn't grab hold of him being in front of me.

"You've got a view of the creek."

I smiled. "I do. I watch it all day while I'm working." From my living room. If his blinds were ever open, I'd be able to see into his bedroom.

A lurching sound turned our attention down the street. A moving truck headed toward us.

"I'll help them back in." Charlie jogged away. I'd forgotten he was listening as I babbled on.

Neil stood by my side and we watched the truck. Even though we weren't touching, his heat radiated, reaching my arm. As if whispering to himself, Neil said, "You live on Cobblestone Lane."

I couldn't tear my eyes off him. He didn't seem like a man who got flustered, but his body language right now said otherwise. We stood there and I watched him push his fingers into his forehead.

All I wanted was to keep watching him. "Do you guys need help? I'm really good at lifting light things. Nobody can carry fluffy pillows the way I do."

He grinned. "I imagine that's true."

The truck's brakes squeaked, and it came to rest next to us in his drive. The mover jumped out. "I don't think I broke anything." His eyes danced to Neil, then me. And another popped out from the truck's passenger side.

"TJ." Neil pointed to me. "This is Tova, my new neighbor. Tova, this is my brother, TJ." TJ had Neil's same blue opal eyes, but with his stockier build, I never would've guessed them brothers. Neil gestured to the other guy. "And my friend Reid."

Reid rounded the bumper, stern, scowling. This one was no model, not with that once—or twice—broken nose. Shaking hands, we said our hellos. It was my very lucky day; TJ and Reid had an air of seriousness that superseded even Neil.

After a second more of speculating glances from this pair, Reid patted the truck and said, "We'll start."

Neil placed his hand on my lower back.

That hand of his—oh my god, the heat permeated, and need tore through me and settled in my chest as he shifted me out of Reid's way. I caught Reid check out my wedding ring as he marched past.

My skin-to-skin deprivation at peak levels, I looked up at Neil. "I suppose you won't be needing my services to lift things."

"Probably not." He gazed at me with fire flashing in those eyes, but just as quickly it disappeared. Neil's face fell, his expression turning austere, then blank. I wished I could read his thoughts. I hated how his face became a mask of control.

I was acting like my dad—or, at least, how I figured my dad behaved. Deep-seated fear rose from my belly to my chest. *I'm nothing like him*, I chanted in my head. "I should go and get out of your way."

The guys came out of Neil's house. I handed the brownies over to Mr. California. What was his name again? "Hey, Charlie, you take care of these. Make sure Neil shares, okay? It was nice to meet all of you." All four men returned the sentiment as I walked away. As I reached the end of the driveway, I could feel their eyes on me, but I didn't check to verify.

I felt lucky. I worked hard for the body I carried around and I liked it just fine. Even though I knew the guys were watching as I walked into my house and even though I didn't want to think about my flirting, I still hoped my ass looked good in my jeans. What can I say? I'm vain.

Neil. Neil lived *across the street.* How was this possible? I flopped onto my sofa, laid my arm over my eyes, and exhaled. Rocco nudged my forearm with a cold, wet nose. No wallowing for me. I sat up and glanced out the front windows.

I wanted to make my marriage work, and now Handsome had moved in across the street. Was I cursed?

"Tova, quick question." Reva, one of my employees, came in, and she followed the direction of my eyes. "*Hello*, look at that view." When I didn't answer, her head swung back to me, caramel-colored hair flowing over her jaw like some shampoo commercial.

Neil and all the guys were still out there unloading furniture. Taking one last peek, I joined her. "I know, right?"

"Can I make popcorn?"

I grinned. Anytime "hot guys"—her words, not mine— were on TV Reva asked to make popcorn and enjoy. She said she had to.

"I could eat popcorn," Astrid piped up, coming to watch out the picture window with us.

Oh boy! "We have work to do."

Reva pointed outside. "Look at that view."

Astrid glanced at the men moving in the driveway. "I see hot guys at the garage all the time." Astrid, in her carefree and honestly uninterested way, ignored them and sat for a second.

"Did I hear *hot guys?*" Vivian, my last employee, asked.

I groaned. "It's work time." *Not stare-out-my-window-and-admire-my-handsome-new-neighbor time.*

"I wondered where the party was." Vivian kept her eyes trained on the men. "We have great news—"

Astrid cut in. "Got a huge order!"

"From who?" I asked, tearing myself away and looking at Vivian.

She wore a vintage, emerald green, A-line dress courtesy of the 1950s. Her strawberry blond hair fell in waves down her back as she pronounced, "Nordstrom."

"Where's the purchase order?" Obsessing over Neil would need to wait. *After all, Tova, you* are *married.*

"On my desk." We trooped back to the studio, and Vivian handed me a stapled stack of papers. "It's a big one."

My three employees waited for my reaction. I flipped through the pages, scanned to note the quantities, and jumped to the back page for the amount. "This is great." I smiled before moving to my chair. "I'm buying lunch tomorrow."

Rocco followed and placed his chin on my foot. Vivian rolled her chair to my side and handed me my messages.

"Hey, I need to ask if I can have Friday off in two weeks." Reva probably had something with her boyfriend. He played drums, and she always sported a concert T-shirt.

"Sure." I remembered then. "It's moving day, right?"

"Yep."

"Did you check with HR?" I joked.

Reva grinned and brought a finger up to her chin for effect. "Uh, I forgot. Let me check."

"Speaking of days off, boss, can I get Friday off in three weeks?" Astrid asked. "I need to look at bridesmaid dresses with the sis."

"Sure. They set a date?" I jotted down the two days off in my calendar.

"Don't make me laugh," she huffed cynically. "Ah...no. So don't ask me why I need to go look for dresses."

I set aside my calendar, clearing the top of my desk, and hid a certain business card again.

It was like someone had brought over gourmet chocolate-chip cookies and left them on my counter. Even though I hadn't asked for a cookie and certainly didn't need a cookie, I couldn't help it. I kept thinking about that friggin' cookie. The temptation loomed.

"Why're you frowning?" Reva asked.

"Just thinking about something Grace told me." *Complete lie.*

———•———

Awhile later, my cell phone went off with Andrew's ringtone. I was on a business call. *He could wait.* How would he react if I didn't call *him* for days and days, like he did to me? Thinking about it made my blood pressure rise. He'd call my business landline—that's what he'd do. Other than his cell, where would I call him? Nowhere.

I closed the door to my studio and went into the kitchen to pick it up.

"Hey, princess." He sounded patronizing. "Glad you could get back to me."

I leaned against the counter. "Seriously, Andrew?"

"Tova, I'm sorry, okay?" Andrew would say my name in almost every sentence, and it always held a condescending note. "I'm busy."

My body shook with anger. "Really, *you're* busy? That's your excuse for not calling? You live with your phone in your hand." Did he think I was stupid?

"After these products launch, we'll go on vacation, anywhere you want."

"It's been two weeks since you left. And you haven't called. Not a word. Two weeks!"

"I'm sorry, Tova. Everything's been really stressful and I'm calling now. I'm checking in." Did he think he should get a prize for that?

I grabbed a mug and slammed the cabinet closed. "You'll go to therapy then?"

"Of course. And don't worry, everything will be fine when I get home." Heard that before. *Find what's real. It's not in words,* my mother used to tell me. When I was younger, I'd never understood what she meant.

"Give it some more time. In a few more months, everything'll be great."

"Let's talk about our fight."

"Don't you trust me?"

Trust. I never knew such a small word could crush me. I poured coffee, splashing some on my hand. It burned. "Let's talk about our fight."

"Tova, I don't have time. I need to get ready. I'll call tonight."

"You called me, Andrew." The conversation sounded like a dream. No. A nightmare. I wanted to look around the room and see if someone was taping me.

"Well, when I called, I had time to talk. Now I don't. I have to go."

"If you just leave, don't call me, and stop answering my texts again, Andrew, that's it, we'll need to get a divorce." I don't know if he heard me. The line had gone dead.

———•———

I took Rocco around to the front yard and threw the ball for him to chase after. The sun started to hide behind the bare limbs of my oak tree. Instinctively, I looked toward Neil's house. None of the cars or trucks sat in his driveway.

Earlier in the day, I saw Max and Mallory, neighbors, bring over a plate of food. Neil opened his front door. I should be neighborly. Cold beer after moving was customary.

To hell with it, I decided. I called out across the cul-de-sac, "Hey, you want a beer?"

Neil's eyes stayed on me as he sat down on his front steps. "Sure."

"I'll be over in a minute." I went inside and grabbed a six-pack of Fat Tire. No ulterior motives other than being neighborly, I told myself.

An opener in my pocket and a big rawhide for Rocco, I walked back. There was the slight chance he'd be a total ass and my little infatuation could die a fast death.

The only modern house on the street, Neil's stood out with its bold lines and intense color. I loved my home, but I appreciated his.

When the Donaldsons were still there, I'd been over, and through, the house all the time; I knew that, except for a length of slightly hidden skylights somewhere in the middle of the house, it bore a flat roof. The whole thing always struck me as a treehouse, what with all the trees in the back. Skylights illuminated the kitchen, and the front of the house held six huge floor-to-ceiling windows. Evidently, he'd bought the place because he liked natural light.

Neil wore black shorts, a T-shirt, and that look of reservation. I handed him a beer. "Here you go." The step, still warm when I sat down, heated my backside.

"Fat Tire, nice."

I smiled, feeling silly and awkward. "Only the best." *I really shouldn't be doing this.*

"I only have time for one," he said, all distant cordialness.

"Okay." I barely quelled the desire to ask, *Why bother?* The recollection of his face shutting down hours before flashed in my mind. Neil'd felt obligated and agreed to a beer—nothing more, nothing less. Rocco leaned against my leg for a cuddle and scratch.

"What's his name?"

I could be the good neighbor and play along. So what if I felt the need to look at him and catalog every detail and he only wanted to have a plastic conversation?

"Rocco. He's my baby." At my statement, Rocco burrowed into my side. "Aren't you, Rocco? You're my sweetie?" He really was. His tail went a mile a minute as I rubbed his back, fingertips disappearing into his shiny black coat.

"He sure is a large baby."

I gave my baby his treat to gnaw on. "Big-boned."

Neil huffed. "He's the biggest Lab I've ever seen."

"He might be."

"'Might' is also an understatement."

"Okay...he's furniture that barks." Neil closed his eyes for a brief second and grinned. I shifted to get a better look at him. "You better not be implying my dog is fat."

He laughed. "I'm not. Not fat. He's a tank."

"Yes, and he's my tank."

Perfect cheekbones and curls showing hints of auburn. I remembered him being gorgeous—perfect, actually—but as I sat there with dusk washing over him in shades of pink, apricot, and gold, I knew the actuality remained better than any recollection. He jarred me to the quick. I couldn't look at him anymore, so I glanced down at his feet.

His naked feet.

"How much does he weigh?"

"Just over a hundred pounds." Even his feet were sexy. Damn him.

"He could take you for a walk."

My eyes rose. He smiled, as though amused with his observation. My mind went right to the gutter. "Who would wear the collar?"

He threw his head back and laughed. "Christ."

Neil must secrete some type of pheromone, something making me behave this badly. I bit my bottom lip and smiled crookedly. Unfortunately, I liked getting such a big reaction from him.

"You're too much," he said, still amused, tipping his bottle up again.

"Really?" I should've been embarrassed, but I wasn't. "You keep giving me the opportunity."

Hmm. Good point.

Why couldn't I stop flirting with him? I needed to stop asking myself that. I needed to switch topics. "How'd the move go?"

He blinked at my change of subject. "Well, I'm unpacked, and none of us threw our backs out."

"You work fast."

"I don't have a lot of stuff. The place is kind of empty." His bottle tipped toward me now. "This is great, by the way. Thanks. You're the welcome wagon.

"I suppose." A thought came to mind. "You asked for a change-of-address form at the DMV."

He ran a hand through his hair. "Yeah."

Even if we hadn't met that day, we would've met today. "Thanks again for helping me."

"It was my pleasure."

I wondered if that guy, Billy, was as dangerous as Neil said. We sat in silence for a minute, but nothing about it seemed uncomfortable. A laugh and a beer cured us.

That was the problem, wasn't it? I felt too comfortable with Neil.

Now he changed the subject. "How long have you and your husband lived here?"

"I bought the house seven years ago. Andrew moved in right before we got married, just over two years ago."

"Were you even old enough to buy a house seven years ago?"

I leaned back against his step. "Fishing?"

"Yeah, I'm fishing, Blue Eyes."

I swooned and stared at him, instantly speechless at the possible nickname he'd given me. Andrew called me princess, but it never came off as endearing. Neil's eyebrows rose, playfully, daring me. His stubbled chin aimed in my direction.

"Take the bait," he said in his honey voice.

CHAPTER 4

TOVA

Every feminine part of me came to attention. I took the bait, all right, hook, line, and blue-eyed-bobber. "I bought the house when I was twenty-four."

"Making me do math?"

God, I liked him. I glanced at his feet again. "Just checking to see if you're paying attention," I said, repeating his words back at him from the DMV.

When I looked up, his face held a thought I couldn't decipher. I wondered if one day I would know what that look meant. "Earlier today you said you work from home. What do you do?"

"I'm a jewelry designer."

He appeared pleased and glanced at my hands. "And you look at the creek all day."

"I do. Did you know Minnehaha doesn't really mean 'laughing water'? It actually means rapid water."

"I didn't even know it meant laughing water. Were those customers who left this afternoon?"

I wanted to tap him on the nose with my index finger. "Very astute, aren't you?"

"I pay attention. It's my job."

I laughed. The cheeky devil. "You're bound to be astute, I suppose. They were my three employees. One is in charge of all of my accounting and paperwork, another helps me create some of the metal pieces we use and does assembly, and the third does everything else. I have a few contract employees, also, when we have lots of orders."

"You have a good business?"

"I do." I drew in a deep breath and let it spill. "I looked up your business."

"And?" he asked expectant.

"Do I sound crackers if I tell you I want to know everything thing about it?"

"Crackers?"

"Yeah, you know, nuts?"

His eyebrows shot up. I laughed. *Oh god.* I wanted to kiss him.

"No, you're not crackers or nuts. It's not as exciting as you think. We do a lot of corporate work, background checks, evaluating security systems."

"Well, it's more active than what I do."

"You mean when you're not jumping in at the DMV, trying to save someone?"

"Touché, Hamilton." He laughed. I loved his laugh. Andrew never laughed at anything I said. "What's one of your most memorable cases?"

"I never discuss cases."

"Really? Come on." I picked up the six-pack and waved it in front of him. "Could I bribe you?"

"No." But he did grin.

"How did you get started in your business?"

"That's a long story."

"I have time."

He glanced away. Maybe he didn't want to tell me. "I really wanted to find someone. While hunting her down, I learned the business. Decided I could do it full time."

My phone buzzed. A text. Cassie wanting me to come over and make her fish tacos. I typed, *No*. An army of little green men would need to carry me away from Neil's stoop.

Neil's hand dipped into the front pocket of his shorts, extracting his phone. "I should get your number…and your last name."

I felt like I knew him, yet he didn't even know my last name.

"It's Hudson."

"Give me your phone I'll put it in." We exchanged identical phones. Thank god I hadn't programmed in his phone number… though I really didn't need to. I'd memorized it. "You can put yours in mine."

Neil smiled. "That's what she said." I laughed despite the stupidity of his joke. "You have a great laugh."

Moths took flight on my insides. He shouldn't be telling me sweet things. "Thanks."

"Hudson, huh?" He lowered his head and typed into my phone.

"Yeah." I asked then question lingering in my head. "Who were you looking for? When you learned the business?"

Neil's head rose slowly. His chest filled with air. "My mom." His eyes cut away. "Your husband's name is Andrew?"

He'd been looking for his mom? "Yes, but his last name isn't Hudson. It's Cain."

That stopped him for a second. Neil looked up. "You didn't take his name?"

"Nope. My business is my name. That's the main reason I didn't change it. Well, that and 'Tova Cain' sounds like a curse for a dentist's wife. Novocain. Tova Cain."

He shook his head. "Funny."

I couldn't help but ask. "Did you find her?"

Neil nodded his head and signaled to the beers. "Can you pass me another?"

Relief washed through me. I didn't want the night to end. I didn't want to think he only agreed to have a beer out of niceties. I felt like I'd reached a goal with his asking. I had a similar feeling once before, but with Andrew.

He opened his bottle, air fizzling out. "Do you have family here?"

"Yeah. My grandmother and aunt live fifteen minutes away in Edina. You?"

"Just TJ, my brother. My parents and two sisters are in Florida." I caught him studying me and fiddled with my bracelets in response. "What about your family?"

"No brothers or sisters. My dad's in New York, and my mom passed away nine years ago." Every time I told someone about my mom's death, I felt like an orphan.

"Sorry," he said faintly. We both set our sights on the setting sun and drank more beer. Then he twisted, and our naked knees bumped. He didn't move away, nor did I. "Did you make these?" His attention stayed on my arm. With only his thumb, he touched me, sliding it to my wrist, giving me visible goose bumps. I couldn't pry my eyes away from his hand on mine.

The mere brush of his fingers excited and unnerved me all at the same time. I really should move my leg. "I did."

"They're cool," he rasped. His finger glided over the cords and chain, his thumb occasionally finding skin. He rubbed the bone of my wrist. Lust surged through my system, my body buzzing. I wanted him to keep touching me. Hypnotized, I fought the urge to lean into him.

I promised myself a long time ago, even before I'd met Andrew, that I never wanted to be my dad. As I sat there, I wondered if he'd found himself drawn to a person so much so that he'd put himself in a position where he could let his marriage vows slide.

I always wanted to prove I was better than him. Maybe I wasn't.

Neil's eyes rose to mine. Something palpable and stirring zapped between us. I likened it to sheet lightning, the way we stared at each other, flashes of light and heat lost in the dark.

"I riveted the leather to the clasps," I said in some drugged state.

"I have no idea what that means." Neil's finger followed the blue vein of my arm. A shiver ripped through me and I pulled my arm away. He let go of my hand and moved away.

In silence, we sat listening to the odd hum of air conditioners, out of context for April. "How'd you guys meet?" Neil focused on my house. Lights on and curtains open, he could see into my living room.

"Andrew and I? We met at a casting class."

"A what?"

"A class for making molds and pouring molten metals." It's a strange place to meet your future spouse, but it was just as strange how we even ended up together.

At first, we would say hi while making eye contact, a cursory greeting at best. Andrew then graced me with an eyebrow lift or raised corner of the mouth to acknowledge my existence. Rather smug, I thought, as this went on for weeks. I'd been okay with Andrew not talking to me. He was a good-looking man—athletic body, a face that any woman would like looking back at them. Naturally, Andrew caught my eye. And his presence, his stance, the ramrod-straight back, the way he carried himself shouted proud and confident. But he looked and acted like a military man—way too stuffy for me. My dad being stuffy knocked that right out of me. So Andrew—although good-looking—had been welcome to keep to himself.

But he hadn't.

Later, I remembered how pleased I'd been to catch his attention, like I'd won a trophy. Similar to how I'd felt when Neil had asked for that second beer.

"Your husband's a jeweler? I thought he was a dentist."

Doctor Andrew Cain. "He was a dentist. Now he's an inventor." He was good at what he did, and his patients loved him. They were really upset when he left his practice.

"What's he invented?"

"He had a product go into production last year for dental implants." Andrew had so many technical questions regarding metals and molds when we started dating. Who didn't like using their skills to help someone else? I got to think creatively and we would brainstorm. "Another three launch in a few months that are—I quote—" I used my hands to emphasize. "—'going to revolutionize that thing that shoots water in your mouth.'"

"I hate dentists."

I laughed too eagerly. Two beers. "Don't we all?"

Neil took the last sip. The bottle sounded hollow when he set it down. "He's not home?"

"No. He's usually home one weekend a month."

"Once a month?" He scrubbed a hand down his face.

"Yep."

"Is he based out of China or something?"

"On the road. All the time." I never dreamed his inventiveness and work ethic would become something I resented. "He goes from hotel to hotel, city to city. But mostly his time's spent in Memphis, Savannah, or Orlando."

"He can't work from here?"

That was a great question. I finished my beer and looked him dead in the eye. "Apparently not."

NEIL

The woman I'd been thinking about non-stop for a week is across the court for me to see every day. Frustrated, I grabbed another beer from my fridge. It took me a year to find this house, and I fucking liked it. And now I had this complication.

I closed my eyes and thought about her skin under my thumb, the edge of her wrist and the bump of bone I kept passing my finger over. More than once, I wanted to reach out and touch her. This was bad. Tipping the bottle, I downed the beer too fast.

She'd asked who I'd found and I'd told her. I never told anyone.

In the past week, more than once, I'd almost looked Tova up for my own selfish reasons. Not for the one I kept telling myself—Billy getting out of jail. Why couldn't I get her out of my head?

The calluses on her fingers made sense. She made jewelry from home. I'd see her all the time. "No, you won't," I told the counter. "You're busy." This would be a good excuse to work more.

Billy's lawyer did a good job at court yesterday. I laughed. Now, I knew where to find her. Didn't even need Reid or TJ to look her up. I'd be getting the call on Monday, I figured, that Billy'd be released.

Do I tell Tova she needs to watch her back? Or in Billy the

Carver's case, her neck. Pretty girls had the tendency to have their throats cut if they knew him. *I wonder if she has a security system?*

And her husband only came home once a month. Christ.

Reid dove in with questions when he caught me unable to look away from her this morning. Like an old woman, he wanted to know all about it; mostly, why she looked at me the way she did and flirted when she wore a ring? Men don't care much about that, but not Reid. I certainly didn't want to talk about her.

Before he left, he'd told me, "Leave her alone, Neil." *No shit.* He didn't want me making the same mistake he had.

I'd seen enough infidelity to know it ruins lives. The way she looked at me and asked if I found my mom. Her perfume floating around me, her soft leg against mine, her pulse ratcheting up under my thumb. Damnit. I'd keep my distance. I slammed the bottle into the trash and went to take a cold shower.

———·———

TOVA

My hands weren't often buried in the guts of my lawnmower, but that afternoon it decided to sputter, smoke. Then it died. I stood and wiped grease on my shorts as Neil came jogging down the court, mopping sweat off his forehead with the shirt in his hands. I stared. Fixated.

He wore shorts. Or rather, only shorts.

His arms pumped at his sides, and the definition of his shoulders and biceps seemed like moving art. What would it take for me to become immune to looking at him? *I'll spend more time around him so I build up a tolerance. That could work, right?*

He stopped in front of me. A thick patch of dark hair on his upper chest thinned and trailed down his model-worthy abs and below the waistband of his shorts.

"Hey, how are you?" I asked.

He did some more chest mopping and said, "Well enough. You?"

"I'm good." I could build up a tolerance. Most definitely.

He reached out and touched my forehead with his thumb. I lost my balance and took a sharp step back. He should *not* be touching me.

"Grease," he said softly.

His freaking shoulders and chest... Cryin' out loud. I wanted to slap him and tell him to put some clothes on. I snapped my eyes back to his. Satisfaction lit his baby blues. I'm sure he knew my thoughts.

Bastard.

He looked down at the mess on my driveway. "What are you doing?"

Trying not to think about you naked. "It's acting up."

He put his hands on his waist as he took deep breaths. "So you took it apart?"

"Well, *now* I'm putting it back together."

"How many times have you pulled apart a small engine?"

"This would be the first. Looked it up on YouTube."

He chuckled. "Of course you did."

"I'm surprised you're not trying to take over."

"Ha ha. Until a week ago, I've never owned a lawn mower." He smiled. "But want some help?"

"No, I think I've got it." What I *wanted* was his shirt back on and for him to skedaddle.

He stayed put. Darn it.

I tightened the last bolt, stood, wiped my hands on my

shirt, and said a quick prayer to the lawn mower goddess up in the sky before pulling on the starter. I got one sputter. Neil looked amused. I had the instant desire to pinch him. Not that I could, what with his flat tummy. "Are you hoping I can't get it started?"

He frowned. "Of course not."

I held the handle one-handed and, with a death grip, yanked the cord harder this time. It roared to life. I smiled like a kid with a new bike—or, in this case, like a woman who'd fixed her own lawn mower.

Neil's whole face grinned. "Is there anything you can't do?" he asked with no trace of mockery.

"Lots. I can't make dog hair disappear." I turned the mower off and continued, "Or sew a straight line, and I can't turn back the hand of time."

He took a step closer. His hand came up. "You still have… some grease. Can I get it?" I nodded and his thumb brushed softly over my forehead. Damn, his finger felt nice. "Why would you want to turn back the hand of time?" he whispered.

Why did I just tell him that? "Maybe I'd like a redo on some things."

When had things started to go bad with Andrew? Were our problems based on my self-containment? I'd just take care of everything. I remembered feeling bitter about him staying up late and working when I lay awake in bed. Had I made it harder with Andrew by not telling him I was upset? I needed to speak my mind and not let things fester. Then we'd decided it was best for him to go on the road. When I'd started to feel the divide it caused, I should've put an end to it. But that made me the dream crusher. And I didn't want to be that woman.

"I think you're right, Blue Eyes," Neil said, cutting into my thoughts.

It was a guilty pleasure that he called me that again. I should tell him to stop.

Eve's garage door opened. Happy with the distraction, I waved as she started pulling out her green garbage can.

"Have you met Eve and her husband, Stan?"

"Yeah. Yesterday she brought over pierogis."

I turned sharply. "Seriously?"

"Yes." He pushed his sweat-soaked hair back.

"That tans my hide. It took years for me to get those little Polish potstickers. And I watered their yard for two weeks and scooped up a dead squirrel for her. She must really like you if you got her little morsels of love so soon." Neil laughed. "I'm serious."

His eyes glittered. "Christ, you're funny."

"You think?"

"Hell, yes."

"Thanks. Flattery will get you everywhere, Hamilton."

With Neil chuckling, I swiveled as the pierogi maker closed in. "Hi, Eve." The neighborhood curtain-snooper wore white pedal pushers and a questioning gaze—at the state I was in? Or how close we stood? I backed away.

"Hi, dear," she said to me. "Hello, Neil." I should've told him to put his shirt back on.

"Hi, Eve. Thanks for those pierogis." He winked at me. "They sure were delicious."

Eve eyed up Mr. Half-Naked. Even eighty-year-old women couldn't help but take all of that in. What if she had a heart condition? After a few niceties, a purple delivery truck pulled up to my curb. I knew this truck; everyone knew this truck. The best flowers in the city were delivered from this business.

The Bach's delivery woman stepped out a side door with two-dozen red roses. Screaming with color, they looked startling awkward.

"Those must be from Andrew," Eve stated.

My cheeks grew hot. "They're the wrong color," I said, instantly embarrassed. Andrew hadn't sent me flowers since we dated. They couldn't be from him; he always sent pink roses.

The woman came at us. "Tova Hudson?" she asked. I glanced at Neil. He straightened, the face he made hinting at him biting the inside of his mouth.

Eve cooed. "Lovely!"

"Yes." I signed her clipboard. Needing to confirm my suspicion, I set the vase on my driveway and ripped opened the small purple envelope. I could feel the heat of Neil watching me.

"They're beautiful," Eve told the driver as I slid out the card. They were.

Andrew, it read. I shoved the torn card into my pocket. Why had he sent red? Was this his way of saying sorry?

"They're from your husband, yes?"

I glanced to her, then Neil. "Yes." I should be happy.

Eve picked up the blooms. They covered her face. "He has great taste." *My husband wants me to forget that he ignored me for two weeks.* "Your birthday or anniversary?"

"Neither." I reached for the vase. "I've got them, Eve."

Neil stepped back and looked away from me. "I should go." With nothing more to say to me, he jogged back to his house. I watched him for a second, and Eve went back inside.

———•———

Later that evening, darkness swept over the sky. Tornado weather. I shut my computer down and moved through the house, closing windows before the rain kicked in. The visual of

Neil running, sweating, and half-naked might be seared in my mind forever.

My cell phone rang—Andrew's ringtone.

I stared at the foreign-looking bouquet on my counter as I answered. "Hi. Thanks for the flowers." I decided not to mention they were the wrong color.

"Hi, Tova." Lightning cracked and broke across the sky. "I've been thinking…" He paused. "I think you're right. Things aren't good between us and haven't been in a long time. We should get a divorce."

Thunder rattled the floor. I stumbled into a chair. "What?"

"I'd rather we end on good terms than arguing every minute." His tone came out even, level. "I'm not enjoying that either."

He couldn't be serious. We'd just talked about getting help. He'd wanted to work on us. Outside the wind howled. Holding onto my phone, my hand shook. "No." This wasn't how it would end; I wouldn't allow it. "Andrew. We'll. Go. To. Therapy." The words came out hard, but I couldn't help that. My grandmother, my mom, and now me—I wouldn't allow it. I was *not* getting a divorce. "No," I said again. He had to give us one last chance.

CHAPTER 5

TOVA

He sounded reasonable. "Tova, therapy isn't my thing." The lights flickered and went out. "I don't think I'm meant for marriage. You should find someone who wants what you do." What I wanted was him to think about what he was saying.

"I can wait. I won't just divorce you, Andrew!" A tear slid down my cheek, and I sunk further into my chair. "You just need to see your new launch through." It had been two years of him on the road. What was a few more months?

"You'll get over me, princess. I'll be back in two weeks to get all my things. We'll talk later." He hung up.

He hung up on me!

I threw my phone. With the protective cover on, it bounced on the hardwood floor and flopped over, face up, glowing on the other side of the room.

I hadn't gotten any candles or my flashlight out. I just sat there, reeling in the dark, staring at the fading light of my cell.

How could he be so cold? I'd given him everything to be successful. For us to be successful. I'd given up my desires.

"Goddamn it!" I shouted to an empty house. After a calm decision on his end, he thought we were over?

It was as though I wasn't worth the trouble anymore.

———·———

Neil parked at my curb. "Christ, Tova, I think you need a hand," he called, hanging out of his Yukon.

I stretched to reach the apex of a branch on my oak. "No. I need a foot." I was in my front yard, trying to cut down a limb that had taken a beating in the storm last night. "Don't you see? I'm too short." I was also trying not to dwell.

"Give me that thing," he demanded. "What the hell is that?" He grabbed at the saw, but I moved away.

"I have no idea, but it helps me cut down branches."

"It looks like a medieval torture device. Why didn't you call me? I would've come over."

I'm not helpless. "I do this all the time."

Neil sidestepped me. He successfully snatched the saw-on-a-stick from my grip. "I know you're more than capable, but just because you can, doesn't mean you should."

"Wow, Neil, feeling sexist?" Deep and mocking, I lowered my voice. "Is this another one of those 'when you see a woman with a tool, you feel the need to take over' kind of moments?" Like I needed another man telling me how it was gonna be.

"One of these branches could knock you out when it comes down."

"I know how to run."

His face held an expression of pure frustration. "Not funny." He wore black cargo pants and a tight T-shirt. A gun, knife, and pepper spray were attached to the thick belt around his waist. He had dark circles under his eyes.

"Were you working last night?"

"Yeah, I came to see if there was storm damage. Did you have any besides this?"

"Just these branches and a little more in the back."

"Let me get changed and I'll help you."

"I'll be fine."

He braced a hand on his hip. *Oh, no, Mr. DMV has to step in now.* "Tova, I'm going to help you."

"I'm fine." I reached out, trying to take back my saw.

He shifted so I couldn't. "Why are you so stubborn?"

What the hell. "Why do you insist I'm stubborn?"

"Because you are." His face fell. "Christ, Tova. Please."

I don't know why I gave in, but I did. "Fine." It took all that to grab the saw-on-a-stick from him. Still reeling from last night, my need to rip something apart sounded like good therapy. "You can help me, but first we'll check your house. We lost power."

Talking to me, he walked backward to his truck. "Give me five minutes."

I set the saw in his yard and ran home to grab two mugs of coffee. I'd made a trip to Starbucks earlier and got a carafe. Like Neil, I was tired.

Wearing a fresh T-shirt, minus the gun belt, Neil let me in. "You know, you can come over without bringing something."

"I thought you'd like one." I held out the mug. "I assumed you didn't sleep last night." *Lord knows I didn't.*

"You're right." The corner of his mouth lifted. "Thank you." He took the coffee from me, and I got the same zap as always when our hands touched.

Neil took a large sip, then ran his thumb over the lip of the mug, watching me.

I figured we could stand there all day. Instead, I passed by him. "Now let's go check your yard. Chop-chop wicky-wicky."

"What?"

"It means hurry up."

I strode through the main level toward the stairs. After all, I knew the layout. The furniture and personal effects were sparse, but he'd warned me of that earlier. You could tell a single man called the place home. The requisite large TV held center stage in his living room, along with a comfy-looking chocolate sectional, but then something made me stop and stare.

"That's a mountain ash," I said, stunned. A large sepia print of my favorite tree hung over his fireplace. "It's gorgeous." The berries, a muted orange, stared back. "I love it."

"Thanks."

I walked to the mantel. "I bought my house because of that tree." Neil came and stood by me. "Did you notice there's one in my front yard?"

"Yes," Neil responded.

"When I was a kid, my grandmother had one in her front yard. I'd lie on my back and run my hands up into the leaves. I thought the berries looked like beads." I twisted to look at him; his eyes stayed on the picture. "I'm blathering. We should check out your yard. I'm sure you're tired."

I strode by him. His kitchen, with rich cherry wood, opened to the casual dining area. I liked seeing a stack of mail on his heavy round table, the two shirts thrown over a chair. Neil was human, fallible—tidy, but not freakishly neat like Andrew.

He led me down some stairs to his near-empty family room and out to the backyard. The space backed up to a wooded area, dense with countless oaks, red maples, and numerous evergreens. His yard rivaled a forest.

We cleaned up a few branches and dragged them around the house to the curb. A light drizzle had started. Spotting Eve and Stan, Neil glanced at me and I instantly knew what he thought.

"Let's get them inside," he said.

"I can take care of their yard," I told him. "You're tired."

Even I noticed I sounded tediously independent but I knew he needed rest.

Neil slid by, calling out, "Hi, Eve, hi, Stan. We've got this. You can go inside." My mom would have been horrified. It's not polite telling someone *go inside your house*, even the elderly or when all you want to do is help.

Whispering, Neil turned to tell me, "There's something you need to realize. I *get* you can do everything I can, but that doesn't mean I'd stand by and let you." He made for Eve, then turned, face grim. "Or be okay with you doing something I'm happy to do for you—or them, for that matter."

Well, he could stuff it. I didn't need another man telling me how it was going to be. At that little speech, I plowed by him and stopped in his way. I didn't care that Eve and Stan might be getting a show. "Get off your soapbox."

He came right up to me. "You're too stubborn to ask for help?"

I know, I'm self-contained. So what?

"You're acting like a bully wanting to make a point?" Andrew understood my need to be self-sufficient. He would joke about not needing to take care of me.

Right then Eve stepped in. "Oh, thank you, Neil." She stepped closer to me and whispered. "We've got more in the back, Tova. You know Stan… he's too stubborn to ask for help." She had to say that out loud in front of Neil.

I reassured her. "Don't worry, Eve. We'll take care of it."

"Dear, isn't it nice having young, helpful neighbors?" Eve asked Stan.

White-haired and stooped, Stan spoke up. "Yes, Evie." I looked at Neil. Did he love that Stan called her Evie, too? "Another reason we should sell this place. Can't even take care of it anymore."

Eve shook her head and her eyes started to glisten. I wanted my marriage work as long as these two had. Stan set his hand on her lower back. His voice sounded gruff, but his words weren't. "Don't cry, sweetheart." Andrew used to talk to me with affection, but I don't think he'd ever put his hands on me to offer comfort. "Come on, Evie." Stan ushered Eve into the house.

I felt the burn of tears in my eyes and turned away. I thought I was cried out.

———•———

NEIL

Silently, Tova started picking up branches. I went to help, and she ducked her head.

I was in the doghouse. I hooked around in front of her, and she did it again. "I'm sorry, Tova." For a flash, she looked up at me with wet eyes. Damn it. "I'm sorry. I sounded like an ass."

She stopped, lifted her chin up and nodded.

"I didn't mean to be a dick." *Yet you were.*

She finally unclamped her mouth. "I'm not stupid. I know you were making a point, but that's not what I'm upset about."

It dawned on me. Stan and Eve upset her. "They've lived here a long time." I stepped closer to her, but she walked to the curb, dumping the wood in her hands.

"Yeah." She kicked at a straggler. "They raised their kids here. Four of them."

"That's a lot of living."

She strutted toward Eve and Stan's backyard. "Yeah, it is." I followed her like a puppy. "They're the happiest couple I know."

Couldn't help myself. "You mean, besides you and your husband?"

"Yeah. Besides me and Andrew," she said it in that sarcastic tone I was growing fond of.

I walked behind her, staring at her ass and hips. Christ, she had a great ass, but her hips—fuck, her hips were fantastic—lean and curvy. I wanted to hold on and—

She twisted and my eyes went up. The rain had stopped. Sun broke through the clouds and lit her up. She glowed despite her mood. "Can you imagine being married that long?" Her eyes didn't break from mine.

I told her the truth. "Never thought about it. Need to find someone to marry first." *Like you,* and where that came from, I'd no fucking clue, but I meant it.

"Well, it's not all it's cracked up to be."

Twisted relief went through me as she ran a hand over her forehead. "Aren't you the cynic?"

Up an old oak tree her gaze climbed. Her eyes and forehead scrunched as she dropped her glance back to me, as though amazed. "I guess I am."

Her off-the-cuff comment meant only trouble in her marriage. If anything, it made me happy to hear. She didn't elaborate, not that I thought she would. But it cemented the idea that she kept everything held tightly.

My feet stayed planted, letting my eyes slip over her. The rain had made her shirt cling to her chest. Were Eve and Stan watching from inside? Tova's hair was up in a clip, and she tilted her head back, the sun caressing her face. I'd wanted to keep away from her, yet here I was, spending time, wondering when it would end.

Nothing more than a huge desire to kiss away the sadness that seemed to be swallowing her.

"I should go tell them the bad news." She pointed. Looking up, I caught sight of it—a crack a mile long in the massive tree.

The smell of her perfume floated to me. "What's the saying?" I asked. "Not everything can weather a storm."

———•———

TOVA

It had been a couple of days, and I still hadn't told anyone about Andrew. Nor had I heard from him. I'd gotten a text from my neighbor, Mallory. She and her husband, Max, had invited me to Crave for drinks. A Saturday night out sounded like the medicine I needed.

In my dark, tight-fitting jeans and a black sleeveless blouse, I walked out of the house. Going heavy on mascara and eye shadow, I'd spent more time on my makeup than I normally did. Lizzy once told me, when your life is crumbling, look your best going down.

As I saw Neil drive down the cul-de-sac, I told myself, *No reason not to invite him. Besides I need to up my tolerance of him and maybe he needs a night out, too.* That is until he stepped out of the Yukon. From a distance, he looked a bit disheveled, but as I got a better view, I changed my mind. Neil's pants were torn at the knees and his T-shirt looked filthy. He'd been fighting.

"What happened?" I studied him.

Neil grinned like a kid. "Hey, Blue Eyes." What the hell? Was he drunk? He braced a hand against the top of the doorframe, his body taking up more physical space than I thought possible.

"Seriously, what happened to you?" He looked like he'd been rolling in the dirt.

"I was looking for someone. He wasn't thrilled with the idea of comin' with me." The drunk look was the high of adrenaline.

It bothered me that Neil could get hurt, but I supposed it

must happen all the time. Still, I asked, "Are you okay?"

He ran his hand through his hair. "Yeah."

"I came to invite you to Crave with some neighbors, to get drinks. Max and Mallory planned it, but I'm thinking you're probably not in the mood."

His eyes twinkled. "I'll come." He closed his door.

"Really?"

"Yeah. I'll drive. Come on in. Let me get you a drink while I shower."

"Okay." I followed. "Was the guy out on bond?"

"Yep. He skipped." Neil strutted to his kitchen, stripping off his torn shirt. "You want a beer? It's that or water."

"A beer's good." I spotted a trail of blood on his neck. "You're bleeding." I reached him and clasped my hand on his neck. Not touching the cut, but following a parallel path along the column of his throat with my thumb, inspecting the injury. "It's not bad..." I run my thumb over his neck once more. Our eyes aligned again, all that heat zipping between us.

He tensed, took a step back. "I'm okay, Tova." There was an edge to his voice. He grabbed a beer from the fridge, tore its top off, and handed it to me without a word.

As he headed to his bedroom, his steps sounded harsh. "I'll be out in a few." He closed the door with a bang.

Was Neil mad I'd touched him?

Thoughts circled, chasing around in my mind. I'd actually thought about telling him what was going on in my life. *Hey, my husband's decided he doesn't want me anymore.* The picture in his living room took on a surreal glow of orange as I waited. Better yet: *Hey, remember when we stood outside the DMV and you asked if I was separated? Funny thing, I might be soon.* That sounded like the winner. Not nearly as desperate and pitiful as my first thought.

Neil opened his door. Three buttons of his white shirt were

undone. He stalked toward me, buttoning one, then another. An image of him *un*buttoning that shirt flashed in my mind. *Gah.* I needed to shake my head, like an Etch A Sketch, to erase the thought. I set my beer bottle on the counter.

Neil closed in and stopped a foot from me. "Christ, you're tall." A Band-Aid decorated his neck, and his drying hair had started to curl at the collar.

I could smell every bit of him and wanted only to get closer and bite his neck. I suppose that's what happens when you're in your sexual prime and haven't had any action in nearly a year. "Do I make you feel short?"

"No." The tiniest of smirks tilted the corner of his mouth.

If I inched forward, our chests would touch. Even our mouths. "I don't wear heels often. I hover over everyone."

"You don't hover over me." He snatched his keys from the counter. "You ready?"

He led me to his truck, his hand low on my back. Part bliss, part torture, that feeling, radiating through me until he opened my door. I didn't experience simple gestures like that often with Andrew. A hand on my back or a door opened for me. Everyday life. If I ever did again, I wouldn't take them for granted.

Looking out the window as he drove, I tried remembering the last time Andrew had touched me with affection. I couldn't come up with one. The only touch lodged in my head was the removal of my hand from his leg a month ago. Would Neil do the same if I leaned over and put my palm on his thigh?

Yes, I decided.

———•———

The Crave lot was almost full by the time we parked. When Neil opened the door, noise spilled out; the place was packed. The restaurant—with its high ceilings, big windows, modern lights, and a large rectangular bar—made for a great mixture of swanky and uppity urban. Neil turned, eyebrow raised. I read his lips more than heard him ask, "This is where you go to relax?"

In his ear, I answered, "Mallory likes it. It's not so bad."

"Do *you* like it?"

I smiled. "It can be fun."

He looked at the crowd and found my hand. "It's a meat market." He led the way through the bar. Half the women turned to gawk as we walked. The rest, I figured, were too drunk to notice.

Glassy eyed and smiling, our party planners—Max and Mallory—wove their way over. Neil had met them the day he moved in. Tate and Gillian joined us. More neighbors. More introductions.

At our table, Max asked, "Ann, are you being a spy?" Ann, another neighbor, was giving Neil the third degree. She loved asking questions and she never had a problem getting people to answer them.

"Neil's the spy," I said, as if revealing a secret.

A lopsided grin appeared on his face. I wanted to snap a Polaroid of it, hang it on my wall, as he said, "No, I'm not."

"He hauled in a guy who skipped bail," I told everyone, recognizing I sounded proud.

Ann reached forward and gripped his forearm. "You did?"

Neil just nodded.

"You should've seen him. He looked like he rolled around in the dirt."

"Had you?" Ann asked. I liked watching him interact with everyone. Including the ease at which he took everyone's attention.

Neil ran his hand through his hair. "I might have."

I pushed at his arm. "I knew it."

Neil excused himself and headed to the restrooms. On the way back, he stopped to chat with a stunning woman with long dark hair. The woman was talking with Gillian. Completely unable to look away, I watched as he smiled, bright and beautiful, for this mystery woman. Tiny to my tall. Tan to my fair. She was everything I wasn't.

He guided the beauty toward me. "Tova, this is Brooke." She wore foolishly high red heels. Four or five inches of toe-smooshing-hell. I hoped Brooke's feet hurt.

"Hi." We shook hands. I couldn't be rude, even though I wanted to. "Nice to meet you."

"Brooke dated Reid a few years ago," Neil told me. The group around us just smiled hello and watched. My shoulders relaxed. Reid, Neil's mover-buddy, his best friend.

We all talked for a bit, then Brooke appraised Neil. "You're sure looking scruffy." She reached up and fiddled with his hair. "You know, we cut guys' hair at the salon." More was said, but I'd tuned out. It was guy code: You couldn't bed a buddy's ex-girlfriend, right?

Ann cut in from the table. "Neil's hair is perfect," she said. "I'd kill for his hair."

Brooke dove into his locks again. "I think he needs a trim," she said, standing too close. I wanted to slap that hand away. He stood there with a blank face, not discouraging her familiarity but not embracing it either. She let her hand coast down his arm, raking her nails down the fabric of his shirt. She wanted to see if he would break the code.

For everything Neil seemed to be, a code breaker he wasn't.

To help him out, I told her, "I met Reid when Neil moved in."

"Was he grumpy and irritable?" Brooke asked.

Surly, I thought. "Maybe." I laughed a little wildly. Two margaritas.

"Some men never change," she stated. "Neil, are you still playing the field?"

He scowled and set an empty beer bottle on the table behind him. "No."

Brooke laughed. "I doubt that." What did that mean? Brook didn't give up. Now she poked his arm with a manicured finger. "Like I said, some men never change."

Did he incessantly sleep around? Out of the corner of my eye, I saw a flash of short, pink hair. I knew that hair. I took a step to the side, my eyes following the vibrant color, but I lost her.

Neil touched my hand. "What's got your attention?"

"I thought I saw the woman from the DMV. Lena, with the pink hair."

CHAPTER 6

TOVA

Neil turned, eyes scanning. "Where?"

I pointed past the bar to the dark corner of the restaurant. "I saw her in the crowd over there."

"Did you see Billy?"

"Who?"

"The boyfriend?"

"No, but I wasn't looking." I hadn't thought to look for him.

"Stay here. Don't leave." Neil said something to Tate before he cut around tables and people. With his height and my heels, I watched him move through the bar area until he melted into the crowd.

"What was that about?" Ann asked.

"It's a long story." My eyes danced around, looking for Lena or Billy.

Tate came over. "I'm supposed to watch you. What's going on?"

Mallory handed me another mango margarita. Leaning in, she lowered her voice, asking Ann, "What's a long story?"

"Tova was just going to tell us," Brooke replied, having stolen the seat I once sat at.

I gave them the briefest version of the incident from the DMV. Like a shiny thing for a person with attention deficit disorder, every baseball hat in the place triggered my awareness as I finished my third drink. Still no Neil. Where did he go? What had happened? I started to worry. Was he all right?

"What's the name of your hair salon?" Ann asked Brooke.

"Tease." *How appropriate.*

Ann rubbed at her jaw, stifling a grin. "Isn't that on Hennepin?"

Instantly, I visualized the illuminated, bright pink sign. "Oh, yeah," I nodded. "I've seen it. It's been there a few years?"

"It's been there for five. I bought in last year."

If Neil found Lena, what would he say or do? I didn't have an answer. But I wanted a do-over. I wanted to help her.

Mallory leaned in. "So you're a partner?"

"Yes, one of the owners."

Beating me to the same question, Ann asked, "How many are there?"

"Five," she said, straightening her back. "Neil, would you mind showing me where the ladies' room is?" Neil came up from behind me. His cheeks were flushed. Brooke stood and twisted into him, rubbing her chest against his arm.

I quelled my desire to growl like a protective dog. "Did you find her?" I asked.

Neil shook his head.

"We'll take you," Ann said, grabbing Brooke by the crook of her arm and simultaneously pulling both her and Mallory off their bar stools.

"What happened?" I asked.

Neil's phone rang. "One sec, okay?" He moved away and leaned against the wall but kept eyes on me. Confidently, he stood there. Gloriously tall, wide-shouldered, filling out his white dress shirt.

He made his own slow study of my body. We stared at each other as though soaking up the sum of each other.

The way Neil looked at me revealed longing. Had Andrew ever looked at me like that?

My thoughts were wrapped in alcohol and crazy attraction. Neil wouldn't do anything and neither would I.

Bathroom, I mouthed to him. I needed to get away before I did something stupid like let my friends catch me gaping at him. That would be great. Considering I knew all of my parents' neighbors gossiped about them, I did not want the same fate.

I cut through the crowd. A guy grabbed my forearm and spun me around. I wobbled.

"Where do you think you're goin'?"

I should've stopped at two drinks. I'd never been known for holding my liquor. When my eyes focused on the man before me, I sobered right quick.

Dirty Hat—minus the hat.

Billy squeezed my arm. "Remember me?"

Without the brim, I saw his gaunt features. The hollowness around his dark eyes. There was a lethal slant to his eyebrows and a scar that ran through one. "You haven't learned your lesson yet," he said.

I pulled back, but his fingers dug in. "Let me go!" Fear crept into my voice. I doubt he heard my alarm with the deafening music, but I'm sure he saw it on my face. Had Neil gotten off the phone? I looked over Billy's shoulder.

"Your husband can't see us." He still thought Neil was my husband. Drunken adrenaline roared through me. My free hand curled into a fist, but Billy took a step back before I did anything stupid. "No one makes fool of me." He stepped into the hall. "I'm gonna find you," he said. "Later."

He disappeared past the restrooms, and I hightailed it back and found Neil in the same spot.

"Dirty Hat just threatened me." I held up my arm. Neil's eyes knifed to my face. "The guy from the DMV," I explained. "You called him Billy."

"You okay?" Neil assessed the crowd as he stepped closer.

"Yes."

"Where is he?"

I pointed. "By the bathrooms."

"Christ, come on." He took hold of my hand, the grip firm but gentle. "Stay right by me."

"Please tell me you have your gun?" I whispered.

He nodded and placed his other hand behind him, at the small of his back. It was then I noticed what his untucked shirt hid.

Neil tugged me along into the men's room. We got a smile out of two guys. I shook my head. They seemed to get the hint nothing scandalous was gonna happen when Neil used his foot to kick in a closed stall door.

Never letting go of my hand, Neil glanced at the emergency exit sign as we reentered the hallway. "He probably went out the back."

He led me back to our table.

Ann took one long look at me and called her husband, Todd, over. "What's going on?"

"That guy Billy grabbed me." Everyone crowded around, listening, then glancing at Neil. Did they think Neil and I were fooling around?

Neil spoke up. "Billy got out of county today. I should've told Tova." A true wedge of fear stuck in my throat; I wanted it to go away. Neil squeezed my hand. "I'm sorry." Ann noticed and Neil let go.

Important pieces of information started to catalog in my head. Billy, out of jail. Had Lena taken him back? He wanted to harm me. And Ann was wondering if something was up with Neil and me. The rush left my throat dry. I glanced around the tables.

Mallory took note. "Here." She handed me another margarita. "This'll help."

I could always count on her.

In the course of minutes, I downed the peach-colored liquid and something shifted. Was it scarier to have a bad guy taunting you? Or friends wondering what you were doing with the hot new neighbor?

"What does he look like?" Tate asked. The tall corporate tycoon rose to the balls of his feet to glance around the bar like he'd spot Billy and drag him over. It must be the Nordic Viking in him. I imagined Tate with a club and an attitude, hauling Billy behind him.

I sat on bar stool. "Skinny and scary."

Neil frowned at the glass in my hand. "He's gone, but I'll text you a picture." Neil had a picture in his phone? The conversation went on in ripples. What was up with this Billy?

"Here, Blue Eyes." Neil handed me a glass of water. I preferred the drinks.

"Thanks." He could've given me a wicked shot of Jägermeister and I would've happily downed it.

Mallory asked, "Why do you call her Blue Eyes?"

Neil drew his gorgeous lips into his mouth and tried not to laugh.

"Okay." Mallory held her hands up. "Dumb question." She wandered off with everyone, headed to the bar. He shouldn't call me that in front people.

"Drink," Neil ordered.

I frowned and he laughed outright. He seemed to enjoy my loopy state. I slapped him on the arm. "Okay, enough already. I might be tipsy." His laugh only grew. After a minute, I couldn't take it anymore. I laid my hand flat on his sternum. "Enough." The muscles of his chest were hard and his skin hot. All too aware that his strong shoulders that I'd been dying to touch were within reach, my fingers pulsed. I wanted to touch him all over to see if he was hard everywhere. I liked the idea of him hard.

Classy. I needed to stick to water.

On its own accord, my hand slid lower. His muscles tensed, and Neil put his hand over mine. "Stop."

What was going on with me? "Sorry." Embarrassed, I drew my hand away. Had anyone seen me? I glanced toward our neighbors. "Thank you for before. For watching out for me."

Neil rubbed the back of his neck. "Why don't you live in the South?"

I blinked hard. "What?"

"Why don't you live in the South with your husband?"

Did Neil think Andrew had a house down there? "Andrew lives out of hotel rooms and my Grandmother Lizzy and Aunt Donna are here. I would never move." And Andrew had never even asked me to relocate.

Neil's eyes lingered on my bruising arm. "I never asked—what did Billy say to you?"

"He said no one makes a fool of him." What did that mean anyway?

Neil worked his jaw back and forth. "You okay?"

"I'm fine."

"You're always fine, aren't you?" He took a small step forward and didn't let me answer. "You have amazing eyes." His voice, husky and warm, wrapped around me. "It's fascinating how

they're dark blue around the edges and light near the pupil."
He shouldn't say things like that. I didn't have the armor. "Even
more blue tonight." His eyes lowered to my mouth. "A man
would give up everything to look into your eyes."

The conviction in his tone, what he said—how could I not
fall for him? His enchanting words were a sad love letter—
sweet, wonderful, and unexpected, its sum too much.

And I'd vowed to make it work with Andrew.

He backed away from the table. "You need to drink that."

I scowled at him.

"Don't give me that look."

"Why not?"

"It makes me feel like your dad."

I huffed. "Trust me. You're not my dad." My dad had no
morals and changed wives every few years. An earlier comment
popped into my head. "Brooke mentioned you playing the
field."

He shifted on his feet. "I'm not a monk, Tova." He lifted
his hand and tapped the water glass in my hand. "Drink."

I drank the water, and Neil walked over to Tate. The pair
stood eye-to-eye. Tate nodded his blond head at something
Neil said.

Off to my right, I saw a baseball hat coming at me and
jerked back. I'd never felt worried for my personal safety, but
now I wondered if Billy could find me again.

Neil came back. Everyone was leaving. "I'm gonna take
Brooke home." Momentarily, I wondered if I'd heard him
right. Why would he take her home? "I asked Tate to drop you
off. Okay?" *What?* Brooke came up behind him. "Okay?" Neil
asked again.

He was just gonna leave? What could I say? *No, you can't.* I
felt sick. "Okay."

"Lock your doors. I'll see you in the morning." He moved

away, ushering Brooke out of the building with a hand to her back as though nothing had happened.

Like smoke from a fire, everything he said drifted, fading away.

———•———

I heard a vehicle, got up without turning on a light, and peeked out the curtain. Neil still hadn't gotten back. Thanks to Tate and Gillian, I'd gotten home an hour ago. I'd been squished in next to a drunk Max and Mallory.

The car turned into a driveway and disappeared into a garage a few houses down. My stomach felt ready to revolt, and my mind straddled a line between jealous obsession and sprouting surreal profanity.

Pathetically, I still wore my makeup. I wanted to know when he came home and couldn't risk running to the bathroom and not hearing him.

He wanted me as much as I physically wanted him. I saw it in his eyes and felt it in his actions—or, at least, I thought I had.

Courts annulled marriages because your spouse should be sleeping with you or fucking you, if you wanted to be crude. And mine hadn't been. The effects of which were getting to me. When Andrew came home, we needed to have sex.

Then I remembered he wanted a divorce.

Eventually, I fell asleep with my rolling pin on the bedside table.

———•———

At the restaurant, Ann had invited Neil on our weekly walk. Not that I believed he would be there. He no doubt was busy getting busy. I wanted to hide under the covers but got up anyway.

Opening the door to the sun catching fire in the east, my hand came up, shielding my eyes. Ann and Neil waited at the end of the curb.

Whaddayaknow? He pulled out and came home.

I followed Rocco out. I could feign indifference. After all, I'd been taught by the master. My mother.

"Jeez, Tova, you look like shit," Ann called.

"Thanks for noticing."

She smiled. "No problem."

I slid my sunglasses down. Neil reached out and stole Rocco's leash from me. His own eyes were tired and that rumpled hair. That insufferable— What grown man has curly hair?

"So, Neil, did you get Brooke's number?" Ann asked.

He didn't bother answering. No shock there.

"She probably shoved it down your pants," I said. Ann barked out a laugh.

Neil worked his jaw back and forth. He did not appear amused. Play around with honey and you might get stung by a bee.

Thankfully, Ann talked the entire time. I wasn't up to holding a conversation. I knew I had no right to be jealous, but my heart said otherwise. All I could think about was Neil breaking the code and sleeping with Brooke.

After our walk, we dropped Ann off at her house and made our way toward mine.

Neil had put his hand on my arm, halting me before we got to my driveway. A paperboy biked past us, tossing my daily news over for me. "What are you so pissed about?"

"I'm not pissed." I kicked a bottle cap. It stuttered on its way to the curb.

"Yeah, you are. Is it because I didn't drive you home?"

Yes. "No." All too grateful for my sunglasses, I still fought to keep my eyes from tearing up. "Rocco, knock it off!" He was sniffing the paper as though it was something worth marking.

"Will you look at me?" Neil touched my chin and made me look. Shocked, I backed up. Neil's jaw clenched. "Brooke couldn't drive."

"I get it." I looked away.

"No, you don't." He grabbed my hand, fumbled, then twirled my wedding band. My heart jumped into my throat. "Don't be pissed at me."

I pulled my hand away, unclipped my hair, and ran my fingers through the strands. He thought I was being a bitch and I hated that. *What could I say? You hurt me?* "I'm in a bad mood. I'm sorry."

"You don't feel well. Take a nap today." If that's all it would take, I'd stay in bed for a week.

I glanced down, the image on the front of the paper drawing my eye. I picked it up and gasped. *Model Found Dead.* "Neil, it's Lena."

"I heard about Lena last night."

Still reading, I opened the front door. "She was found in St. Louis Park, not far from Crave."

Setting the paper on a table, my thought was, *Why hadn't he told me?* "We need to call the police. I saw her."

When I looked up, Neil frowned. "I don't want you getting involved. Billy doesn't know who you are. If you go to the police, he'll find out your name."

It hit me then. "He killed her, didn't he?" My stomach rolled. I sat down, hand over my mouth. "I could've helped her."

"There's nothing you could've done." Neil sat next to me.

I shifted to look at him. "Why didn't you tell me?"

He stared out the window. "I wanted to know more, and I knew you'd be upset."

"Did you see her last night at Crave?" He didn't answer. "I need to call the police." If they'd held him, Lena might still be alive.

"I'll talk to my friend." His eyes came back to me.

"Neil," I said, upset—with this news, with him.

"All you did was see the back of her," he reasoned. "The police would question you and it'd prove nothing. Besides, Billy grabbing and threatening you wouldn't amount to anything either. It'd be his word against yours. Please."

He had to go throw out that *please*. "How was she killed? Do you know?"

"Stabbed." He rubbed his temple. I felt myself cringe. "Please, Tova, you can't get involved. Not yet at least."

I knew he was right, but I hated it. I nodded. "Okay."

A large breath of relief escaped him. Neil stood and paced around my living room. "You don't have an alarm."

"No. But he doesn't know who I am. You said so yourself."

"You need to be careful. Stay aware of your surroundings."

———•———

A week later, the day before Mother's Day, I pulled into the parking lot of a three-story modern brick building. Donna, my aunt, smiled ear-to-ear, her sunny disposition always catchy. The dynamic duo waited for me, purses dangling from forearms.

Lizzy, my grandmother, stood proud, a woman with life experience to back up her posture. "Hi, Grandma." I gave her a kiss on the cheek to go with a hug.

"Hi, sweet girl." She looked me over. "You're so thin. Are you feeling all right?"

"I'm fine."

Lizzy tucked my hair behind my ear. "You'll never get pregnant if you're too skinny."

"I'm not too skinny. And I'm not trying, so no need to worry." Lizzy wanted great-grand babies.

"Time is ticking. You need to stop lollygagging."

"Mom, leave her alone." Donna smiled at me. "She looks great."

"Thanks," I whispered and gave her a hug.

I took them to Benihana's. The modern Japanese teppanyaki restaurant, known for the enormous flattop grills, was bustling. The chef stood nodding as he cooked our meal in front of us, entertaining the table with his knife skills and jokes.

"The usual?" Lizzy asked, looking at us. The main reason we came was for the Japanese beer. In agreement, Donna and I both nodded and Grandma ordered. After the waitress set out our drinks, we raised our glasses of Tsingtao, my mother's favorite, to toast her on Mother's Day. Every year got a little bit easier. Eventually, I wouldn't cry.

Lizzy started us off. "To a wonderful lady. She raised a wonderful daughter and made me a grandma."

"Thanks, Grandma."

Eyes twinkling, Donna lifted her glass. "To the best bridge partner." Donna always said they'd played bridge, but I'd never witnessed it. Now I wished I'd gotten to eye them from the top of the stairs. What a memory that would have been. I wondered what they'd talked about?

"To my muse." Just three words before I choked up a bit.

I could say my mom let her husband walk all over her, I could say she was depressed, but no one could ever say she didn't have the greatest taste.

"To Ingrid, my cooking student," Lizzy shook her head. We all chuckled. One Thanksgiving Mom tried deboning a turkey, which was way above her cooking skills. I wondered what concoctions we'd be eating today if she were alive?

Donna winked. "To Ingrid, the best martini maker." That's the toast that got me right in the chest and muddled my eyes. No longer me watching at the top of the stairs. A week before she died, Mom had sat me down in her living room and given me my first martini—with an olive. "All others," she'd said, "were silly."

I still have her cocktail shaker.

I'd like to make her a drink right now. If she sat here with us, would my mom know what was going on in my life? Would I have the guts to let her know?

Probably not.

That made me so sad. I'd never told Andrew I met him on the anniversary of my mother's death. I'd wanted my life to progress, and that meant getting married.

"To Ingrid." My eyes watered. "Even though she hated to ride a bike, she still taught me how."

Andrew and I had acted impetuously, marrying months after we met. But the aphrodisiac of falling for someone does that. Doesn't it?

He'd said we'd work on our goals together. Oh, had Andrew wooed me.

After we got married, he'd included me in his business, but then as things got rolling, he'd stopped. Maybe that was our problem? I no longer was included in that very important aspect of his life. He'd cut me out.

When he asked me to marry him, he said we made a good team.

I believed him.

Would Mom have understood any of that?

CHAPTER 7

TOVA

The next day I woke up early and went to the gym. I tried to stay busy on Mother's Day.

No word from Andrew, but I hadn't called either.

I wondered if he called his mom, who lived on a farm in North Dakota. Of course he did. He couldn't go a day with speaking to her.

I worked out and worked on the great divide growing between us. How come I hadn't done something sooner about us? To not be my dad and make my marriage work no matter what? The thought came crashing in as I drove home.

I entered the house from the garage. "Rocco," I yelled as I came in. He normally waited in the hall, tail knocking furiously on the wall.

He didn't come.

Had something happened? My heart knocked in my chest. I dropped my purse and keys on the floor and rushed down the hall. A closet door stood ajar. A box lay spilled out, splattered on the floor like a smashed egg. Was someone in the house? Billy? Frantic, I looked around. My ears strained for any evidence.

Rocco scratched at the sliding door. Relief washed through me for a quick second. He must have gotten out to the yard somehow. Had I been that spacey? My hands trembled on the door's handle as I went to let him in. That's when I saw it— jewelry scattered all over the floor of my studio.

I grabbed Rocco and ran for the front door.

———•———

NEIL

"Neil!" Tova yelled.

Opening the door, I found her there, pale with fear. "Someone broke into my house. It must be Billy. He could still be in there."

"Come on," I led her inside. She wore yoga pants. I wanted to groan when I saw her ass.

Not that I planned on telling her, but Wade had been following Billy; there was no way he could've been in her house.

"How do you know someone broke in?" She looked like she wanted to hit me with an idiot stick or sic Rocco on me. "Sorry."

"Billy did! A display was knocked over. Rocco'd been put outside. And a box that had been in my closet was all over the floor. Someone broke in."

"It's not Billy."

I called my contact at the St. Louis Park Police Department. Walked to my bedroom for my gun and tucked it into my pants. She stood in the middle of my kitchen, rubbing her forehead as I came back to the living room.

"You're bringing your gun?" *Amateurs.*

"Stay here. I'll come get you when it's clear."

Tova hunched down. Slow and methodical, she rubbed Rocco's ears. Simultaneously, she worried her lower lip, then told her dog, "Calm down." I read those bottled nerves on her face. Always so tough. Looking up at me, her dark blue eyes full of worry, she said, "Be careful, okay?"

A pang of want collided with need in my chest. "Lock up."

I ran over, studied her front door. She'd never closed it. No damage to the casing.

They'd probably come in the back. I drew my gun and moved down the hall. Two feet from the closet lay an overturned white banker's box. She was right. That hadn't fallen on its own. I reached up and into the closet. I could've easily grabbed it.

Did it fall because the intruder couldn't get their hands on it?

Tucking my gun in my pants, I moved to her studio. Half the contents of a big table lay all over the floor. I glanced at a desk area. Two huge computers still sat there, so was theft not a part of this?

I stopped in her bedroom. A drawer lay open and her underwear littered the floor. My eyes swept over a red pair. I'd bet my truck she wore those the day we met.

Ignore the hawkables, but mess with a lady's lingerie? Who the fuck would want to make *that* statement?

The jewelry box on her dresser looked untouched. I took out my knife and flipped it open, stirring what they'd left. Expensive-looking rings remained.

It didn't make sense. Valuables left alone. A box from a shelf and underwear? Did she have something in her drawer that they took?

Downstairs, I found a shattered pane in the double doors and the lock flipped. Easy in, easy out, and nothing looked odd. My eyes swept over the wall as I headed to the stairs. Then, shoulder-high—a smear of blood caught my eye. Just a dot, but fresh on the surface.

The idiot cut themselves, left me a present.

I got back upstairs to see that the police had arrived. Nate, my buddy, was at the door.

"Hey," I said, gesturing him in. I took a quick look over to my place. Tova stood at the window, her hand on the glass.

"You move into the neighborhood and you're already bringing trouble, huh?" he said with a grin on his tired face.

I looked over again and realized, *I can't help myself.* "The intruder left some blood behind."

He took out his notepad. "Where's the homeowner?"

"At my place."

His eyes darted around. "Where's the blood?"

"On the wall downstairs. Will you make sure it's not Billy or one of his cronies?" His questionable friends were dealers and wannabe thugs.

"Not a problem. Go get her. I need to ask her some questions."

Tova unlocked the door and held it open as soon as I started up my driveway. The sight of her waiting knocked the air out of me. It was bad enough when she'd told me to be safe.

"What happened?"

"Everything's fine. My friend at the police department has some questions for you. Did you go into your bedroom?"

She swallowed visibly. "No. Why?"

"Clothes on the floor." I went for vague, knowing she'd get worked up.

Her face paled and her arm flattened against her stomach. "Did they take any of my jewelry? My mother's ring is in there."

I took a step and reached to calm her. Her soft skin met my palm. "No. I checked. Typically, they take everything, and your jewelry box was still closed. I looked inside, and my guess is everything's still there."

Tova bent slightly at the waist and closed her eyes. "Thank god."

My hand slid down, and I grasped her hand. "Come on. Nate needs to ask you some questions."

Nate walked out of the studio as we came in. Tova glanced toward her bedroom, no doubt wondering what waited for her. Nate took the opportunity, looking her up and down. He raised an eyebrow to me, but he waited for me to introduce her.

"Tova, this is Nate. He has some questions for you."

"Of course."

"What time did you leave the house?" he asked.

"I'm pretty sure it was around eight."

"Where were you?"

"At the gym."

Tova gave her statement, and all the while she wore those damn yoga pants that hid nothing. She gestured to the closet or studio as she answered, giving me a glimpse of a black sports bra under her loose tank. I knew Nate—he enjoyed the view, too.

The crew from Hennepin County came, and she watched them head downstairs with big tackle boxes of evidence-collecting equipment.

"Neil said they were in my bedroom?"

Nate looked up from his notepad. "Yeah."

"Can I see?"

He slid a glance over to me and told her, "Let's finish here then you can." He tapped his notebook. "But you can't touch anything."

When Nate finally let her check out her bedroom, she paced in front of her panties, blushed, but her stance straightened. "Well, perfect. Everyone gets to see my underwear today."

"Did you have anything of value in the open drawer? Hidden?"

She blinked. "No." She peered into the jewelry box I'd left

open. "I want to take my mother's ring and also grab a chain."
She turned, asking, "Is that okay?"

I understood why this was important.

"Nothing was taken from there?" he asked.

"No."

"Yeah, that's fine."

She dove into the box, grabbed a gold chain, slipped a diamond ring onto it, and clasped it around her neck.

Nate and someone from the team walked her through the rest of the house. Tova kept repeating, "I don't think anything's been taken" and "Looks like some damage and a mess."

Yeah. Her brave face and briskness didn't fool me.

Damages: a swipe at a large display. Her stuff tossed here and there. The window on the door. I counted it all up as we walked room to room. Enough damage to definitely cause someone a panic. What a mess. I nearly missed her telling Nate the box they'd strewn in the hall belonged to Dickhead.

"It held some files," she admitted when he pressed her about it.

None of it made sense. When Nate asked her to call her husband, Tova said, "Oh! He's busy. Does he have to be bothered?"

What *could* he be bothered for, I wondered?

The bedroom bugged me. Her underwear all over the floor.

Nate left me alone with her. "You should call your husband." I wanted to know why she wouldn't. What if something from that box was missing?

Her face twisted up. "Why do that?"

"Why wouldn't you?"

She grumbled, took her hair down, re-twisted and clipped it. Did she know that was a tell she had when she evaded? Christ, she looked sexy with her hair up. But she looked even sexier with her mother's ring dipping into her cleavage. "Well, doesn't he need to know?"

"Trust me, he won't care."

What the fuck? Should I tell her she'd better not repeat that to Nate or he'd get suspicious? She got up from her chair, took out two glasses, and filled them with ice.

I took another approach. "They broke in through the basement door. You sure as hell can't stay here after what they did. You need a security system."

She set a defiant hand on her hip. "I'm staying." She glanced around. "It's my house, I run my business from here. It's Rocco's home."

Tova gave stubborn a run for its money, but egging her on wouldn't get me anywhere. "I can get a system in fast. And get the glass replaced." I'd carry her back to my house and lock her in my guest room if I had to. Either that or I'd tell her how freaked out this was making me, about her underwear strewn on the floor.

As she filled the second glass, her attitude fell away. I saw it in her eyes. "What kind of system?" *Thank Christ.*

"Sensors on your doors and windows. An alarm you set when you go to bed or leave. I could have it partially installed today and finish it tomorrow."

Her next question was, "How much will it cost?

Nothing, but no way she'd go for that. "Not much. I won't charge you labor."

"That's ridiculous."

No. Ridiculous was me giving it to her for free so I would know she was safe. Worst case scenario, it was Billy. He wanted to know who she was. But I'd learned that he'd figured out I wasn't married. And he knew his mystery woman wore a ring. Probably made his head hurt, trying to put the puzzle together.

He had vengeance on his mind, and the punk was persistent.

If it wasn't Billy she still needed an alarm. The panty raid was too odd.

Thinking on it, Tova stared down the hall.

"Blue Eyes, you can't stay here alone without it."

She blinked, then nodded. "Okay." *That's my girl.* She pointed her glass at me. "You're charging me full price. Can you finish it today, so my girls won't be bothered?"

Always the boss. "Sure." It would fucking kill me and I'd owe Charlie, Gabe, and Leland, but none of us had plans with our moms. We'd get it done. Tova agreeing to a security system felt like I won the fucking Super Bowl. *What kind of woman will stay in a house that's been broken into, as though it's no big deal?*

One of the investigators told me the blood hadn't come from the glass. It was from her studio. When they knocked over the display, the perp had sliced a finger.

—————•—————

Charlie showed up with everything. He and I started unloading his truck full of equipment as Gabe and Leland pulled in. Watching intently, Tova held the door for each trip we made.

I carried a box, wondering what she was thinking. "That's Gabe and Leland. They're here to help."

"Anyone else coming?"

I smiled down at her. "You want more?"

"That's not what I meant."

"Good 'cause that was a lot of favors to call in."

"Neil." Her face fell. "I'm sorry. I'm totally putting you out, ruining everyone's Mother's Day."

"Gorgeous, you aren't ruining my day." Leland set his

toolbox down and ran a hand over his shaved head as he smiled at her.

She looked him over. "If you say so, Dimples." *She flirted with everyone, not just me.*

Leland cleared his throat. "Call me Leland."

"I'm Tova," she said, eyes skating over his frame. It pissed me off.

"You made us brownies."

"I did! And after this…" She threw her hand out to her living room. "…I'll owe you more."

Enough. I bumped his shoulder. "Knock it off."

Gabe came through the door next. An unlit cigarette hung from his lip. "You're not smoking in here," I barked.

"I know." Gabe placed the cig behind his ear.

"Tova, Gabe does wiring and electrical, and Leland's my computer tech. Brothers."

"Thanks for helping." After Gabe and Leland had made spectacles of themselves grinning at her, she asked, "What's the plan?"

"Figuring out where the panel goes. Running wire. That'll take an hour or two." The guys had just come back in with their last load, including ladders. "We're also installing motion sensors. Does Rocco stay in your room at night?"

"Yes." The outline of her barely visible nipples drew my peripheral vision away from whatever Charlie was pointing at.

"Good, we won't worry about him setting anything off."

"I'm gonna owe you lots of brownies." She bit a fingernail.

"Yeah, you are." She sucked the tip of that finger into her mouth. My dick turned to stone. *Excellent.* I wanted to feel every part of her at once—her mouth, her hands, her body against mine. I cleared my throat. It didn't help.

At that moment, Reid's ugly mug walked in the front

door. I guess that's why Charlie pointed outside. "Tova, you remember Reid?" Charlie must've squealed.

"Hi, Reid." She glanced at me, her face screaming, *I thought you said no one else was coming,* but she was too nice to say it out loud. Reid watched us, uptight as always.

"You should clean up the mess in your studio, Blue Eyes." Her eyes got big and Charlie came over. "They took what they needed."

She glanced from me to Reid. "Okay."

—·—

TOVA

The frosted glass door to my studio closed behind me. I'm pretty sure Reid shut it.

I knelt down and plucked earrings from the pile first. Did Neil feel the need to constantly tell me what to do? Seriously, I needed to have a come-to-Jesus talk with him. If his friends weren't there helping me, I would've told him to cool it.

Neil's voice rose, then Reid's, as I reached for a necklace.

"Kind of bossy," Charlie said.

"He can't help but boss her," Reid replied. *Were they talking about me?*

Neil hissed, "Shut it."

"Well, he needs to help it." Even though I couldn't see them, I looked toward them. I didn't even pretend not to be listening. "Blue Eyes?" Reid said it like a snarly question.

As much as I liked it, I knew Neil shouldn't be calling me that in front of other people. Hell, he shouldn't be calling me that at all.

Neil spoke next, but I couldn't hear. It came out a low grumble, the tone angry.

"Don't care," Reid said. Did they really think I couldn't hear them? "Just 'cause your mom needed your help doesn't mean you go chasing trouble."

What? Our conversation from the night he moved in replayed in my head.

"Fuck off." Through the glass, Neil's larger form stalked off.

"Reid," came from Charlie. "You need to give him some slack." I wanted to defend Neil, too. From what, I didn't exactly know.

"He's pissed because he knows I'm right."

Charlie sighed. "This is different."

"Not the way I see it. Same problems, different woman." What the hell did that mean? "Don't want him making the same mistake, man." With that, Reid clapped Charlie on the shoulder. "I'm heading out. Keep an eye on him so he doesn't do anything stupid. I'll call if I hear anything."

What did Reid mean? And what did Neil's mom have to do with any of this?

———·———

NEIL

She came out of her office an hour later. We'd moved furniture, thick bundles of cables sat on ladders, toolboxes lay open, drills going, and Tova was having a non-verbal freak-out looking around.

I walked up behind her and laid a hand gently on her shoulder. "Don't worry, we're not going to destroy your house. We'll be done by tomorrow and everything will be back to normal. Okay?"

"Okay."

"There will be a few panels, but they'll be inconspicuous."

I slid my hand low on her back, happy to have an excuse to touch her. "Let's toss the ball to Rocco for a minute."

I led her outside and gave her the ball. She pitched it into the lawn. Charlie was wrong. I didn't boss her around. I gave suggestions. Reid, on the other hand, needed to mind his goddamn business. I wasn't trying to save Tova. I wasn't repeating my past with her. If anything, I wanted a future with her. But that's the thing wasn't it? Sometimes what you craved most, you didn't get to have. Life's irony. Because really, there are no happy endings.

"Did you call your husband? Is he gonna come home?"

She frowned. "I haven't called him, and he *won't* be coming back."

Why was she with him? "Can you stay with someone tonight?"

"Neil, I'm not leaving my house. It was just some kids. They didn't take anything."

Rocco brought the ball back. I held my hand out, and he came to me. I threw it clear over to my house.

Her hand went to her hip. She put her hand there when she wanted to tell me off. "Then who was it? Whoever they are, they're mad. You piss anyone off lately?"

"Besides Billy, no. Do I seem like I might piss someone off?"

Yeah, me.

She asked, "Are you sure it's not Billy?"

"I know it wasn't him. But, Blue Eyes, he could've sent someone." Dread slackened her face and I backpedalled. "I don't think he's involved, though. It's not his style."

"What is?"

Kidnapping and killing you slowly. "Not this." She frowned. I changed tactics. "Can you think of anything odd?"

"No." Rocco waited, looking up at her. She looked down at him, patted his head, and lobbed the ball.

"What was in the box?"

"Old papers of Andrew's. Research stuff."

"Can I have a look?" Knowing it could hold the key, I held my breath waiting for her answer.

"Sure."

CHAPTER 8

NEIL

Back inside, Leland, Gabe, and Charlie stood on ladders. They pulled wires through her ceiling, communicating with few efficient words. I considered installing cameras 'cause the underwear thing—that had stalker written all over it.

Gabe and Leland let their eyes follow her as she went to the kitchen, and they smiled at each other.

"Don't," I said, warning them as I followed her. They nodded, but I needed her to get out of that tank and those damn pants. "We're finishing this job today."

She brought me a refill on my glass of water.

"You should change."

Her cheeks turned pink. "How embarrassing. I probably smell."

No. "You don't smell. I figured you'd be more comfortable." She smelled fantastic, and if it'd just been the two of us, she could've stayed in that outfit all day.

Instead, she changed and made the crew cookies while I looked into all of her husband's files. I didn't find anything out of the ordinary.

She invited us all to an annual party she was having in a week. Charlie asked, "Will your husband be there?" I could tell he was just as curious about him as I was.

"Nope," she said. "He's back the next day." She has a party before her husband is home? I didn't get the two of them.

———•———

TOVA

I opened the cabinet and stretched on my tiptoes, reaching for the high shelf and my very girly, clear glass plate with pink iridescent glass loops along its edge. My mom's cookie plate. Now my cookie plate. A recurring dream flashed in my head.

We were standing in the kitchen, gathered around Lizzy's fancy mint-green mixer. My mom accidentally started up the machine on high, and it let out a poof of white, encasing us in a fine layer of flour. It looked as though someone had come by and sprinkled us with powdered sugar. We broke into laughter, and my mom grabbed my hand and danced me around the kitchen.

God, what was that all about?

Neil came up behind me. "I got it." His voice became a texture behind my ear, abrading the skin of my neck, and his hand fastened onto my waist. I'd made cookies to distract myself. I'd made cookies because Leland said I could make him something sweet. Neil's other hand claimed the fragile glass as his rock-solid body brushed me from shoulder to thigh. My butt nestled at his groin, and I stilled.

A heavy rush of anticipation tore through my veins and converged in my chest and sex.

Dust particles shimmered, fragments in the light. All too aware of his hand, I swallowed.

This wasn't good. Could two people get closer with clothes on?

Neil set down the plate, so slowly I briefly wondered if he was trying to stop time. Fingers grazed lightly over a sliver of my belly. I sucked in a gulp of air. *Not good at all.*

Recurring dreams, *now this.*

I could feel all of him, his heat, his size. "There you go, Blue Eyes."

Married people don't put themselves in this position. But I couldn't pull away.

I don't know how much time passed as he boxed me in. Seconds. Minutes. I wanted to lean into him, to reach up and pull his head toward my mouth. Kiss him as though life held no happiness without all of those wondrous things. But I didn't move. Then, ever so lightly, his right hand grazed mine, his thumb gliding along my pinky finger, explicitly innocent.

I swayed. *Like with that nickname*, I thought. *This isn't what married people do.*

Neil mumbled and pulled away. I held onto the counter for dear life, hoping to clear my head. Why did I keep doing this with him?

When I finally turned around, he sat on one of the stools, staring at the floor. I watched him work his jaw back and forth, then grab for the back of his neck.

Charlie, Gabe, and Leland came into the kitchen, ending our awkward silence. They tore into the cookies as though starved.

It would've been so easy to lean back against him, grab him by the neck, make something of it. But really, he'd helped get a plate down, that was all.

A glass guy Neil knew came over, and everyone but Neil left the kitchen. Depositing two cookies on a plate, I shoved the rest in a container. "Here, for you."

His eyebrows pulled together. That little vertical line

appeared in the inch of space between his eyes. I adored that line. "Keep them. You hardly have any left."

"Didn't you like them?"

He smiled. "They're great, Blue Eyes."

"Good. Then take them home." I put my hip against the counter. "I don't need them. I'm trying to get into my skinny jeans."

Why had I said that? I could already get into my skinny jeans. I glanced down and thought of my dream from earlier. Thoughts cycled through my mind, but this time they included off-limit orange berries. The crisp visual of those plump waxy orbs were etched in my core like the stamp of an inky tattoo.

I saw myself that day, on my way to the grocery store, and without reason, I'd followed a few signs for an open house. I'd been a ship, following a beacon to safety on a majestically gray day. Seeing that tree and the lush yard had brought me right back to the dreamlike days spent at Lizzy's house.

My mind cleared. Neil stood so close I could see light splintering through his gem-like eyes. He got my attention when the pads of his fingers nipped at the flesh, this time of my hip. "You can eat cookies." Like cold water, his touch was a shock.

"Please, Neil." I winced at the pleading tone of my voice. "Take the cookies." I didn't listen to his answer. Instead, I turned and washed my hands.

Another visual from the day I found my home invaded my thoughts. I'd stepped inside to see dated wallpaper, an old kitchen, and carpeting needing to be tossed, but it hadn't mattered. The yard was so wonderful, and the bones of the house so perfect. The house would help shape my future, and every fall, I'd gaze at those citrus-colored berries hanging in dense clusters of waxy, forbidden flesh and remember that simple childlike joy.

Enough!

I heard Neil's long sigh, but didn't bother looking. His footsteps followed.

Hours later, they finished everything, going home a little before midnight. They wouldn't need to come back, or so I thought.

———•———

Andrew texted me he was coming home in a few days. I had one last chance to make him give us another chance. The thing was, I didn't know if I wanted to put the effort in anymore. Time and distance faded my desire to hang on.

"Come on, Rocco, let's go outside." I opened the front door and stepped out rather ungracefully. My hair flew back, and Rocco raced the wind in front of me.

Cassie and Grace had taken me out earlier, and I'd overindulged on margaritas. I'd told them every separate thing on my mind: Andrew, my possible divorce, Lena at the DMV… What a week. Then the newspaper and the break-in. They'd gotten me thoroughly drunk and home safely. I'd figure out what the neighbors might think if, or when, any of them came and asked.

Out of habit, I looked over at Neil's. I hadn't seen him in days. Two black trucks were parked at the curb. Neither was his. The moon illuminated the road and a smattering of fireflies flashed in the darkness. I threw Rocco his green tennis ball. The heat had settled. My clothes no longer clung, but the wind lifted my skirt off my legs. Another storm.

Rocco trotted back with his ball. A vehicle's lights struck his tag. *Neil's truck.* A flash from the metal glared in my eyes.

My skirt whirled up off my legs. I shielded my eyes with

one hand and patted my skirt down with the other as Neil pulled his Yukon up next to me.

Vanity caused me to run my fingers through my hair and tame the mass—or mess, depending on the wind damage.

He lowered his window. "Hi."

"Hi." I peered in. "Hey, Charlie."

Charlie smiled. "Hey, Betty Crocker." Too cute. I liked Neil's friends.

"That's funny." I cocked my hand on my hip for Neil's benefit, though I kept my eyes on Charlie. Who wouldn't want to feed this one something sweet? "Did you enjoy the treats?"

"I did. You make a mean cookie."

"Thanks."

The back driver's side window eased down. "Hi, Tova, I'm Wade."

"Hi, Wade." The cut of his cheekbones showed in a play of shadows and light.

"I liked them, too."

"Great."

He peered at the tennis ball. "You hopin' to start a game out here?" He had a pretty mouth for a man.

"You wanna play?"

He glanced down my body. "I could play—with you." He gave me a hot look that said, *And I'd like it.*

Trying to keep a straight face was useless. I laughed. "I'm sure you could." My sixth sense told me he flirted with every woman he met. Neil cleared his throat, switched off the truck, and stepped out. He wore a dress shirt and scowl.

"What were you up to tonight?" I asked the group but kept my eyes on Neil. The wind carried his scent toward me. I breathed him in, hoping no one saw that.

"No good," Wade answered.

I whipped around a bit unsteady. "I'm not surprised."

Again, Neil cleared his throat. "Blue Eyes, why throw the ball around for Rocco at eleven at night? In heels and all?"

"You like?" I performed a twirl and my skirt whirled out. Surely they'd get a kick out of this.

Coming back to face them, I spied one loose curl lying perilously close to Neil's narrowed eyes.

"I just got home. Been gone since late this afternoon. We're out here to get Rocco's wiggles out."

Neil studied me. "His wiggles out?"

"Yes. He needed to get the wiggles out."

From behind him, Wade added, "We should've joined you."

I twisted. "It would *not* have been fun." I meant that. Neil listening to me whine to the girls about my marriage imploding—talk about a barrel of monkeys.

Behind me, Wade laughed. Neil latched onto my hand, grabbing the ball and throwing it clear over to his house. He could've been a professional ball player with that rocket launch.

"Jeez, Neil." For a second, my body was in control instead of my brain. I went over, reached out, and brushed the lock of hair away from his eyes. My hand dropped to his shoulder. The overwhelming need to touch him took over, and my hand drifted down his arm and stopped on the solid muscle of his bicep. Thick and hard, it twitched under my hold. I slurred my speech, even though I felt every word I said, "Thanks again for everything the other day."

"Are you drunk?" he whispered.

"Most definitely." I smiled. "You coming tomorrow?"

"Yes." His hands went to his pockets.

"Did you invite Wade?"

His eyes flared. I had the uneasy feeling he wanted to say more. "Yeah…"

I looked to Charlie and Wade. "It starts at eight."

"We'll be there," Wade assured me, a hint of a laugh as he said it.

"Great. Well, I should go. Rocco needs his beauty sleep. It was nice to meet you, Wade." I waved. "Bye, Charlie. Next time I see you, I'll be sure to wear my apron." I looked at Neil last. *Oh, god.* "Sleep well."

I wove my way to the door and shifted to usher Rocco in. The guys may have been watching. When I looked back, Neil whipped around, took a step toward Wade, clutched the doorframe, and said something low that I missed.

"'Night," I called out.

Neil twisted. "Set your alarm. Don't forget."

"Aye aye, Captain."

NEIL

I slammed the door. Wanted to kick Wade's ass for looking at Tova like he wanted to fuck her.

"Nothing's going on between you two?" Wade asked again as he got out of my truck.

"No." Wade had his own problems. Why did he need to dig into mine?

"You sure don't act like *nothing's* going on. All I said was I wanted her number."

Charlie scratched his chin but couldn't hide a grin. "Wade, why yank his chain?"

Wade threw his arm out in my direction. "'Cause look at him. He's pissed. Neil's never pissed, especially over women."

"You might be right." Charlie looked me over.

"You realize you stared at her the entire time we were out there, right?" Wade poked at me.

I wanted to punch the both of 'em. Next time we got some

shitty job, those two were gonna be on it. I took out beers and set them on the counter. "Take one and shut up."

Wade twisted the top off his. "Please tell me she doesn't dress in skirts like that all the time. 'Cause if she does, I'm moving in."

That goddamn, up-to-no-good grin on her face. She was drunk. I slammed my bottle down. Suds bubbled over my hand. "No, she does not wear skirts like that all the time."

Wade glanced at the mess on my hand. "You should call Brooke." Charlie laughed.

I never should have told him. "Christ, why do that?"

Wade leaned against the counter. "'Cause, *Captain,* you need to get laid."

"Like you should talk." Charlie tipped his bottle back.

Why'd Tova touch my hair? Brush it out of my eyes? I fought not to touch her. Not to grab those fingers gliding across my skin. I dreamt of getting hair out of her face all the time. And then she goes and does it to me.

I'd never forget how she looked. That red skirt moving around her mile-high legs. Shorts and the yoga pants were one thing, but that red skirt... Fuck me, I wondered what she wore underneath? Thinking that redirected my brain to the scattered underwear from the break-in, a train of thought where one thing leads to another.

Wade knocked the counter with his knuckles. "See, Charlie? Lost in space."

———◆———

I'd flipped the covers back on the bed more than half an hour ago. I slept for shit, with all the images of Tova and her husband sharing a bed again. In two days, he'd be stripping off her clothes and I'd be getting shit-faced drunk. The dickhead had appeared smug in their wedding photos. A good-looking hardass. That's exactly what he looked like. A hardass.

I grabbed my jump rope, but the constant slap of it on concrete sounded like a good fucking. I dropped it.

Dickhead never smiled in any of those pictures lining Tova's hallway. Everyone else smiled in the photographs—her family, her friends—but not the dickhead. Nope, just a smug, pleased-as-shit face staring back at you.

I hit my punching bag. The smug bastard should be fucking thrilled. What could possibly make him grumpy?

She never said much, other than the few offhand remarks that didn't flatter him. There must be something. Why would she stay?

Every blow to the bag did nothing. I switched to cross punches and reached some satisfaction when my arms started burning.

He was never home. She didn't need him. What did he offer? Christ, I hoped it wasn't sex. My arms exploded against the bag with harder crosses. I kept at it until sweat poured off me.

Borrowed time had ended. I needed to stay away from her. Only one problem with that: I didn't know how.

———•———

TOVA

I'd dreamed of Neil again. Getting out of bed, I turned off the alarm and opened all my windows. All three of my apple trees were in bloom. Pink blossoms coated the dark limbs, making them sag. The sweet scent drifting off the branches wafted toward me.

Vivid memories of my mother doing the same came at

me in a barrage. Our house had always smelled of baking bread, and that crisp breeze would blow in, mixing with the yeast, making a memory. On days like that, we'd head to the downtown farmer's market. Going to Minneapolis held its own delight. Growing up in a suburb and then traveling to the heart of the city with all of its grit and graffiti left me wide-eyed and feeling a bit sophisticated.

Making a day of it, we'd plan dinners and sample produce. I loved every minute.

It had disappeared too fast.

Waves of grief took over as I showered, tears pouring out of me and down the drain. I wish I'd grabbed one last hug, one last morning picking vegetables. But wishing was hopeless. It would never happen; it would never come.

And tomorrow, Andrew most likely would be gone, every last bit of him.

———•———

Cassie and I were in the bathroom, freshening our makeup before everyone came over.

Grace came in from changing. "How are you doing?"

I leaned against the counter and lowered my mascara wand. I'd been saying this all morning. "I'm okay."

She picked up my left hand. "When did you take it off?"

I set the mascara down, then rubbed at the ring's tan line and the slight indention on my finger. "This morning."

"Don't think about it tonight, okay?"

"Wasn't planning to."

"Good." Grace had changed into a yellow sleeveless dress. It didn't appear too dressy, but considering I expected we'd end up outside by the bonfire, it might be. She eyed me for a second. "Don't worry. I have a change of clothes and sensible shoes in my bag."

"To hell with sensible shoes, I'm wearing heels tonight," Cassie said.

———·———

Guests started arriving. I stood next to the dining room table. "How are you doing, Chris?"

"Great, now that I see you made steak."

Ann smacked him on the arm as he stalked the table like a hungry tiger.

We hung around my long farm table, so heavy it had taken four men to carry in. Vases of lush white peonies sat on the surface, along with tea lights.

"Do you need me to do anything?" Chris asked, picking up a steak bite and tossing it in his mouth.

"No, all is good."

"God, these are good, Tova," he said through a full mouth.

Ann turned to me. "We should've come over earlier."

"We had it under control." I motioned to the kitchen. "The two of you should grab a drink."

"Good idea," Chris replied and took Ann's hand, leading her away.

People gathered in different parts of the house. Some lingered over food in the dining room, a few engaged in a heated discussion on baseball in the kitchen, and a bunch of ladies discussed shoes in my living room.

I'd switched the music to Grace Potter and the Nocturnals as Neil came through the front door, and damn if our eyes didn't meet and hold. I swallowed and took in his rolled-up sleeves, then his shorter curls. Ridiculously sexy, he wore dark jeans and a black, long-sleeved dress shirt that opened at the throat. He'd gotten a haircut. It didn't fall over his collar anymore. As usual, though, I wanted to run my fingers through it.

I started moving toward him. "Neil?" Cassie asked from behind me.

Charlie stepped into the foyer, a dimple appearing on both cheeks. When Wade came in, I swear I heard Grace moan from somewhere to the left. Both of my friends had followed me. Last night I'd gawked at Wade from the shoulders up. Tonight I could see from the waist down. I appreciated him just as much.

"Hi, guys," I said. "Glad you could make it."

I hugged Neil. I don't know why I chose that moment to, but I did.

His arms went around my waist. "Hi." His voice flowed into my ear.

My pulse fluttered, as light as paper lifted by wind. I stepped back. But he reached out, fingered a few strands by my ear. "Haven't seen it straight before."

Charlie cleared his throat. "How are things, Crocker?"

"I'm good. How are you, Brownie Boy?"

"What's this? No apron?" Charlie reached for my wrist, then stopped, laughing.

I smiled. "Give me time, give me time." Cassie settled on one side of me, Grace on the other.

Moving over to Wade, Charlie gave me a smirk. "Do I get a hug?"

"Of course. I want to introduce you. Guys, these are my two best friends. Cassie runs her own graphic design business." I laid my hand on her shoulder. Then I turned to Gracie. "Grace is in charge of fundraising for the local chapter of Habitat for Humanity. Ladies, this is Neil, my new neighbor, and *his* friends, Charlie and Wade. Charlie likes my brownies, and Wade's a mischief-maker."

Charlie and Wade laughed, along with everyone else. I hoped it'd cracked the ice. "Come on, let's get a drink." I turned and led them into the kitchen. Grace whispered, "I like mischief."

The guys grabbed beers from the iced-down sink, and we all leaned against the counters.

"So how do you all know each other?" Grace asked after a sip of wine.

Wade spoke first. "We've known each other for years. Neil and I grew up together. We met when he broke a kid's nose for me. Charlie and Neil met at a gun training class."

"Gun training class?"

Neil took a long pull on his beer, and I watched, fixated on his throat. He broke a kid's nose? That didn't sound nice.

Charlie answered Grace. "Yeah, the kind for picking off people from far away." Sniper training? That didn't sound nice either. He asked Cassie, "How do the three of you know each other?"

"Tova and I were roommates." Cassie set her glass down. "In college. Grace roomed next to us. We've been bubbas ever since."

"Bubbas," Wade murmured with a wicked grin.

"Bubbas," Grace proudly confirmed. "Friends."

CHAPTER 9

TOVA

Wade aimed a grin at Grace. "I've met some bubbas, and the three of you don't look a thing like them."

Grace smiled. "So you're a private investigator, too?"

Wade took long lingering look before another drink. "Yep."

"What does that mean?" Grace looked away for a second.

Wade did a fuller sweep down her body. "We investigate. Or we're retained by one-half of a couple when they suspect the other's cheating."

"What do you do?" Cassie asked.

"I'm more or less a bounty hunter, and Charlie here—" Wade whacked Charlie's arm. "—he's an investigator, working with our corporate clients."

Grace shifted her hair back. "Interesting." When her eyes met Wade, he winked and she blushed.

He zeroed in on her pink cheeks and murmured, "Not as interesting as some things."

———•———

A little while later, Cassie tugged us into my bedroom and shut the door. "You got some explaining to do," she said to me over her shoulder. She marched us into the bathroom. "And I know Grace's knickers are in a twist over Wade."

"Cassie," Grace admonished and frowned.

"Don't look at me like that. He hadn't even said a word, and you were drooling. Then he spoke, and I noticed *you* about fell over."

Grace fussed at her hair. "I did not almost fall over."

"There are more of them," I announced.

Their eyes cut to me. Cassie blinked a few times. "There's more of them," she repeated.

"Yep, Neil's best friend Reid. Scary hot. As in, he could growl at a pit bull, make it fall over and beg for mercy. I think he's coming later. Then there are the two brothers that helped put in my security system. Leland and Gabe. They're so devilishly cute and sexy, you kind of just wanna pinch 'em."

Cassie's eyes lit up. "I need to hang out at Neil's house."

"No lie," Grace said.

Cassie adjusted her cleavage. "Maybe I need to find myself in some trouble so I can hire a PI." Giggles ensued, and my cheeks hurt from laughing. "Damn it's good to hear you laugh," Cassie said. Her tone got serious. "You realize you and Neil have off-the-charts chemistry." Her attention turned to Grace. "You agree?"

"Absolutely," Grace confirmed.

Cassie fiddled with her lipstick. "Nothing's been going on with the two of you, has it?"

"No." Did I believe that?

Cassie opened the door. "Just checking."

We left the confines of the bathroom, and I went in search of a cold drink. Neil was pulling the top off my favorite beer. He tilted his head. "Want it?"

"Yes, please." We drifted toward the dining room and

ended up alone. He gazed at me with a warm smile. My belly fluttered in response.

"Thanks for inviting us tonight."

"That sounds like an exit statement."

He shook his head. "No. I couldn't pull the guys out of here if I tried."

"Really?"

Neil's eyes went to Grace and Wade, and mine followed. "Yeah."

Gracie laughed and flashed her incredible smile at Wade. He hung on every word falling from her mouth. Cassie and I gave each other a knowing smile from across the room. Grace hadn't been on a real date for months, and even worse than that, her bed had been empty for a year.

"I think you might be right," I told Neil. "I wanted to start the bonfire, but we should stay inside."

"The guys and I will get the fire going. You don't need to get your hands dirty."

My fire-making palm went to my hip. "That's twice you've made some comment about that. Since when do you think I don't like getting dirty?" *Here I go again.* I changed tack. "Never mind. Let's get something to eat and sit down. I need to get off my feet."

Neil focused on my nude slingbacks. "Okay." His eyes climbed upward slowly, not caring that I saw him getting his fill. My pulse skittered and took off. Wondering if my friends or neighbors were watching, I nearly stopped him, then decided they couldn't care less what Neil and I were up to. When his eyes met mine, he held me, tethered.

I gazed at his throat and the hollow of skin at the base of his neck. My tongue wanted to dip into the space and taste him. Then Rocco barked and bolted for the front door.

Andrew walked into the foyer with his suitcase in tow.

Stunned, I set my plate down. Andrew never came home early. Or unannounced. He hadn't shaved, and his skinny tie sagged at the neck. He glanced around, trying to figure out what he'd walked into. From the hard line of his mouth, I'd say he'd forgotten about the party. Did his coming home a day early mean something?

With the heat of everyone's eyes on my back, I crossed the living room to the foyer.

"Hi." I stopped a few feet from him. His face, hard and blank, held no warmth. *Probably not.* The only thing racing in my head was: I hope he doesn't kiss me in front of Neil.

He cocked his head to the side, and his eyes traveled the length of me. "You actually look hot tonight," he whispered.

My head whipped back. *I* actually *look hot tonight? What the fuck?* Anger and tears warred within me. I swallowed my tongue, not wanting to make a scene with everyone watching… with Neil watching.

My chest rose and fell. It required all of my fortitude not to tear into him for saying something so cruel. My fingers rolled into a fist.

Did he want to rile me up? He slipped on a fake smile, turned, and lifted his head to the guys in the kitchen. "Hi, everyone," he shouted. The crowd hollered their greetings, and without another word, he walked away from me.

What did I ever see in him?

He grumbled to Chris, "I just need to get settled after the long drive, and I need a beer." Chris handed him a bottle from the ice. The men gathered around him, his return like a hero back from war, something to be celebrated, certainly not scrutinized. Which I was doing. Which I could feel Neil doing from across the room. I didn't dare look at him.

Andrew wiped his beer off with a paper towel, said more of his greetings, and headed toward the master. The wheels of his suitcase clicked on the wood floor, growing louder instead of dying, the unforgettable click-clack resonating in my ears. I heard those wheels in my sleep. Those wheels came and went. Not that I was sad about it, but after the weekend, I'd never hear them again.

———•———

"When are all of these people leaving so I can get some sleep?" Andrew whispered in my ear. He'd finally left the confines of the bedroom and snuck up behind me.

I smiled brightly. "It'll be hours."

He glared and went to get a plate of food.

We were acting like children around one another, as though we'd crossed a threshold and were trapped into being the kind of people I thought we'd never become.

Andrew stood next to me. He ate, drank, and texted, but couldn't manage to talk to me. He accepted a call, stepped onto the deck to answer, then abruptly turned coarse and went into the garage for privacy. *Who takes phone calls for work at this hour?*

My feet led me to the studio. My guests were all doing fine without me. Cutting lengths of rawhide, I hovered over some trays of beautiful ribbon and leather.

"Is this a party of one?" Neil asked quietly and closed the glass door.

I did my best to smile. "No." I snapped the scissors at him a few times. "Have you come to rescue me?"

He came right up to me, his chest connected with my shoulder. He gazed into my eyes. "Do you need to be rescued?"

"Yes," I answered honestly.

He leaned forward, a substantial portion of his chest grazing my arm. He lifted a piece of red silk from the puddle below my hands, held it up, and studied it. With deliberate purpose, he guided the ribbon over my wrist and forearm, lighting my skin on fire. He lit everything in me on fire.

I burned and fought not to close my eyes. Goosebumps on my flesh rose to the surface. He trailed the ribbon up my arm, into the hollow at my elbow, and back toward my fingers. It made me feel naked.

Needing to know his intentions, I glanced at him. His mouth opened and he wet his lips. I wondered what his tongue would feel like. With rapt attention, he watched the slide of silk along the ivory part of my arm. His eyes, dark and needy, cut to mine. They fell to my mouth. He must sense my own desire. How could he not? I'd never been more aroused.

Struck with a punch of clawing need, I dropped the scissors and grabbed a long scrap of leather. I captured his wrist, brought it toward me, and flipped it palm up. "Hold still."

Surreptitiously, I tucked the soft piece of rawhide under his outstretched hand. My fingertips grazed the tender flesh on the back of his wrist. I couldn't help but wonder if he would make a sound if I kissed him there. Or passed my tongue over the blue veins that fought under his skin.

My pale hands contrasted against his darker olive tan. Concentrating as though threading a needle, I tied a slipknot, then held his arm for a second, not saying anything and definitely not wanting to let go. Instead, I wanted to push myself forward, collide with his chest and mouth, and let Neil's arms wrap around me.

"Why did you break that kid's nose?" I asked, needing a distraction.

"A bully," Neil rasped. I was getting to him. "Messing with Wade. I stepped in one afternoon. The kid had me in a hold. I whipped my head back and stomped on his foot at the same time."

I tied the last knot in the leather and looked up. "Why stomp on his foot?"

Neil grinned. "Stunned him. It also helped so he couldn't chase after me." *Wise.*

"You can take it off if you want." I showed him how the band adjusted and pulled it loose. "See?"

I watched his mouth as he opened it. "Tighten it."

I'd never touched, much less kissed his mouth, but I swear I knew the texture of his lips from staring. Neil focused on my face. A potent combination of alcohol and longing passed between us.

"Look who we found," Charlie said, opening the door to the studio, breaking the cocoon we'd wrapped ourselves in. Charlie's step faltered in the doorway, and he studied us with a question in his eyes.

With a heavy dose of lust and madness, my heart hammered in my chest.

Over Charlie's shoulder stood Reid. He narrowed in on our hands. I dropped my arms and stepped back.

Neil exhaled audibly, leaning against the table with a strange grin as he told Reid, "You made it."

"Yeah. Finished up early." He looked plainly from Neil to me.

"Hi, Reid. Did you meet everyone?"

Reid's narrowed eyes made me feel guilty of a sin. "Yeah."

"Tova's been making jewelry since college." Cassie came in, guiding more people into the large room.

"Yes, but technically I started before that," I added. A

minute longer, alone in the studio, and I would've kissed Neil. I would've kissed him with a house full of guests, my husband nearby, and with no remorse.

Cassie looked from me to Neil, then Reid. "Hey, everyone, I forgot about the Jell-O shots, back it on out." She held her hands out and reversed out of the room, giving me a silent I'm-saving-your-ass look.

I glanced at Neil. He focused on his bound wrist. Then he pointed at my two workbenches. "What's all of that?"

"That's where Reva and I make the metal parts we use on my higher-end pieces."

Reid motioned to my acetylene tank, doubtful. "So you know how to use this torch?" He arched an eyebrow at me.

"Do you want me to prove it?"

"Sure." Reid and Neil answered in unison.

I slipped on my heavy, canvas apron. "Tell Charlie I'm finally in an apron," I said to Reid. He took a step closer and glared at me, or maybe it was just his normal scowl. Kind of hard to tell with his fist-like face. Then I remembered he hadn't been there for the joke. *Damn it.* When my eyes slid to Neil, a pleased grin graced his mouth.

"I'm surprised you came," Neil said to Reid.

"I gotta keep an eye on you. Wouldn't want you getting into trouble."

Boy, that was subtle. I dropped a piece of sterling into my pickle pot.

While the silver cleaned in the acid, I textured a small piece of copper on my bench block. I got my work area ready with a heat-resistant piece of sheet metal and two well-worn kiln bricks. I looked up at Reid's nearly bald head. "You and Neil better step back. I wouldn't want to singe your presumptions."

Neil laughed but not Reid, who, on the whole, seemed

offended by me. *What's new?*

Without thinking, I turned on the tank and winked at Neil. Blue as the hottest part of the flame, his eyes flashed.

Something about Reid watching me with a laser-like gaze made me nervous. I braced my arms against my sides so they wouldn't tremble. Seconds later, the pieces joined.

I attached a charm to a key ring and handed it to Neil. "You can throw your new house keys on there."

We filed out and went into the kitchen. Reid grabbed a fresh beer, and Charlie said, "I'll start the bonfire."

The house emptied as Cassie waved marshmallows in the air and led everyone to the backyard.

Andrew was back in the bedroom. Needing a minute, I didn't follow everyone outside. Instead, I drank wine and sat on the couch. The alcohol hit too fast, and I closed my eyes. A hand grazed my shoulder, near my neck. My eyes popped open.

"Is he always like this? Ignoring you and on the phone?" Neil asked from behind me. He sounded angry.

Still tingling from the alcohol, I was slow to absorb what he'd asked. *Andrew? He barely tolerates me.* I shifted.

He rounded the sofa. "Does he have business calls this late all the time? It's ridiculous." Neil sat across from me and clenched his hands. His eyes, persistent, held mine. My subconscious flashed on my dad's often irate and disappointed face. Neil had that look.

"He hasn't seen you in weeks. And your house was broken into."

I never did tell Andrew about that.

I didn't think anyone could see the farce playing out between Andrew and myself, but of course, Neil would notice. I couldn't look him in the eye. He stayed silent; the question lay stagnant between us. I suppose I should've been outraged he'd ask such an intrusive question and expect a reply, but I couldn't garner that emotion.

From the depths of my belly, the words poured out of me. "He's made an art form out of ignoring me." I looked up to see Neil's jaw tick. Liquor would fix this. "I need another drink. You want one?" I got up, not paying attention to whether he answered, and plopped some ice into a tumbler, along with a liberal amount of whiskey.

He followed. "How long?"

"More than half our marriage."

Neil's fury spiraled in the air, but the click of shoes on the hardwood ended that conversation.

Andrew sauntered into the kitchen and took a beer. Before opening it, he wiped it off. "Hello," he said to Neil.

Had he heard our conversation? Did it matter? I decided I didn't care.

He stepped toward Neil and offered his hand. "Andrew."

Neil simultaneously coughed into his broad palm.

I wanted to cackle. His clever little tactic to avoid shaking hands had to be the most poignantly funny thing I'd ever witnessed. Especially since he didn't know what a germaphobe Andrew could be.

Neil tipped his chin up in that very male greeting. "Neil," he acknowledged.

Andrew tucked his arm around my waist and pulled me toward him. "How do you know my lovely wife?"

Twisting out of the hold, I poured another inch of whiskey.

"I'm your new neighbor."

I peered at Neil. Pure frustration glimmered across his face. I swallowed half of what I'd poured.

"Oh? Which house?"

Neil's eyes tapered. "The brown one across the court."

Andrew's phone buzzed, then vibrated. He drew it from his pocket and glanced at the screen. "I need to grab this, princess. Work." He strode away, muttering something to whoever was on the line.

Work, my ass! No one does business at this hour. I'd be stupid to think that's what the call was about. If it was business, he wouldn't need to run away.

Embarrassed, I opened the pantry door. This must be how my mom had felt. "I'm gonna grab another bag of marshmallows. Would you take them out to Cassie?" I asked. "Tell her I'll be down in a bit."

I needed him to skedaddle so he wouldn't hear me going nuclear. Instead, Neil surprised me when he shut the pantry door behind us. He took two paces and caged me with his arms. His head came down, eyes piercing. "What did he say when he came home?"

"What?"

"I saw your face. What did Dickhead say?"

Anger swelled in my belly. I nudged at his arm. "Please take the marshmallows."

His eyebrows slammed together. "He didn't kiss you. What did he say?" He asked as if I had no choice but to answer him.

I couldn't stifle my temper. "Why do you care? I take it you haven't seen Brooke lately, huh?" As soon as the words spilled, I wanted to run.

His head yanked back. "You've got to be shittin' me. Why do you think I care?"

"I have no idea." The hoity-toity was unmistakable in my tone.

His body moved closer. "He hasn't seen you in weeks and he doesn't kiss you?"

My grip on the shelf behind me unlocked, and my palms landed on his chest. I pushed at him. "You don't know what's going on."

Neil's jaw worked back and forth. "I have a clue, but you don't." Considering Andrew had been on his phone all night, I had an idea. It certainly couldn't be about work.

Neil stared at my mouth. "I'd kiss you, Tova." His words lost their earlier bite. Instead, they sounded pained.

Tears welled in my eyes. I knew he'd kiss me, just like I knew I'd kiss him. "Then why don't you?"

He grabbed both of my hands from his chest. His thumb and index finger rubbed, probing where my ring should be. Bewildered, he looked down, finding it bare. A question furrowed his brow.

He stepped back, ran his hands through his hair before dropping them to his sides. We stared at each other. My blood raced through veins suddenly too small to hold everything I felt for him.

The vulnerability in his eyes crushed me.

CHAPTER 10

TOVA

So what if I was drunk? I took a step, raised my hands to his chest. He felt better than I thought he would. "Just kiss me, Neil," I whispered against his neck.

Maybe he shifted—or maybe I did—but either way, my lips made contact with his ear. It was warm and smooth, like I imagined his mouth would feel. He let out a stuttering whoosh of air. The sound became the drug I wanted to get high on.

I glanced at his closed eyes. His thick lashes lay on his cheeks. He held so still I thought he'd willed his mind from his body.

I leaned my head against his clavicle and breathed him in, my arms around his shoulders. "How come you smell so good?" *How come he* felt *so good?*

"Christ," he said softly. He stepped back, making me lose my hold, and tilted his head toward my ceiling. "You're drunk."

"Not that drunk."

His head came down, and he grasped my wrists. "Tova, I can't do this. You're drunk, and you're—"

"No, I'm not." He was gonna say *married*, and in that second, I decided to tell him. I needed to tell him so bad it throbbed.

He dropped my hands and spun on his heels, opening the door. "No, Tova."

My voice never came as he left. My fist slammed down on the kitchen island. Steps weaving, I marched down the hall on a mission. Maybe I was drunk. A border crossed, a threshold broken, the door bounced off the rubber stopper and nearly slapped me when I threw it open.

Andrew sat on the edge of the bed. "I gotta go," he said into the phone and hung up.

"Who's that?"

"A client."

"Really? It's eleven at night."

"Yes, Tova. Really."

He thinks I'm dumber than a box of rocks. "Yeah. Sure. I believe you."

He slipped his phone into a pocket. "Don't then. When are you going to kick all of these people out? I want to get some sleep."

He was the one who came back a day early. "You're such a prick. It's one night. Could you *not* humiliate me?" *I'm not gonna cry.* Needing to get away from him, I stomped from the room.

Two steps into the hall, and a hand bit into my shoulder and spun me around. Andrew held me against the wall. "Don't you ever talk to me like that!" Both of his hands dug into my biceps. "Do you understand?"

"Let. Me. Go."

Out of the corner of my eye, Charlie came at us. "Get your hands off her."

The hall charged with a volcanic hum. Andrew dropped his hands as though my flesh burned white-hot.

Charlie's eyes flickered to Andrew and back to me. "You

all right?"

I nodded. "Yes."

"Everything's fine," Andrew said. He was making light of the situation, trying to woo Charlie. He did that with everyone. "Nothing for you to worry about, friend."

Charlie glared. His chest expanded, and his body grew larger as he got closer. "I'm not your friend. My friends don't toss their wives against walls."

Andrew's tongue passed over his upper teeth. My humiliation kicked in. "Get the hell out of my house, Andrew."

"I was out of hand," Andrew allowed. "I'm sorry."

"You're packing up tomorrow. You're not staying another night."

"Wasn't planning on it." He turned and went into the bedroom, coming out with his bag a minute later. "I'll be back in the morning."

Charlie and I watched from the kitchen as Andrew steered his way to the garage door with his bag. "What's this?" he asked, pointing to the alarm panel.

"Someone broke in."

"When?"

"It doesn't matter, Andrew, nothing was taken. Just go."

He slammed the door, marking the night with an exclamation point. My shoulders slumped, and I dropped my head. I started to sway.

Charlie tagged me at the waist. "He hurt you?"

"I'm okay."

"Sure you are."

"I walked away from him."

"Is that all? No big deal then. Maybe we should invite him back."

"Charlie…"

"Don't." He motioned to a stool at the island. "Sit down. You need some water. You've had enough to drink tonight."

I scowled, but he never saw it. He got a glass filled and handed it to me. Then he poured himself a large shot of my best whiskey.

"I'm surprised I didn't beat the shit out of him." My eyes went wide as Charlie emptied the glass in one gulp. "Don't look stunned—he grabbed you. Pushed you."

"Charlie…"

"Don't try and explain." He pressed his fingers into his forehead. "What the hell, Tova? The only reason I didn't clock him was because I figured you're too smart to put up with that shit." He looked directly at me. "Please tell me you're too smart."

"Never, Charlie." Andrew might be an ass, but… "He's never done anything like that before."

"Thank god. Otherwise, I would've hated myself. *And* Neil would've kicked my ass. I mean, really. Kicked. My. Ass." His body relaxed and he shook his blond head. "I'll go and get Cassie and Grace."

When did my life start looking like a soap opera? With Grace on her heels, Cassie tore into the kitchen. "What's going on? Charlie just said to get our butts up here."

I bit the inside of my lip, trying to figure out how to put it. "Andrew and I got into it. He grabbed me and kind of held me against the wall. Charlie walked right into it."

"Tova." Grace's mouth dropped open.

Cassie eyed the hallway. "That asshole. Where is he?"

"I kicked him out."

"Good," they said in unison.

Grace took my arm, making me get up. "Come on." She led the way to my room. "I'll stay here. I've got a change of clothes."

I said it all the way down the hall, but they didn't listen. "He's gone, I'm fine. Tomorrow he's coming to get his stuff."

Cassie motioned for me to sit on the bed. "Where did he grab you?"

"My arms. I'm fine."

"I'm going to kill him the next time I see his pompous ass," Cassie stated.

Grace sat next to us. "What happened?"

I went over the details and now the expletives flew.

A knock interrupted us, and Charlie said, "Everyone's gone. I put out the bonfire. And as much as I hate saying this to three beautiful women on a bed, but you need to get up 'cause I'm tired."

We all went to various parts of the house and finished cleaning. Cassie and I dealt with leftovers, Grace and Wade got my furniture back together, and Charlie did god-knows-what.

"You could also come stay with me," Grace said, coming up next to me.

"I'll be fine. They changed the locks."

"Where did where Neil and Reid go?" Cassie asked.

"I have no idea."

"I agree with Grace," Cassie butted in. "You should stay at her place or mine. I'll sleep on the sofa."

"I'm staying here."

"Okay, I'll stay with you," Cassie stated.

Grr. "No."

Charlie joined us. "Can I talk to you?" His look told me that *no* wasn't an option.

"Sure." I wanted a reprieve.

He led the way to the foyer. "You're not staying here tonight."

"Yes, I am, Charlie. It's my house, not his. I won't leave. And for god's sake, you just put in an alarm system."

He frowned. "Where's your phone?"

"In my pocket."

"Good, keep it there." Rocco scratched at the front door. I let him out and threw him a ball. All the lights were out at Neil's. Not that I looked. "Set your alarm. I pushed the chair that's in your bedroom near the door. Lock it, then block it with the chair. Got that?"

I blinked and tried taking all of that in. Charlie knew I wouldn't budge, and he'd checked to make sure I'd be safe.

"Crocker, you got it?"

"Yeah. Yeah, I got it."

"He's coming back tomorrow. Keep your phone in your pocket at all times."

"I will."

He held his hand out, palm up. "I want your phone. I'm putting my number in there."

"Don't worry about me." But I did hand it over.

"Impossible, Crocker." Charlie's expectant grey eyes held mine. "Promise to call if anything happens, or Neil will kick—"

"Your ass. I know. I promise to call."

Charlie and Wade had left, and Grace tried once more to talk me into going back with her, as did Cassie. "No," I said again and promised to call them when I got up.

Grace asked, "Should I come over tomorrow?"

"She knows we're here," Cassie reminded her, then to me, "Whenever you need us to, we'll be here."

I knew they worried and I was being selfish, if only for the fact they might lose sleep wondering if I was okay, but I wasn't going to let Andrew make me feel unsafe in my home. No way.

The girls left. I locked the door, led Rocco into the

bedroom, and set the alarm. I also pushed the chair against the door frame like Charlie asked me to.

Wired, I kept re-fluffing my pillow and flipping it over to find the cold side. I wanted sleep to claim me, take me away, but my mind kept replaying parts of the evening.

I called Rocco onto the bed and finally fell asleep.

———·———

The doorbell woke me. Rocco's protective side came out in a handful of gruff, meaty barks. My eyes popped open to the dark. Then I heard Neil shouting.

"Tova!" He pounded on the front door. "Tova!"

One of the guys must've told him what had happened and he'd come to gloat. I got up, slipping a robe on over my underwear and tank top. Through the accent window that ran the door's length, I could see two silhouettes.

Pouring in through the small panes, a ribbon of light from the street lamp lay on the hardwood floor. *Bam bam bam.* Neil knocked again.

"Knock it off, man, you're going to wake the entire neighborhood." It sounded like Wade was with him.

I switched off the alarm, turned on an overhead light, then opened the door. Neil shaded his eyes, and Wade frowned.

"Don't the two of you have better things to do? Like, sleep?"

"I'm sorry, Tova," Wade said. "He's been drinking."

"So you brought him to me?"

Wade grinned. "No, he—"

Neil interrupted. "I'm not drunk!" He leaned in, and his eyes traveled to my toes and back up again. He'd done that earlier, when he'd still respected me. "Wade, I got this."

I laughed.

"You've seen her. Now come on."

"Wade," Neil bit out. Even drunk he could argue. "Time to get lost. I need to talk here."

"There's nothing to talk about," I huffed.

"Yes, there is," Neil ground out.

"You're making an ass of yourself," Wade warned. I agreed.

Neil shifted away but didn't stagger. "I'm not." *Enough.*

"How much have you had to drink?" I asked.

Neil's grin was that of a boy who knew he was in trouble and didn't care. "Plenty." *No shit.*

I turned to Wade. "Is he a mean drunk?"

"No," they both answered.

I ran my hand through my hair. May as well get it over with. "It's fine, Wade."

"You sure?"

"Yeah, you can go."

Wade bumped Neil on the arm. "Behave." He headed to his truck.

"Wade!" I called out. He swung around. "Next time you deliver a drunk to my door, I'm kickin' your ass."

He smiled that cocky little grin of his. "That'll be fun."

"Won't it."

Neil growled. "Stop flirting."

"I'm not, smartass." Praying for patience, I looked down the length of him. "Can you walk?"

"'Course, I can."

I pointed to the living room. "Then get to it. I'm tired." He took two steps, stopped, and shut my front door with a kick of his foot.

"I like that door. Try not to break it."

He held my eyes and closed the distance between us. "I'm sorry."

I knew he wasn't talking about the door. His sincerity made my chest hurt.

"Shoulda been here." He reached and moved my hair from my shoulder and bruised arm. Startled, I flinched away and bumped into the wall. "Hey." He moved in closer, his eyes growing fierce, his jaw straining. "He hurt you, didn't he?"

"I'm fine."

"Then why'd you jus—"

"I'm fine."

"Charlie told me Dickhead wanted t'kill you." That was extreme. How drunk was he? Neil got so close I could feel the heat of him. "Gonna beat the crap out of him." He could, too.

I shifted on my feet. "I'll make popcorn."

His hand dropped, reached out, and came to rest on my hip. "He ever hit you before?"

"No!"

Neil glanced at my mouth. "Good. Charlie said something about him not staying another night." *What an ass.* "Is he here now?"

"No, there's no way I'd let him back in tonight."

"But are you letting him come back?"

"Aren't you full of questions." Neither of us looked away from each other. His mouth turned grim, and I had to respond. "He's just coming to collect his stuff. He'll never stay here overnight again."

He closed the inches between us. His mouth hovered over my ear. "Why didn't you tell me?"

Was I supposed to confide in him my marriage was sand slipping through my fingers? I had my pride. I didn't want him to know my head was all over the place. I certainly didn't want him to know I'd been holding onto my marriage because I couldn't accept failure.

I also didn't want him to know that I was behaving like my dad. For god's sake, I'd begged Neil to kiss me!

The short whiskers on his face scraped my neck. I shivered and shook my head. *Damn him.* He lingered by my jaw, lips hovering. "Ask me to kiss you again."

"That's not going to happen." I shouldn't be kissing anyone. I was a mess.

His hand at my hip slipped around my back and gently brought me forward until our chests aligned. He felt so good my eyes closed. "I've been thinking about your mouth since I met you. Weeks."

Why did he have to tell me that? He held me lightly enough that I could get away if I wanted to. But I didn't. I looked up, caught in the net of his opalescent eyes. He nearly sighed. "I'm sorry, Tova."

His admission and scent made me foggy. The searing heat of him awarded me a case of marionette head. I laid my cheek on his chest. Part of me hurt from what Neil had said and how he'd reacted in the pantry, but the reasonable part of me understood.

"Please tell me you forgive me?"

Unable to deny him, I whispered, "Yes."

Then he finally kissed me.

He tasted like whiskey and pent-up lust. A languid sweep of his tongue and the greed of his mouth pulled at the wanting part of me. I succumbed and kissed him back. It was a dance, a fight, and finally, surrender.

My hands went up his torso and chest slowly, to feel the muscles under my palms. He felt better than I'd imagined, and I'd imagined *a lot.*

I grasped his thick shoulders and did the one thing I'd wanted since the day I'd met him—delved my hands through his hair, giving a tug.

A growl came up out of his throat, and he kissed me harder, pushing me, leading me to get as aggressive as I wanted. And I wanted. I attacked his mouth and bit his juicy bottom lip.

His hands skated over the silk on my butt. He lifted me off my feet and ground the soft part of me against the hard part of him.

I groaned.

Neil groaned.

My head fell back. He took the opportunity and let his mouth travel my throat. I felt his whiskers everywhere. He found the hollow at the base of my neck. In the most wildly illicit move, he licked it with his flattened tongue. My sex clenched. I wanted him too much and moved restlessly to prove it.

Almost willing the other to bend, we both kept pushing at each other. We were bound to snap.

What in the hell was I doing? I'd just kicked Andrew out. I pried myself away. "I need to get my head together." Neil let go and my feet hit the cold hardwood floor. My head shook. "No," I said, gazing at his mouth. His chest rose and fell. I'd been thinking about getting naked with him for weeks, and the night I kick my husband out, I'm making out with him. It made me want to face-plant into a pillow.

He took a step back, rubbed his hand down his face, then nodded.

I went to the kitchen. "Can you make it back to your house?" A stupid question. I knew for certain his feet could get him there.

"I'm not leaving."

I whipped around. "Yes, you are. Did you think you'd sleep in my bed?"

His body stiffened. "I'm staying."

"Don't be ridiculous."

"I want to make sure Dickhead doesn't come back tonight. And when he does, I want to be here." He locked my front door. "I'm staying. Please don't give me that attitude. Not tonight." He sounded genuine. "I need to know you're okay. I'll sleep in your guest room."

Appeased and tired, I gave in. "Fine then. Make yourself comfortable." I walked to my room, Rocco followed, and I closed my door.

CHAPTER 11

NEIL

"Tova!" I held her arms, so she'd stop the thrashing, and not hurt herself. "Calm down." She jerked, finally opening her eyes. "You're dreaming."

I let go of her. Elbows to the mattress, she scrambled back against her headboard. A horrified look of shock flashed across her face. She started crying.

Getting onto her bed, I gathered and held her. I ran my hand down her arm. "You're safe." I kept my voice low. "I'm not gonna let anything happen to you. Everything is gonna be all right." I needed to calm down right along with her. When she'd screamed, I'd grabbed my gun. Not thinking Dickhead had come back, but you never knew.

Thank Christ Rocco hadn't leaped at me when I'd opened her door. I'd been serious enough to shoot.

"Please stop crying, Blue Eyes." I could listen to anything but hated hearing my strong girl break down.

She swallowed a sharp breath and burrowed in close, her cheek on my chest. The sigh she let go warbled across my neck, then stopped. She curled further into me. Her bare thigh slid along my ribs, and her chest rubbed against mine. That didn't calm me down. I jostled her and moved my hips back. She wore nothing on her legs except moonlight. Her soft skin made it impossible to stop touching her. I let my eyes close. My hand on her shoulder skimmed down, but I accidentally brushed her breast. My eyes opened. *Fuck.*

"You got my heart rate going," I joked.

She whispered, "Sorry."

I'd rather she apologized for not telling me her plans about Dickhead. "No need to be sorry." Her skin smelled of flowers and her hair like coconut. My thumb on her hip caught on the silk and lace panties she wore. Rookie mistake. "Do you want to talk about it?"

"Lena," she said and held on to me.

Here I'd thought it was over Andrew.

"We're gonna get evidence on Billy." The booze had faded, but not my wanting her. Her hand came up over my heart, and she made absentminded circles on my chest. When I'd walked in on her cutting cords, her hands a flurry of activity, I'd wondered what those fingers would feel like moving on me, moving over my skin.

She made another pass across my nipple. I dropped my hand over hers, halting her fingers. Neither of us said anything. My mind weaved around, fighting with itself. It was the hardest thing I'd ever done, but I told myself tonight all I could do was ease her mind. Rocco sighed. I held her like I'd wanted to for weeks, and at some point, we slunk down into the sheets and fell asleep.

———•———

TOVA

It was another delicious dream about Neil. My hand—over his heart—slid down his chest, belly, and muscled abs. He felt ridiculously warm, unbelievably good. I followed a line of hair and ventured inside his boxer briefs. My hand gripped and stroked. He was hard, hot and thick. Perfect. His hips bucked, knocking me from my rhythm, but I didn't want the dream to end before he finished. I pumped with purpose. He pulsed and groaned, becoming liquid heat in my hand.

The groan, though, sounded too real. I hadn't realized there was a hand on my back until it dove into my panties and cupped my bare bottom. My eyes popped open to a wall of chest. Neil's chest. My hand disengaged. I wiped it off on the sheets. Did I really just do that?

Neil's dark lashes lay thick and lovely on his cheekbones. I watched his torso rise and fall. I'd dreamt of this. Okay, not quite this. But waking up with him. How could I end up in bed with him hours after telling my husband to shove off? Then I remembered—a nightmare about Lena. I couldn't catch her, and Billy had gone after her. I couldn't save her. And then Neil woke me.

My breathing accelerated, my pulse wildly taking off. I sunk into the mattress. I couldn't move my limbs, but I could feel my blood stuttering in my neck. It tasted like a panic attack.

Neil moved. Getting up on an elbow, he smiled. "That was unexpected." *No kidding!*

His hair stood on end. Before I knew it his tongue dipped into my mouth, and with a graze of hand, he touched the side of my breast. He stroked back and forth, not taking more than a curious caress.

He broke away. His index finger dipped into the valley of my cleavage. He peered at me with half-lidded eyes. "You're beautiful." He drew his finger over the swell and slipped it underneath the strap of my tank top. I just gave Neil a—I couldn't even think about it.

The sun lay over us, making our skin gold. My white blankets covering us reminded me of cotton candy, but I didn't feel sweet. Anger rumbled through me. "I'm not sleeping with you."

"Too late for that." A teasing smile winked from the corner of his mouth. "You did." He would have to be literal. He focused on my breasts again.

I sunk down into that panic warring in my head. "Don't make me that woman, Neil."

His eyes sought mine. "What woman is that?" Wonder thickened his honey voice.

"The woman in bed with another man the day after she kicked her husband out. The same husband who's coming back soon."

He swayed back, keeping his focus locked on my face. Shock registered in his eyes. "You're not taking him back, are you?" I suppose he thought I might be the type of woman who lived in an abusive relationship. *That didn't bother me at all.*

"God, no." Better to have him question me than have a discussion on what I'd just done. His shoulders relaxed. "Did you really think I'd want him back?" His dubious eyes skirted away. I yanked from his hold and got out of bed. "He's gonna be here soon."

Neil sat up, grabbed his gun off the nightstand, stood, and aimed himself at my bedroom door. Good thing I didn't know that was there all night. "I'm staying until he leaves." I wasn't going to argue. I wanted him here and felt relieved, not mad. He got up and started walking out. "Please, for the love of Christ, put some clothes on."

He only wore black boxer briefs. "Back at ya." He faltered, then shut the door behind him.

Not long after, a car door outside slammed. My heart

jumped into my throat. I peeked out the window. It was Eve. She got into her ancient gold Buick.

It went unsaid that I was sleep-deprived. That term seemed inadequate. More like a shaky, nerve-revved adrenaline was coursing through me.

I ran through the shower, barely standing still enough for the soap to wash away. The replay kept at me as I washed him off my hand. *I'd given Neil a hand job. Who does that?* I heard Neil in my guest bath as I texted Cassie and Grace. Hearing Charlie's words from last night, I pocketed my cell after getting dressed.

Wanting Andrew gone as fast as possible, I gathered his things, dropped all of his clothes into garbage bags, and lay them near the door to the garage. His clothes getting wrinkled would piss him off, and to help expedite that, I may have stomped on them a few times.

Just about everything in the house belonged to me. Andrew had lived like a nomad before we'd met. He literally could fit his life into his ridiculously expensive BMW and never need to come back. With that thought, I didn't want to miss one item belonging to him.

I pulled down the last of his unpacked boxes, including the one spilled on the floor from the break-in, when my phone beeped.

My hands shook when I read the message.

I'm on my way, Andrew's text said.

"What's it say?" Neil asked, making me jump.

"He's on his way."

He squeezed my hand. "I got this." He went to the window and watched. Minutes later, the garage door sounded.

Neil came up to me and cupped my cheek. "Calm down and let me handle this, okay?" He'd said something similar the day we'd met.

He propped the door open before Andrew even got there.

I stayed behind him near the kitchen. Rocco leaned his big head against my leg, and I hid my shaking hands behind my back.

Leaving room for Andrew to get into the house, Neil backed up. His legs locked shoulder-width apart.

Andrew stopped and processed Neil in his way. "Nice, Tova." He crossed his arms over his chest. Flabbergasted, his eyes cut to me. "Where's the other one? In the fucking bushes?"

"He wouldn't be here if you hadn't hurt me."

"I see you're not wasting time." *Nice.*

"Watch it," Neil barked.

"You're the one who wanted a divorce," I said. *That didn't sound right.* "I don't want a fight and I don't want an argument."

"This isn't how I saw this going. I lost my temper." Was this Andrew apologizing?

"You did and it doesn't matter anymore. It's over."

Andrew's brow furrowed. I wondered if he couldn't grasp the situation.

"The way this works," Neil explained, "is you're gonna put your shit that Tova so nicely gathered into your car and be on your way. I'll even help. 'Cause you're not hanging out."

Andrew shook his head. I could tell he was sucking on his teeth. "You've got to be fucking kidding."

"Nope." Neil took a step forward. I wished I knew what was running through Andrew's head. "You're not stepping foot in the house again. Got me?"

Andrew didn't respond. I figured one of two things could happen. Either he'd realize Neil would beat the living daylights out of him and wise up, or he'd get so pissed he wouldn't care.

Trying to defuse the situation, I told him, "I got everything.

Even the boxes from the closet."

Taking in what was on the floor, he looked down. A nerve twitched in his neck. "Good." With that, he grabbed the banker's box that had fallen from the closet. "I've got it," he told Neil. "You've helped enough."

In less than twenty minutes, Andrew was backing out of the garage. Neil went downstairs and took Rocco out to play fetch.

A heavy weight on my shoulders lifted. Andrew's absence was a physical relief. When the doorbell rang five minutes later, I prepared myself for it to be the girls or Andrew telling me he forgot something. Instead, a supremely thin woman with long dark hair stared back at me through the glass.

Unfortunately, I opened the door.

"Get the fuck out of my way," she said, coming through. I don't know why, but instinctively I backed up. "Drew, where are you?" she yelled.

I latched onto her shoulder. "What the hell are you doing?"

She backhanded me across the cheek. "Let me go, you bitch." The hit rattled me enough that she launched into my house. The sting came a second later, and I touched my cheek. Blood coated my fingertips.

She made for the kitchen. "Drew!" she bellowed.

"Tova!" Neil came running up the stairs from the basement.

"Who the hell are you?" I asked.

She came to an abrupt halt, seeing Neil. "I'm Josie, Drew's girlfriend. Where the fuck is he?"

I finally got it. Andrew was Drew. Drew was Andrew. "Not here," I said, sidestepping her.

Neil's eyes fell to me. "She hit you?"

I touched my cheek, my paralyzed senses coming back. "Yes." He drew the gun from the back of his pants, pointed it at her, and propelled himself toward her. "Sit down," he yelled.

"Holy shit," Josie said, retreating.

"Oh my god, Neil, put that away."

He pointed the gun from her to my island. "Sit," he growled. She did and he walked to me, grabbed his shirt by the bottom, and used it to wipe my face. "You okay?"

"Yes." Not really, but what could I say? My soon-to-be-ex had a girlfriend. I figured this might be the case last night, but this seemed different. She'd just decked me and was now sitting at gunpoint.

Neil got on his phone.

I took another look. Her pupils appeared larger than normal, and she twitched a few times. Guns can do that. But then she blinked wildly at nothing.

Perfect. She's high.

"You need to hear what I have to tell you. I want you to know Drew and I have been together for years." *Different all right!*

High as she might be, I didn't doubt her. I took her in. Everything about her said sultry—her eyes green emeralds, her hair wicked black. I could see what Andrew must have seen.

She shifted on the stool in her all-black outfit of sexy stiletto boots and a too-short skirt that rose to an indecent level. "I don't want you gettin' any crazy ideas about taking him back 'cause he's mine."

"What?" *As if I'd want him now.*

She got up and came at me, but what could she do in her thin, long-sleeved T-shirt that clung to her surgically enhanced chest? "You heard me, Drew's mine."

Beyond the dark exterior and the addiction, I could see pretty.

Neil, still on the phone, got in front of me. "Sit. The. Fuck.

Down."

She did.

Her smile twisted between sly and malicious. "I know he wasn't fucking you." She gestured to me. "I can see why."

I couldn't answer. I suppose Andrew told her we hadn't had sex in a year. A *wahp-wahp* from a cop car sounded from outside, and Neil brought me into the foyer. The view of my marriage changed, dramatically.

"Tell me this isn't happening," I blurted.

He opened the front door. "Oh, it's happening, sweetheart."

I stumbled to the living room. Taking in the crowd, the vehicles, and Josie's cruel words, the veil of keeping my shit together disappeared, and since I couldn't spare myself the humiliation, I started crying.

Just great.

Neil abandoned his post. "Don't."

"I'm trying." Wade walked toward us. I yanked on Neil's shirt. "You called Wade and the cops?"

"Wade called the cops." I made a horrible gasping sound as I took in a big breath of air. God, I hoped she couldn't hear me. "Sweetheart, please stop."

I waved a hand at the window and toward the kitchen. "It's not like I'm enjoying this. Do you think I like slutty, twitching nutjob seeing me cry?" I saw the corner of his mouth lift. "Are you grinning?"

"You're one of a kind, Tova."

I controlled the sudden urge to kick him and frowned. "Really? You chose this moment for an insult?"

"It's not. You're the only woman I know who'd convince me she's trying not to cry and I'd wholly believe it."

What? I blinked and stopped attempting to figure out what he said as one of the cops came through the door.

"She's high, isn't she?" I whispered to Neil. He nodded.

"I'm Officer Dean. I need to get a statement from you, Ms. Hudson."

I told him the gritty details, and then he thanked me and asked to speak to Neil privately. From the front window, a different officer stuffed Josie in a squad car. Her long dark hair moved like a raven's wing, jet metallic as the wind stirred it up against her pencil-thin frame.

I should be upset that Andrew wanted her over me, yet I wasn't. I only felt a fool.

"Mrs. Hudson, do you want to fill out a no-trespassing order on Ms. Lawson?" Officer Dean asked.

I remembered when my mother had unintentionally woken me up yelling at my dad, telling him to keep his dick in his pants. She'd put up with a lot, but she'd never gotten a restraining order on some woman.

I turned and held my head up. "Yes. She's bonkers."

He cracked the smallest of smiles. "I'll be right back."

I sat on the sofa and Neil joined me. "I'm proud of you. I'm guessing not going after her took supreme effort."

"She hit me. I was dazed."

He put his arm around me, clutching my shoulder. "She's got an impressive record."

"What kind?"

"I'll tell you later. I'm gonna get a clean shirt. I'll be right back." He got up and I followed him. "I'm sorry I bled all over your shirt."

"I don't care about a shirt." He tucked my hair behind my ear. "But you know that. I made sure Wade called Grace. She and Cassie are on their way." My eyes widened. "Blue Eyes, you know you want them here."

I swallowed. "You're right."

He winked again, stopped, and smiled. "Just remember that."

———•———

"I can't believe that pig," Cassie repeated. She made her way over to me with a wet paper towel. Grace, Wade, and I were perched on kitchen stools listening to her rant as Neil strolled in with a fresh shirt on. He sat next to me.

Then Cassie started at it again. "He leads his girlfriend to your house so she can bitch-slap you." She leaned down and began patting at my cheek. "That doesn't hurt, does it?"

"No. I'm all right."

She pointed in the direction of my studio. "You should singe his balls off with your torch." Wade winced. Cassie saw that pained expression. "Yep, that's what you should do. The next time you see him, light his fucking dick on fire."

"I'm sure it is already," Wade muttered. Neil reached around me, knocking Wade on the arm.

The gravity of it hit, a blow to more than just my dignity. Andrew was sleeping with her when he was sleeping with me.

"I need to go to the doctor." This was what my mother went through.

Cassie put an arm around me. "Honey." She squeezed me tighter.

This realization made me one of those women. The one labeled *ignorant wife*.

Strong arms gathered me in—Neil's arms. He led me to the bathroom and made me look in the mirror. I took in the dried blood smearing my cheek.

"Wow, I look great." If great meant vulnerable and overwhelmed.

Tenderness painted Neil's face. He shifted a touch closer, saying, "This is going to pass. You're going to be okay."

"How do you know?"

"Because I do." And for whatever mysterious reason, I believed him.

I remembered once as a teenager walking out of the girls' restroom with my skirt tucked into my underwear. *Not pleasant.* I'd always thought *that* was my most embarrassing moment, but my dirty laundry unfolding in front of Neil seemed exponentially worse.

He leaned into me and turned on the warm water and wet two washcloths. Gently, he wiped my cut cheek. He dotted on ointment and placed a large Band-Aid on my face. He took care of me.

I hadn't been taken care of in a long time.

Exhaustion set in and I slumped against my sink. "Thanks."

His arms wrapped around me. "Did you know?"

"I just need a minute."

Neil's arms tightened. He breathed deep, his chest expanding and pressing into mine. "All the minutes you need, Blue Eyes—they're yours."

I burrowed in closer, my hands going around him. "I'm not devastated. Don't think that. Things between Andrew and me were a mess for a long time. I'm upset because you're so sweet to me."

"Tova," he whispered and clutched me tighter. With a finger, he tipped my chin up. Softness washed over his features, the thumb of his right hand passed over my lips, and he kissed me.

CHAPTER 12

TOVA

Cassie was waiting when I stumbled out of her bedroom after a three-hour nap.

"We're going to paint our toenails," she said. She and Grace had packed up Rocco and me and we'd all come here to her condo.

"Pick a color, Tova." Grace held out a tray of rainbow polishes.

I chose black. It reflected what I kept seeing: snippets of the past two years playing out in grainy segments. Had those dark signs been there all this time? Had I ignored them? Closed my eyes in delusion? It made me stupid and gullible.

"I've had my fill of men," I announced. "The Hudson women remain cursed. I'm continuing our tradition."

"Andrew's the one who lied!" Cassie said.

But I'd lied to myself. I'd kept it to myself.

Grace patted my thigh, practically reading my mind. "He wasn't the right one." Between the three of us, she remained the romantic. I wanted to tell her to take her optimism and throw it over the railing.

"My father's a serial adulterer, my grandfather cheated and was abusive, and Andrew... Andrew made me a patsy!"

I took a gulp of my drink. "*Tea?*" I frowned at Cassie. "You know generally we drink alcohol?" She shook her head. "Really, Cassie, *I'd* give *you* booze."

"Yes, but I'm a nicer drunk than you are."

I glared. "I'm instituting a moratorium on men. I'm not going near another man again. A fucking moratorium!"

"You mean a *fucking* moratorium," Cassie replied. "Don't get so worked up about him. Soon he'll be your was-band, not your husband."

I frowned. "I'm not going near another man again," I said again, completely adamant.

Cassie broke out laughing, then Grace.

"Sure you are," Cassie said and took a drink of something I'm sure contained alcohol.

I reached out and tried to grab her glass. She moved it. "I'm serious." Even I knew I sounded childish.

Cassie raised a questioning eyebrow. "What about Neil?" I glared at her again. Her face broke into a huge smile. "Tova, I hate to tell you this, but the two of you look at each other like you can barely keep from tearing each other's clothes off."

That made me sound like my dad. How embarrassing. Was that how Neil and I appeared around others?

"We do not." I glanced over at Grace for confirmation.

Grace nodded. "It's true."

Gah. What happened in my studio and pantry came flying back. It angered me how I'd behaved.

"I know you're devastated and heartbroken, but that doesn't mean you just throw in the towel."

Devastated and heartbroken? Hardly! I hovered between humiliated and furious. Cheated on. I'd proved to be just like my mom.

"Have you wondered why you met Neil?" Cassie asked.

I hadn't thought about it. "No."

Cassie took a sip of her drink. "I think there's a reason."

I remembered thinking how if we hadn't met at the DMV, we would've when he moved in.

"Neil kissed me." Now that I'd been opening up, may as well let it rip.

Cassie threw her hands out in front of her. "See."

"When did he kiss you?" Grace asked.

"He came back after the party."

Cassie leaned forward and put her elbows on her knees. "Why did he leave anyway?"

"Neil asked if Andrew always ignored me. Then he cornered me in the pantry and wanted to know what Andrew said when he came home."

"What did he say?" Grace asked.

"He said I actually looked hot for once."

"That ass," Grace said. Cassie called him other choice words. "What else happened in the pantry?"

"Neil told me he would've kissed me. I told him he should. I made a pass at him, and he left, pissed. When he came back drunk, it was with Wade, so I suppose he and grumpy-ass Reid went drinking."

"When did he kiss you?" Grace asked. "I'm lost."

"Neil and Wade showed up at two a.m. It sounded like he'd insisted on seeing me after he heard what happened."

"I adore him," Cassie blurted.

Grace whacked her on the leg. "Stop interrupting. Go on, Tova."

"He showed up, but I was still mad at him. Anyway, at some point, he kissed me."

Cassie smiled. "How was it?"

"Good." *Great, actually.*

Cassie laughed. "You're such a liar. It was better than good."

I ran my hand through my hair. "Do you think I'm attracted to him because I haven't had sex in forever? What if I'm lusting after him because he's hot and I'm under-sexed and overly turned on by him?"

Cassie glowed. "The chemistry between you two is combustible."

"He wouldn't leave the house. He told me he was staying."

Grace's tone came across clear. "Where did he sleep?"

"The guest room…" I cringed just thinking about it. "… until I had a nightmare and he got into bed with me."

"And?" Cassie asked, grinning wildly from her cheeks to her golden eyes.

"Nothing happened." I covered my face with my hands. "Until I woke up giving him a hand job." I looked up at them. "I'm a mess. What if I'm making another mistake?"

Cassie got up and patted my head. "There is no way that man is a mistake."

———•———

Cassie and Grace dropped me off. That night, I couldn't sleep. Why had Andrew been with another woman the whole time we were married? Was I not enough? Did I suck in bed? Probably.

I got up and cleaned and purged. I got rid of any photo or object reminding me of him. After carrying a bag to the garbage, I rewarded myself with a drink. I gutted shelves and took a drink. I moved furniture and took a drink. My garbage cans burst and I took a drink. So many drinks that I called Andrew.

He didn't answer, go figure. "Hey, *Drew*, that's what you

go by now, right?" I laughed. "Call me back so I can find out where to send the divorce papers. Oh, and if you don't get your own loan in three months, I'll send my lawyer after you." I finished with an upbeat, "Say hi to Josie."

Over the following week, I worked to distract myself. The girls called. They came by with matzo ball soup—the Jewish penicillin, as Cassie would say. After the work week, both Grace and Cassie offered to cancel their plans for the weekend and hang out with me.

I told them no. I wanted to be alone and wallow. Not even Neil had come by.

For better or worse, I needed my moratorium. The benefits of celibacy could not be clearer. I never wanted to feel the insidious need to question myself again.

Today, I wanted to be alone, but Neil decided to ring my doorbell. He probably needed a cup of flour.

Rocco barked. I grabbed and shushed him and then hid behind the wall, hoping he couldn't see me. I didn't want to see or talk to anyone. I wanted to stay holed up in my house, but Rocco kept barking and Neil kept up the ringing. Then switched to knocking.

"Tova," he shouted, "I know you're in there." He knocked again, louder this time, which caused Rocco to bark louder. I let go of my brute of a dog, and he bull-rushed the front door.

When Neil rang the doorbell several times in quick succession, Rocco whined.

Damn Neil.

Damn dog.

To hell with it. I walked out into the foyer.

"Open the door Tova or I'll kick it down."

No, he wouldn't. "Don't you dare kick it down or I'll kick your ass." As soon as I opened the door, Rocco swung his body against Neil's and wiggled back and forth, bumping his leg, wanting some attention. "I love this door."

Neil stood there in running pants and a black T-shirt. Material hugged every delineation of muscle. He looked divine. But with my no-man-ever-again philosophy, I decided what he held—an iced venti latte with my favorite green straw—was infinitely more attractive.

He offered it to me. "A gift."

I snatched it away and inhaled half. Neil bent down and patted Rocco's head. I stopped sipping. "Thank you."

He glanced at me. "I lied."

I eyed him warily. *"About?"*

"It's not a gift. It's a bribe."

"You're bribing me?" Did he know I hadn't left my house, not even for Starbucks, except for my doctor appointment? I survived off my Verismo in the kitchen, a sad substitute. Maybe that's why I had a constant headache.

"I need a walking partner." He kept petting Rocco.

I groaned. "Good try, Neil. I'm not in the mood."

"Rocco needs a walk."

"Trying to guilt *and* bribe me?"

"If it works, then yes." His head tilted to the side. "You'll feel better after getting some fresh air."

Knowing it looked bad, I smoothed my hair. "Afraid I'm turning into a hermit?"

"Not yet."

"Thanks, Hamilton." I grasped my drink. "Would you take my drink away if I said no? Because—" I took another pull. "—I wouldn't let you wrestle it away from me, just so you know."

He had to go and smile, and that crease near his eyes showed up. He gestured to the door. "Come on, Blue Eyes, let's go."

"I'm horrible company. You don't wanna hang out with

me. I'm depressing."

"I don't give a shit. Come on."

"You're worried I'll become a shut-in and start wearing housecoats—or worse, muumuus?" I shook my head to dislodge the disturbing visual.

He laughed. "Come on."

I sighed. "Okay, okay, hold your horses, I need to get my shoes on." I sat on the bench by the front door, grabbed my Nikes, and started putting them on.

He dropped down in front of me. "You can't wear those socks."

I looked down. I wore fluffy, bright pink socks. *I suppose not.*

While I got ready, Neil got Rocco on his leash. He shut and locked the door behind us, and we headed to the trail. The sun tried to break through the flat gray clouds.

"What have you been up to all week?" May as well ask—I wanted to know.

"Among other things, I've been looking for Billy."

I'd been so lost in my own upheaval I'd almost forgotten about Billy and Lena. Then again, I wasn't going anywhere, so I didn't feel the need to look over my shoulder every time I left the house.

"How are you doing?" Neil asked as we walked side-by-side.

"I'm fine." I asked myself if I believed Neil. Was he staying away because of work?

"You're always fine. Would you tell me if you weren't?"

"Probably not." We walked for a while in silence until we made it back to the outlet of the cul-de-sac. "I'm sorry. I told you I wasn't good company."

He shrugged. "Doesn't matter."

"Thanks again for the Starbucks and everything." I tried

not to let emotion lace my voice.

We reached my front door. Neil got closer, reached out, and moved a section of hair out of my face and over my shoulder. "Not a problem. Glad I could help."

"You need to get me a bill."

He nodded. "Mmm."

He'd made a similar sound when we'd kissed. Did he remember our kisses? He didn't bring up what happened between us. And in the back of my clouded mind, I figured he wanted to keep his distance. Who wouldn't after knowing my life's sordid details?

"Have you heard from him? Do you know where he is?" The sun came out.

"I never knew where he was when he said he loved me. I sure as hell don't know now."

Neil winced. "Do you need help with anything?" he asked. I shook my head. "You'll let me know, right?"

"Yes," I scraped out and cleared my hoarse throat.

He tipped his head to the side and studied me. "I'll come get you next time I go for a walk."

I nodded a response, fearing my voice would waver. Highlighted in bright light, he turned and strode away. I watched, unable to shut the door until he got into his house. I lost a week in my depressed daze. With the heat of the sun radiating, I vowed to get over it and wake the fuck up.

I just needed to figure out how.

———•———

NEIL

I walked back to my house. The whole time I wanted to turn around and kiss her.

Get her out of her house, take her on a walk, and prove you can spend time with her without wanting to tear her clothes off. That's what I repeated to myself when I went over there.

Thank Christ, I could hardly see the cut on her face. I never wanted to hit a woman, but that addict, screwing her husband, almost forced my hand.

Tova, vulnerable, sitting there putting her shoes on as if they would work with big fluffy socks, and then—like a punch to the gut—she slipped them off and her cute little toes with black polish waved hello to me. The need to lay down with her, hold her, and make her smile became too much. It didn't matter that coffee stains spattered the front of her shirt or that she looked run down. She was so fucking beautiful.

Her face looked thinner—she'd lost weight, which pissed me off. I wondered if she did it on purpose. What she needed was a friend, and I wanted to be her friend. I decided to give her time. I'd waited a week—the longest week of my life—and went to see her. I'd given her time, not pursuing her, but I couldn't leave her alone. Suppose it sounded contradictory.

Every time I closed my eyes, she was draped over me again, warm and soft, my hand on her back. I should've moved away, but I couldn't as her hand had played with my chest hair, tugging, then going lower.

I'd become obsessed with the memory of her calloused finger tips on me.

Her hand had ducked beneath my boxers, wrapped around me, only to reach lower to hold me before stroking again. My blood had pumped faster than her hand. Before I could say stop, I came in her grip. Then she'd been so mad at herself and me.

How long would it take for her to get over him?

I sure didn't like hearing she'd tried saving their marriage while he wanted a divorce.

Dickhead had proved to be a bag of mixed nuts, and it would take more than a little digging to get a clearer picture of him. I knew Tova would be pissed when she found out, but I wanted to know everything I could about him—including his whereabouts, which turned out to be Minnesota and not the south like Tova had said.

He'd lied to her about that, too.

———

TOVA

I yawned into the phone. "Hello, Neil."

"I'll be over in five. Get your shoes on minus the pink socks."

"Huh?"

"I'm coming over in five minutes. Get your shoes on."

Jesus, he could be pushy. "Um, it's Monday. I have to work."

"You have time." He chuckled and hung up.

He came over in three minutes.

"What's so funny?" A bit of a zombie, I'd opened the door to his unnerving look of amusement.

"I was just thinking about how you answered the phone. You need that coffee in the morning, don't you?"

I slapped his arm. "So what if I do? I'm not a morning person." Inwardly, his teasing made me smile. Outwardly, he couldn't tell. I sat down and put on my runners.

"Staying up late?"

I tied my shoes. "I haven't been sleeping so well. I moved furniture last night."

"Why were you doing that?"

His tone told me he'd take my pseudo screwdriver away.

"I couldn't stand looking at anything that reminded me of my soon-to-be was-band."

He grabbed Rocco's leash. "Please don't move furniture by yourself. I'll do it."

"Worried I'll throw my back out and you won't have a walking partner?"

"Yes, that's it," he said sarcastically. He waved a hand at the panel. "Get the alarm."

I keyed my code in, and Neil shut and locked the door behind us.

"I can get one of the guys to help, if I can't do it myself," he explained.

"Don't worry. I decided last night I'll buy some new furniture."

He handed me my keys but kept Rocco's leash as we walked down my driveway.

A year ago, I'd called Andrew to tell him about my shitty day, relaying that I'd changed a tire on the highway. His response: "Well, if anyone could do it, it would be you." I bet Neil would think otherwise, and in a non-Gloria-Steinem-way, I loved that about him.

"We could have another bonfire and roast my sofa." It could go up in flames just like my marriage had.

He glanced my way. "I'm surprised you didn't mention roasting it with your torch."

I couldn't help but grin. "That was Cassie's idea. My conscience gets the better of me. I'm going to donate it to a charity."

"When are you going shopping?"

"I don't know. I haven't gotten that far. Why?"

Neil's tongue darted out and wet his bottom lip. "I need some stuff, so we could go together. It would be less painful."

I laughed. "On who?"

He smiled. "How much stuff was his?"

"Nothing. He took everything the other day." The idea Neil wanted to go shopping with me made me happy for a flash, but that turned to personal loathing. How could I let his attention affect me so much? How pathetic.

"Why are you getting worked up then?"

"I want my house to feel like it's mine again, so I'm going to part with some stuff and paint walls. I mean, I bought a new bedroom set before he moved in because he didn't want to sleep on anything another man had." That comment got Neil's signature eyebrow raise. "I rearranged for Andrew, gave things away he disliked. I even stored artwork and changed room colors. He thought things looked too effeminate."

"Fair enough."

We walked through the park. All the picnic shelters looked pathetic and lonely under their dark roofs.

I was sad to admit that I'd started wondering if Neil would kiss me again. Did he *want* to kiss me again? He probably thought I had cooties. It wasn't until yesterday that I knew for sure I didn't. The test results from the doctors came back okay. At least I didn't need to worry about that anymore. I had other things on my mind.

CHAPTER 13

TOVA

Lena, for instance. I'd been having dreams about her every night. Honestly, they were more nightmares. In one, I befriended her. Another, I helped her get a steady job. Usually, though, the dreams ended where I failed.

After I'd run unsuccessfully after her, I'd wake sweaty and tangled in the sheets. If I had to do it all over again, what would've I done differently?

"What's going on with Lena's case? I feel like I could be doing something. *Should* be doing something."

Neil grabbed my hand and stopped me on the path. "You can't get involved." He shook his head. "I can see your wheels spinning. You'd be putting a target on your forehead, Blue Eyes."

"I let her down. I could've done something. I was complicit." I'd been passive in regards to Andrew, even my own happiness, but I had to make amends.

"She'd been with him for years. She was beyond the help you could give her. She didn't even want to help herself." Neil's chest visibly moved. "I have two guys working on finding him." He did? This was news. "Billy's a fuck-up. I promise you I'll find him." He squeezed my hand. "Come on, you badass, time to get you home. I hear it's Monday and you have to go to work."

———•———

NEIL

The following Wednesday, I called again. She didn't give me the first word.

"What if I wanted to sleep in?" she snapped into the phone. I loved her morning voice, rough around the edges.

"You're up. Just cranky." I was halfway across the court and could hear her rustling around. I wondered if she was in bed. *Naked.*

"That's not nice."

I also loved that fire in her voice. It meant she was getting better. Excited to see her face when she saw what I'd brought, I knocked on her door. "You can yell at me when you open up."

When she peeked through the window, I held out a Starbucks cup and smiled at her.

She opened the door with a swoosh, her robe swaying around her legs. It was the light gray one she'd worn the night of the party, and it held center stage in too many dirty dreams. Being her friend while she got her head on straight was the stupidest idea I'd ever had.

She took the cup. "I forgive you."

I shoved my hands in my pockets so I wouldn't be tempted to reenact the night of her party when I'd come back drunk. She inhaled half the latte before looking up. When she did, I saw mournful circles under her eyes. "You look like hell. Did you sleep last night?"

She scowled. "No, I didn't. And thanks for telling me I look like hell."

"Were you moving furniture again?"

Her guilty eyes slid away. "Maybe."

I'd been joking, but when I walked by her, the sofa was on it's side, feet pointed at me.

How could she move on with me if she wanted to tear apart her living room? I whipped back around. "What the hell, Tova? I told you not to move any more furniture. You're going to hurt yourself." *And you didn't listen to me.*

"I know," she said, defeated. "I couldn't sleep. Then I got frustrated."

She didn't know the half of frustrated. Every time I closed my eyes, her hand was on my dick. "Get your credit card ready." I ran a hand through my hair. "We're going furniture shopping tonight and don't try to get out of it."

"Why would I try?"

"You like to be difficult." Was she ready to move on from Dickhead?

"I do not." At her indignant tone, my anger flew away and I smothered a laugh. "Are you trying to piss me off?" The look on her face when she got mad, like she wanted to jump me, made me realize I *did* like riling her up. But I wanted her to win this argument and I didn't need to push her around.

I locked the door. "Maybe."

Her blue eyes turned stormy. "Neil. I. Am. Not. Difficult. That's ridiculous."

"You're right." *Even though you're so stubborn and full of pride you can't see the obvious.*

She marched ahead of me. "I've been in a black mood."

"Well, sweetheart, it's time to find gray."

———•———

TOVA

"Morning," Grace said into the phone.

I tossed a gray shirt on the bed and smiled. I'd show Neil gray. It was my gray top with tons of grommets, snaps, and zippers. "You sound chipper."

"Yeah, ah…" She hesitated. "Wade and I met up for a drink last night."

Did she think I wouldn't be happy for her? "Really? I want details. Wait, didn't I talk to you at eight last night?"

"Yeah, Wade called half an hour later and asked me out. To Redstone."

I smiled. "Like a bootie bar call. I like it."

Grace sighed. "Tova, I'm in such trouble."

"Why's that?"

"It just is. I like him too much."

Oh, Grace. "What happened? Did he kiss you?"

"He wanted to know about my job and how I decided on my career. The only kink in the night was running into Brad."

I sniggered, happy for her even though she seemed to downplay the whole thing. "Did you say kink, Grace?"

"Tova, did you hear what I said? I ran into Brad. The lost puppy who followed me around after I dumped him."

"Okay, so what happened? Did he lick your heels?" I got her—she chuckled.

"Wade saved me. He came over and slipped his arm around my waist. You should've seen Brad's face. Looked like he sucked a lemon."

"Nice." Neil hadn't touched anything on me but my hand lately. I severely missed his lack of interest in anything physical. When we'd danced around each other for a month, I'd gotten more action. I wondered if Neil even found me attractive anymore. Maybe he'd seen enough to decide we should just be friends.

"He makes my hair curl."

I chuckled. "Okay, get to the good stuff. Did Wade kiss you?"

"Kind of. He walked me to my car. I thought he was going to say goodbye with no kiss…so I kind of jumped him."

I barked out a laugh.

"I did, and it was worth every ounce of pride because he took over and pinned me to the car."

"Wow, okay then."

"Wow is right. It was by far the best kiss. He made my toes curl."

I laughed. "I thought he made your hair curl?"

"Yeah, that, too."

Neil made my toes curl. There I went again with my sex-starved brain. Talk about conflicted. I didn't want to break the commitment to my moratorium, yet I wanted him to put the moves on me. I sounded nuts. "Guess what?"

"What?" Grace asked.

"Guess who I'm going furniture shopping with this afternoon."

"Neil?"

"He's upset I've been moving furniture in the middle of the night. Since he needs some new stuff, he suggested we go together. Says I have great taste."

"Does he know that's because I went with you when you bought half of your furniture?"

I laughed. "Are you jealous I have a new furniture-shopping partner?"

"I am. Do you still have the hots for him?" *Yes.*

"I'm on a men moratorium."

"Poppycock. Why can't he go shopping with Wade?" At that, we broke out laughing. "Tova, you sound happy. You know it's okay if you want to be more than friends with Neil."

I frowned. "I know. I don't think he's into me anymore. Actually, I know he's not. He's been working a lot." *Almost as much as Andrew did.*

"Why do you think that?"

"He hasn't done anything to make me think he is."

"You mean besides seeing you every day?"

"We're neighbors. I'm pretty sure he thinks I've got cooties." *Who wouldn't?* "Who'd want me knowing Andrew stuck it in there?"

"Tova!" Grace said, half-shocked, half-laughing.

What I didn't tell her was that I felt confused and half-swooning around Neil.

"Neil is being a good guy. Maybe you need to kiss *him*."

She made a good point. At least I'd know one way or another.

Ten necklaces hung from my left arm as I filled an order with Astrid. My phone rang. Andrew's ring tone. Astrid held out her paler arm and took the jewelry. I took a deep breath and answered while I walked down the hall to my bedroom. My employees didn't need to hear me yelling.

"Why are you calling, Andrew?"

"I just got an interesting letter in the mail from your lawyer." His tone was sharp. "I get ninety days to find a new loan?"

It wasn't my fault. He sure wasn't getting free use of my money anymore. I imagined his face red with anger, and it gave me some satisfaction. I was bitter. I knew it.

"I want my name off your loans."

"Tova, I have appointments, sales calls. It's not as easy as picking up the phone and saying I need a loan."

I sat on the bed. "You wanted to be with her. Your bed's made. *And* I don't care about your schedule and I definitely don't care about your excuses."

"When did you become such a bitch?"

I decided to list the top three. "After you lied to me, used me, and wasted two years of my life. That's when I became a bitch. Don't call me again."

I hung up.

———•———

An hour after Andrew called, I sat in Neil's Yukon. He stole a glance at my top as he drove. "You're quiet. Something bothering you?"

I twisted toward him. His perception unnerved me. "How do you do that?"

"I take it you heard from Dickhead?"

"He called after he got a letter from my lawyer."

"What did he say?"

"He ranted about needing to secure other financing. I told him not to call me again."

"You need to keep a record of the call."

"I already did."

We got to the furniture store, and Neil headed to the beds. He wore a black T-shirt and faded jeans that accentuated his long, muscled legs and did great things for his ass. It was an ass that defied gravity. It was an ass I'd seen with just boxers on and it was awesome.

He bent over a mattress and patted it. I wanted to go up behind him and smack, slap, and fondle that great butt. Pretty much if it involved his world-class behind, I wanted to do it.

Screw furniture shopping, I need the vibrator store!

"We could block his calls." He laid down on the mattress. Even though I hadn't planned on buying a bed, I tortured myself and joined him.

I stared at the ceiling. "You don't need to, but thanks. Guess what I did today?"

Neil propped himself up on an elbow and looked down at me. The last time he'd done that he'd kissed me. "What's that, Blue Eyes?"

I'd never get sick of that nickname. "I got two bids on repainting a bunch of rooms."

He frowned, and that sexy line converged in the center of his brow. "Don't. I can get Charlie and Wade to come over and we'll do it. You'll just need to feed us."

"I'd never ask you to come paint my house. That's like asking someone you just met to help you move. Besides you're too busy and I'm not that needy." *Well, not that kind of needy.*

The frown deepened. "You know me well enough to ask me to help you paint."

"We met two months ago."

He chuckled. "It's been eventful."

I laughed. "You think?" I poked him in the side. "You're just a teddy bear, aren't you?"

Maybe you need to kiss him, Grace had said. Should I? Neil wasn't on the menu at the men moratorium restaurant. When I looked at him lying next to me, I wanted him there. Possessed, my finger skimmed down his abs.

He halted my finger. All joking ended. "I'm not a teddy bear."

"I think you are."

"Is that what you think?" He brought my finger up and aimed it at his mouth, as though he planned on biting me. I wanted him to.

"Are you shopping for beds?" a saleswoman asked. I could've thrown the flat pillow at her.

Instead, I ordered a bed and we moved on to living room stuff. Even though we weren't planning for our purchases to co-mingle, I got great joy out of furniture shopping with Neil. It seemed so domestic, even though we were shopping for two different households, and unlike anything I'd ever gotten to do with my soon-to-be *was-band*.

"You want a chair and a sofa?" I asked.

He sat in a classic club chair in cognac-colored leather. "Yeah. I suppose I need end tables, too." He propped his feet on the matching ottoman and looked like he should be holding a beer in one hand and cigar in the other. "What's the price of this one?"

I checked. The tag said he had great taste. "You don't wanna know."

"I'm taking it anyways."

"Seriously, you might want to think twice."

He captured me around the waist and yanked me onto his lap. "I don't need to think twice."

My legs hung over the arm of the chair and my butt nestled in his lap. My face flushed. "What are you doing?"

He grabbed a zipper at my shoulder and pulled. The tines rasped as he opened my sleeve. His head dipped. "I like these zippers." His breath sent a chill over my skin. He nuzzled my nape. What was he doing? His whiskers abraded and caused a tingle to slide down my back. Even my sex clenched. He kissed my shoulder and instantly turned me on. I swallowed, wondering if I should try turning it off. He grasped me tighter. "Christ, you smell great."

I shifted in his lap. "Neil."

"Careful," he whispered.

I felt his hard-on against my hip. "What are you doing?" I repeated, turning to see his face. I'd kill him if he turned this into a game. His eyes ran from my mouth to my chest and back again. "Are you staring at my chest?"

"Yes."

I said the first thing I thought. "Since when are you interested?"

His head snapped back. "Since when am I interested? Are you *shittin'* me?"

"No, I'm not *shittin' you*."

He swallowed and worked his jaw back and forth. He shifted me away from his erection. "Why would you think I'm not interested?"

I didn't answer and tried to wiggle free, but he held me tight. "Let me go."

He huffed a laugh. "Never." My pride on the line, I glanced away. "Look at me." He put his hand on my chin and pointed it in his direction. "You know, Tova." His face softened. "You've known for a long time. I've been interested since you called me *cheeky*."

"You haven't kissed me since the Josie incident," I whispered.

"I wanted to give you time." He leaned in. "I feel your hand on my cock every time I close my eyes," he said gruffly but touched me gently on my back. "You're feeling frustrated." His index finger dipped into my cleavage. "I know all about frustrated. It starts with you wearing a shirt that's begging me to take it off." Oh, god.

He lowered his mouth and slowly kissed my upper lip, then slid his tongue into my mouth. I didn't move for a beat, too surprised. When I did, my fingers dove into his hair and I kissed him back with all the want that had been building in me. Neil pulled me closer, my chest against his. Our kiss ran deep and with purpose. But it ended all too quickly.

"Miss, I've got your receipt." Our saleswoman had found us.

"You kissed me."

"I did." A glimmer of a smirk tilted his lips. "Now get over it and go sign your receipt." He moved me onto my feet. "Your moratorium is over by the way," he called out as I made my way back to the mattress counter.

The saleswoman—who'd had an eyeful—smiled as though I was the luckiest woman on earth. I smiled back.

For the rest of our shopping, Neil clasped my fingers in his or kept touching me. Afterward, he drove us to La Cucaracha for dinner. We sat in a booth with a curved back, and he casually placed his arm on the high cushion.

My margarita hit my lips, and I relaxed against him.

"Good?" he asked.

I nodded, and since he was right there, I kissed him. After all, his bottom lip looked so neglected. He tugged on the main zipper of my top, lowering it a good inch.

"Neil…" I batted at his hands. "I don't have anything besides a bra underneath here."

A devilish smirk graced his face. "I know." Then he kissed me quick and ran a finger down my arm. "I need to tell you something."

"Okay."

"I'm doing what I think is best."

"Okay…" I agreed, confused.

"I know where he is."

"What?"

"I know where Dickhead is."

"What?" I repeated, stunned. I'd been thinking about

hiring Neil, but why would I want him knowing all that crap?

"It's what I do, Tova."

It wouldn't have been easy to find Andrew. Neil hardly knew anything about him, but I suppose Wade could've gotten information from Grace. Still, he'd searched for him without asking my permission. "Why didn't you tell me?"

"You didn't need to know."

That was such a man thing to say. "Of course I needed to know." Did he not think I could handle it?

He locked his jaw. "Why is that?"

Why is that? "You shouldn't hide things from me."

"I'm telling you now."

"You hid it from me." I didn't want any secrets. And I sure in the hell didn't want any more surprises.

"No, I just didn't tell you."

My anger swelled. "That's bull." Shaking my head, I looked away from him. So much I could have said, but not the time to try saying it.

He cupped my chin and pointed it in his direction. "Stop looking away when it gets hard, sweetheart. I had to know more about him. I wanted to make sure you were safe."

Sugarcoating his deceit with an endearment wouldn't work. "Don't call me sweetheart and think that makes it all right. You should've told me. You should've asked."

His eyes fired. "I'm trying to help you! And I'm sitting here now telling you."

"Well, it feels like you're trying to hide something from me, and I don't need that again."

A muscle in Neil's jaw ticked. I could feel his anger coming at me before he even said a word. "Don't confuse what I did—wanting to look out for you—with what Dickhead did."

"That's not what I meant."

"Yes, you did."

"I'm used to taking care of myself."

"I know you are, so I'm helping."

"That's easy for you to say and hard for me to do."

"That's why I didn't tell you right away. You're so damn stubborn."

CHAPTER 14

TOVA

I knew I was stubborn and my pride could fill a stadium, but I didn't want Neil disappointing me. I loathed the idea of him keeping something so big from me—and worse, saying why. We needed to communicate. I didn't want a repeat of Andrew.

"Don't keep secrets from me. You can't keep—" But I could trust him. Neil wasn't Andrew.

He rubbed the back of his neck. "I'll tell you everything, but I'm keeping a man on the case." I nodded my head. "What financial stuff of his are you linked to?"

"I secured two business loans."

"Is he on the house or your Rover?"

"No. They're both in my name."

"I'll send you an email list of stuff we'll need."

"Are you gonna send me a bill?"

He screwed up his face. "No." *To think he called* me *stubborn.* "There is one big thing I don't think you know."

My stomach dropped. "What's that?"

"Dickhead's been living here, in Minneapolis, with Josie for the last three years."

Blood roared in my ears. Neil chewed the inside of his mouth.

"In Minneapolis. Three years." I repeated. But we'd only been married for two of those years. He was with her when we met. Not just dating her, but living with her. He'd claimed he'd always been married to his work until he met me. When he proposed, he'd said he couldn't picture his life without me. Then he'd spent all his time with her. The thought knocked me in the chest.

He nodded. "He wasn't there all the time. He probably did live out of his suitcase, like you said, but he lied to you in more than one way."

Had Andrew ever loved me? Had he ever cared? "I see. What else have you found out?"

"Nothing else. Yet." *Is he looking for something specific? Something criminal?*

We ate dinner; well, Neil did. I picked at mine. When we walked out, the heat hit us. A few people passed us on the sidewalk. Some with groceries, others with oversized messenger bags cutting their torsos in half.

"Hey, Hamilton," a man shouted from across the street. We both turned. Billy leaned out of the passenger side of a red pickup truck, his sneer pointed at us.

Neil pushed me behind him and simultaneously drew his gun. He didn't aim it at Billy but held it between us, waiting.

Billy's soulless, raging eyes marked Neil. "Funny seeing you two here, quite the coincidence." Neil's stance changed. Using his body, making a shield, he spread his legs wider and his shoulders drew back. To protect me. Fear knocked inside my chest. "I'm surprised you're not hanging out in your part of town." Billy dropped his chin. "St. Louis Park has gotten dangerous."

This was what Neil worried about, what lingered in the back of my mind after he'd put the thought there. Billy knew where we lived.

Billy stepped out of the truck, his boots hitting concrete. He kept his hands at his sides and leaned against the shiny red frame puffing out his chest. "But the two of you don't know anything about that, do you?"

"You're threatening us?" Neil questioned, his tone thick with disbelief.

"Just reminding." A woman in tennis shoes, a beige skirt, and a suit coat crossed in front of Billy.

"Billy," Neil said, "if you know where I live, why didn't you find me there?"

His eyes narrowed, and he returned to the truck. "You two drive safe. Wouldn't want either of you to get in an accident." With that, the engine fired and Billy sped off.

Neil tucked the gun away and turned. He wrapped his arms around me. "We're fine, Blue Eyes." But his chest rose and fell like he'd run a marathon. "I won't let anything happen to you." He took my hand and led me away, phoning every one of his contacts while we headed to his truck.

"Did he follow us here?"

"I don't think so. Sometimes coincidences happen." He still held my arm. "This neighborhood's questionable at best. We could've been spotted by someone." He unlocked the Yukon. "If Billy knew exactly where either of us lived, he would've waited for us there." Neil helped me up and buckled me in, as though I couldn't do the simple task myself.

"I'm worried." My hands shook.

He kissed my cheek. "I know. We'll stay at a hotel tonight. Who can take Rocco?"

"Grace. She's taken him in the past."

As I texted Grace, Neil called Wade and drove us home.

He went over what happened with Wade. "You need to

find that pickup." Neil rattled off the license plate and told him, "Call in Leland and Gabe." He also kept a keen eye on the rearview mirror as he drove us west on the interstate. "You can take the dog to Grace?" he asked Wade. He waited for the answer. "Thanks."

Neil hung up and put his hand on my knee. "When we get back, pack up enough stuff for two days."

"I need to get ready for my business trip to New York. Plus, what about the girls coming to work?"

"We'll figure out the rest in the morning." Neil pulled off the highway, took a bunch of turns through residential streets, then finally steered into my driveway.

Wade sat in his truck at the curb. He stayed with me while I packed. Neil hurried to his house to do the same.

I'd set my overnight bag by the door and was gathering Rocco's food when Wade came into the kitchen. He leaned against the wall, ankles crossed. "Neil will catch Billy. We have a perfect record."

"What has Billy done before? Neil hasn't told me."

Wade's chin rose. "It's best you don't know." He unglued himself and opened the deck door. Rocco came bounding in.

"Take good care of him." I knelt down and gave Rocco some love. "He's my baby."

Wade smiled. "I see that."

Neil came through the front door. "Ready?"

He drove us to a hotel near Lizzy and Donna's. I could've walked over to their building if I wanted. He asked for room with a king-sized bed, and hand-in-hand, we took the elevator up to our floor.

"This isn't how I saw our date ending," Neil mused.

"Tonight was a date?"

He smiled. "Sort of."

He hadn't asked if I wanted my own room. He'd just gotten us the one. I took off my shoes and tried to remember what underwear I had on. Did I want my blockade to end?

The click of the door shutting and automatically locking behind me forced a memory. Black and sexy, I finally recalled. I set my bag on the floor. The air in my lungs rushed out as Neil strode toward me with purpose. The look in his eyes said my blockade was indeed a goner.

"Relax," he whispered when he put a hand on my hip. "I just want to kiss you."

That I could do.

He lowered his mouth. My hands ran up his hard chest and held onto his thick shoulders. I loved his shoulders. His lips were soft. He took his time, and it felt so, so good to be kissing him. I couldn't stop my roving hands as they slid down his chest and over to his lats and arms. He drew me to him with a hand that swept down to my ass. The last time we'd made out seemed hazy and long ago. This time, I wanted to savor every nuance. Like the way his breath hitched when I grabbed at his shirt, how good he smelled, and how hot his body felt against mine.

"I've wanted to kiss you every day," he murmured against my skin. He laid kisses down my throat, his whiskers tingling every place his lips visited. I tilted my head and sighed. *Neck kisses.*

I ended up against a cool wall. His mouth became insistent and so did I as my fingers snuck underneath his shirt and stroked his back. I grabbed at him and ventured over to his ear and bit the lobe, smiling at his indrawn breath.

"Tova," he said as one hand took a slow journey down the center of my chest. "We should stop."

No way. "Not yet." My fingers grazed and toyed with the

edge of his jeans. "Just a few more kisses," I said and went after his mouth. How could I stop kissing him? He palmed my breast, his thumb and index finger finding my nipple. "Ahh… that feels great." I was grinding against him. I too played with his nipples; after all, fair is fair. His shirt needed to go. Pronto.

He yanked the main zipper of my top. *Okay, mine could go first.* "I've wanted to do that all night."

I started dragging his shirt up and walking him toward the sofa. He tore off the tee by grabbing it behind his neck and yanking. The muscles of his arms stretched before me.

"I love that." I reached out and stroked the thatch of hair on his upper chest. I pushed him to sit. "And I love this." I gave the hair a tug.

His hands on my thighs grasped and pulled until I straddled his lap. There was no way we could stop, I needed him too much. He parted the fabric of my top, his gaze scorching as he took me in. He bracketed my ribs, then caressed my tummy with the back of his hand. Finally, he plumped and cupped my breasts. I arched into him, wanting more, needing more. Teasing, his thumbs passed over my nipples.

"Damn," he murmured.

Mesmerized and restless, I couldn't get close enough to him. He lathed my nipple, his warm, wet mouth over silk. "Ah god, Neil, that feels good."

"I said just a kiss," he whispered.

"We're kissing."

His phone rang. He sat up straight and smirked. "You're right."

All too quick, he placed me on the sofa, got up, and answered. I held my breath. "What is it?" He listened. "We're fine. I'll call you tomorrow."

"Is everything okay?"

"Fine." Neil hung up and picked up his shirt, starting to put it on.

"Don't," I said.

"You sure?"

I smiled, got up, and kissed him. I'd never been more sure about anything.

He moved my hair over my shoulder, stepped behind me, and kissed the nape of my neck. One palm rode the curve of my side as his other held me against him. "I love your hips. They drive me crazy." He squeezed the rise of bone, emphasizing his point.

I turned. Took a step back. Let my top drop to the floor. I should've been self-conscious, but I wasn't. Not with the hungry gleam in Neil's blue eyes. He swallowed, making his Adam's apple bob. My hands went behind me, fingers unhooking my bra. Next, the button on my jeans opened. Except for our breath—a low hum—only the rasp of my zipper filled the air. I eased out of the denim and stood there in my black lace hipsters.

He reached out and watched his hand glide over my waist and hip. "Christ, you're beautiful," Neil said. Back and forth he went, stoking the fire in me.

His mouth went to my mine, and our bare chests, at long last, met. We kissed again, our tongues teasing and finally getting serious. He delved under my panties. "Fuck," he said and gripped my butt. I palmed his erection through his jeans. He growled and drew my hand away. "Nope, I've been hard for hours." *He had?* "More of that and I'll come before I get in you."

I reached for him again.

"Tova." He laughed and gave me a little shove, sending me to bed. "No."

"Neil…"

"There'll be time for that later."

I'm sure I scowled. "Fine, but you need to get naked."

His cheeky eyebrow rose. "I do, do I?" He said this while slipping off his shoes.

I wet my lips and let my vision travel the landscape of his body. "Mmhmm."

He unsnapped his jeans, and I swallowed. He made a show of lowering his zipper, and I leaned up on my elbow, watching. He slid long fingers into his waistband, eased everything off. *Wow.*

Neil got on the bed, leaned over, and lowered his head to my breast. I wiggled closer, my hands going right to his butt and clutching. He flexed and I fondled. With a soft wet tongue, he licked and captured my nipple, teasing me. Seconds later, I moaned his name and the sound triggered something.

He rose up on his knees, grabbed hold of the lace at my hips, and stripped me. He growled as he stared at my sex. "Fuck." His hand stroked the inside of my leg. He leaned down and kissed my hipbone. Then shifting, he bumped my legs open with his knees and slipped between.

A wicked gleam grew in his eyes. "I bet you taste great."

Five words and no lie. I think I came.

He held me still and licked the crease of my leg from center to hip. He played, with his hands, fingers, and finally his mouth. Even though I had dreamt of this, the sight of his curls between my thighs, his eyes on me, became too much. I clutched at the sheets, his hair, and then, without warning, arched off the bed, bursting.

Languorous, I floated down. He lifted his head. I couldn't take it any longer. I wanted him in me. "Come up here and kiss me."

"I don't think I can," he murmured.

I tugged on his hair. "Yes, you can."

He grinned and prowled up the length of my body. His chest against mine, I gripped him. "Tova, you're killing me."

I smiled. "No, I'm not. I'm loving you." He gave me a look I didn't recognize in my catalog of Neil faces.

Then he kissed me. I stroked him, then remembered about protection.

"Please tell me you have a condom in your wallet?" He nodded. "Thank god."

"You're excited."

"I haven't had sex in forever."

He reached down to the carpet, grabbed his pants, and threw two condoms on the bed.

I looked him in the eyes, I needed him to know. "Neil, my tests came back okay."

"I know, sweetheart."

"I'm on the pill, but…"

"It's okay, I understand. Relax, okay?"

"Okay." He grabbed the protection, opened it, and stroked himself once, twice. The word erotic didn't do the sight justice, and it ended way too fast as he sheathed himself.

His fingers feathered up my side. He lowered himself over me, caging me between his biceps. I felt him right there. He looked in my eyes, marking the moment, and smoothly guided himself into me. He felt so right, so good my sex pulsed. He eased out and pushed back in, going further but still not all the way. He did this until in a flash of utter madness I grabbed his ass, planted my feet in the mattress, and arched into him until I felt the knock of his pelvis.

"Tova," he groaned.

"I had to." My sex contracted, then did it again.

Neil's gaze went from belly to breasts. "My Blue Eyes." His whole upper body shuddered. "That's amazing, but you need to stop." But instead of me stopping, he did. He stilled.

I ran my hands down his chest. "Neil?"

"I need a second." A glaze of sweat broke out on his skin. "You're gorgeous and feel too good." When he put it like that, I could wait.

He closed his eyes for a moment, and I leaned up and bit and licked the column of his throat. The salty tang of his sweat met my lips. I couldn't get enough and licked from the base, over his Adam's apple to the stubble of his jaw. "I want to make you into my very own lollipop."

"Sweetheart, after this, you can lick me all over."

Naughty Neil.

He reached down and circled my clit in a delicious little swirl.

My back bowed. He needed to move. "Neil. Please," I begged again.

His jaw tensed, but he got the point and started thrusting, hot and heavy, his eyes on mine, drifting down my form. He pulled almost all the way out of me and glided back in with a nice bump. Desire spread from my core to my chest. I'd imagined this moment for too long, and the reality shattered any conjured scenarios.

"I'm so close," I said on a moan.

Inelegantly, his head twitched and he bucked into me. His breath strained, inciting me.

He reached down. His thumb circled my clit, once, twice, and then the overwhelming force of my orgasm hit. *Spontaneous combustion.* My sex contracted in rapid waves, awash in the most incredible, body-wracking—I went off with an echo of Neil's name bouncing off the walls.

Neil's eyes pinned me to the bed. I started to come down. He concentrated so hard, his face screwing up in that *don't come yet* grimace, I had to hide a grin.

His turn. I pushed up on my elbows, kissed his chest. "You feel so good." I slid my hands down his abs and gripped his behind. He locked his arms at my sides. Transfixed, I watched as his eyes closed, he threw his head back, and a ragged groan escaped.

After he came down from his high, he bent and kissed near my ear. His whiskers rasped against my cheek, and he reached out, squeezing my hand.

"Christ, why haven't we done that sooner?"

I smiled. "We've been busy."

———•———

NEIL

I woke in a haze to the stretch of Tova's body against mine. I twisted the hair off her neck. My fingertips trailed the bumps of her spine. I couldn't stop touching her. My hand kept going up and down her back until I put my mouth to the juncture of her neck and shoulder and bit. Last night I'd found out she liked to bite, and now I wanted to, too.

Last night she also said she was loving me and I knew she meant it.

"Morning," she moaned and wiggled against me. The vibration sent another spike of blood to my dick. She twisted to the side and kissed me with her sweet mouth.

"Morning." I held her tight and ground my hips against her incredible ass. This was what I'd been waiting for—to wake up next to her. There was no going back now, I wasn't letting her go. My hand slipped down, grabbed her thigh, and lifted her leg over mine. My fingers wandered. "You're so wet again."

She moved restlessly against me. "I can't help it."

Did she think I didn't like it? "I fuckin' love it." I wanted to hear her come, feel it, and know I was the one doing it.

She rocked against me and whimpered a little bit. "Right there," she whispered.

Her leg twitched, her stomach contracting in a jolt. A few more strokes and she stretched her taut torso, feline and seductive, as her body gave.

The naked press of her body and the noises coming out of her became too much. I tucked my hand between her thighs and laid a trail of kisses to her ear.

"Neil." She reached back again and grabbed my ass, the clutch making me falter.

Had to get inside. I found the extra condom and put it on. I eased into her, my hand on that curve I loved, and she started working her hips. I went slow. I'd told her last night I'd last longer on round two. I think I lied. I reached between her legs and found her sweet spot.

"Neil." She tensed. "Oh… Oh god, don't stop."

She stiffened from head to toe. "That's it, sweetheart." She arched back, clamping down on me. "Fuck, I feel that." My hand clutched her so hard I marked her. I thrust into her and stayed as I came.

We lay there panting, our legs tangled. I rolled to the side. A loveable enigmatic smile graced that pout of hers. "Now *that* was a great way to wake up."

I held off telling her we would be waking up every morning together.

We got ready and stood by the door waiting for Charlie. I wrapped my arms around her. I never knew my heart could expand to the point of this. I worried about her. We needed to get Billy off the streets.

She slipped her hands into my back pockets. "I wish we could stay in bed all day."

Sure would be safer. "Me too." I bent down and kissed her, then patted her butt. "I'll pick up dinner tonight."

———•———

TOVA

"Where are we going?" Charlie asked. We made our way out of the hotel to his truck.

"I need to pick up an order from a vendor in Minneapolis. I've been waiting two months for it, then we can head back to my house. I just need to get some stuff to work on and grab my laptop."

"Sounds easy," Charlie said. "I have one stop in between."

We ran my errand and then got onto I-94, passing the beautiful basilica with its copper top. The Lowry Tunnel lay ahead, carved into a hill and nestled in-between buildings. Before blue sky disappeared, the Sculpture Garden's white spoon and cherry broke through tall trees.

Entering the tunnel, harsh yellow lights illuminated dirty subway tiles. Charlie took the sharp turn—and then we jerked forward. Someone had run into us. The sharp sound of metal ripped through my ears. Charlie swore. My hands flew in front of me.

That damn hill rose from the earth. People died if they hit that grassy hill.

We were hit again. My shoulder banged off the window. Airbags released. My knuckles slammed into my face—

Blackness came too fast.

TOVA

"What's your name?"

Sucked into a foggy dream, I heard a voice, yet wasn't able to open my eyes. Why was someone asking me that? Something vise-like trapped my head. Pain radiated through my body. When I moaned, it sent panic flaring though me. Finally, I opened my eyes to see who was asking my name.

The guy, an EMT, hovered over me, again asking, "What's your name?"

Why wouldn't he stop? I got it already. Fuck, my head hurt. "Tova," I grated out. Glancing down, I saw the stretcher below me. "I'm Tova Hudson," I said with more clarity.

"You've been in an accident, ma'am."

No shit. He smiled, then winked, and I realized. "Said that out loud, didn't I?"

"Sure did."

I recalled hearing the impact, then the throbbing pain reverberating in my head. I tried to move but couldn't. "Is Charlie okay?"

"Ma'am, you need to stop wiggling around."

"Well, stop calling me ma'am. I'm, like, five years older than you. Is Charlie okay?"

"Charlie's fine." He examined my shoulder. I examined his hair. *Too blond to be natural.* "Do you know what happened?"

"Someone ran into us." My heart leapt into my throat. Billy. Was Billy responsible? "Where's Charlie?"

"On his way to the hospital. He put up a fuss not being able to wait with you." *Oh, Charlie.* "Is there someone we can call?"

"Yes." Blondie jotted Neil's name and number down. My hands came up from my sides and I tried to do a pat down. I groaned, then remembered I got knocked into the widow.

"Shoulder again?" he asked.

"Yeah, it hurts. What's wrong with me?"

"Might have dislocated your shoulder. In a second, I'm checking if I need to pop it into place. Otherwise they'll do it when you get to the hospital. I bet you have a concussion, too. The rest are bumps and bruises. The airbag helped."

"What's wrong with Charlie?"

"I think he broke his arm."

"Did he roll the truck?"

"Luckily, no. The cops'll have some questions when you get to the hospital. Did you see who hit you?"

"No. Why?"

"They ran."

———•———

"She's in here?" I could tell the questioning voice belonged to Neil. He opened my curtain, his face panicked and pale.

"Hey." I shifted a bit higher on the bed, smiling at him.

His worry cleared after he looked me over. "Christ, you scared me, Blue Eyes." He bent and kissed my forehead.

"I'm fine."

He cupped the side of my head and lingered, looking at me. "You're always fine. I bet you feel like shit."

"I'm a little sore. Banged up my shoulder." *Thankfully I didn't dislocate it.*

Neil's thumb passed over my bumped head. "And this? What's this?" He sat on the edge of my propped-up bed.

"I think my head hit the window. How's Charlie?" I skipped over the ache from the seatbelt.

"He's okay. Let discuss your head."

"I feel fine." Was Charlie really okay?

"The airbags messed with his hands. Nothing's broken." He moved my hair over my shoulder. "I want to wrap you in bubble wrap."

The doctor came in to evaluate my concussion symptoms, and our moment ended. Then a nurse led a detective into my tiny space to ask me questions. Unfortunately, I had no answers to help solve who'd hit us.

Charlie came to see me with bandages on his wrists. "Airbags," he said.

"Oh, Charlie." I waved him over. "Come here." I gave him a hug. He sat down in the empty chair next to Neil. "What did you see?"

Charlie talked to Neil. "A woman with short, dark hair driving a white van." Then he looked to me for confirmation. Could it have been Josie? "I was checking to make sure we weren't being followed. I saw the van behind us on Broadway. She got on the highway. But I didn't think much about her. I was on the phone." He shook his head. "Maybe I was distracted. I must've been 'cause she plowed into us like she meant it." Charlie reached out. "I'm sorry, Crocker, I could've gotten us killed."

"You stopped them from forcing us up that dangerous hill.

We would've flipped."

My doctor poked his head back into the cubicle. "We're releasing you in another two hours. Have to watch you for a bit. But we'll send you home with some good pain meds."

"We're going to your house," Neil informed me.

"It's safe?"

"Word on the street is Billy's still running his mouth trying to find out your name. Besides you'll sleep better in your own bed."

———•———

I called Grace once I got settled at home. I wanted to check on Rocco. I sat on the bed and told her, "Don't freak out, but I was in a car accident. I'm okay, though."

"Jeesh, don't do that. I hate it when you tell me not to freak out and then tell me you've been in an accident. That is not nice!"

I laughed; it hurt. "I'm sorry."

"Where are you?"

"Home. Neil came and got me for the hospital."

"You were in the hospital?" She sounded shrill.

"Yeah, but I'm fine. I messed up my shoulder." Thank heavens I wasn't busy making things for a new line right now and I could let my arm rest. Neil walked in, shaking his head. He brought me a glass of water and signaled for me to hand him the phone.

"What?" I whispered.

"Let me talk to her."

"Really?"

"Yeah. Take the pills the doc gave you."

He held out his palm, and I gave him my phone. "Hi, Grace. Yeah, she's okay." I wished I could hear what she was saying. "Yeah," he answered. Gracie talked again, and Neil frowned at me. "No, she didn't *just* hurt her shoulder. Tova has a concussion and she's banged up."

I heard Grace cuss through the phone and cringed.

"Okay," he answered her. "Yeah, I'm staying with her." He listened. "You're welcome."

He ended the call and set my phone on the nightstand. "Just hurt your shoulder, huh?"

"I didn't want her to worry."

He sat next to me. "Tova, you don't need to hide what's going on so people don't worry about you. It's okay for them to worry. And for you to accept help."

He was right. I did have a problem taking any type of assistance. Bump me around and I just got worse with it.

"When your friends need help, you don't see it as a weakness. Do you?"

"No. Of course not."

"So how come you can't let them do the same for you?"

He was right. So right it bothered me. A lot. I rested my head on my good shoulder. "Point made."

"How are you feeling?"

"Like a truck hit me."

He scowled and laid his hand on my head. "I want you to nap, but first do you have it in you to tell me what you did today and what you remember from the accident?"

"You heard all I said to the detective. The only thing to add is my head bounced off the passenger's window, and I passed out."

"Do you think Charlie was speeding?"

"I doubt it."

"And you never eyed the car behind you?"

"Nope. You heard the cop. No one saw a license plate. Only an outline of a woman."

"TJ's getting me a copy of the tapes." He touched my cheek again, and I wondered what he might not be telling me. "I wanna know it wasn't Billy."

My pulse spiked. "You think it could be him? The other witnesses thought a woman drove the van, and Charlie thinks a woman drove the van, too. You don't think it could be Josie, do you?"

"It could be anyone. First thing we're gonna find out what kind of vehicle she drives."

She'd already proven she was unstable when she barged into my house. Was she really so crazy that she might try to kill me over Andrew? I'd already agreed to divorce him. What more did she want? Besides, he wasn't worth it.

"We'll get some answers soon. I know you said you're still planning on leaving for New York in three days, but I want you to think about canceling or sending Reva and Astrid without you." Did he think he could run my life?

"Neil…"

"That's what employees are for."

"You don't understand!"

"*You* don't understand." He took a deep breath. "Let them do their job, sweetheart. This is exactly what I was talking about earlier. Let them do what you pay them for. Take the help."

Damn it, he was right. My lips pinched together. And I nodded.

———·———

A few hours later, I got up from my nap. Neil had started dinner, which involved getting Thai food delivered.

"I got it," he said, sidestepping me after the doorbell rang.

"The least I can do is pay for dinner."

He didn't respond. Instead, he answered and paid the

driver.

"That's clever, Handsome." Neil looked over his shoulder, smiled, but didn't answer, just handed me the takeout bags and signed the receipt. I itched to go get my handbag; it was my house after all. He was the guest. But I resorted to my usual snappy comeback. "What? You think if you just give me a sexy smile, it's like I didn't say anything?"

He chuckled as we headed into the kitchen. "You need to get over it."

"You're as stubborn as I am."

"You know the saying, 'It takes one to know one'?" he asked, walking by.

"Yeah."

"Well..." He lifted an eyebrow.

I laughed. "You are," I said emphatically.

He reached to grab plates. "No, I'm more."

No kidding. I sat and watched him get out silverware and open the takeout containers.

"Iced tea?" he asked. I nodded. That sounded great. Looking pleased, he got me a glass and opened the fridge. As he reached to grab the pitcher of tea, the muscles of his back pulled and flexed. I recalled them flexing last night. Heat rushed to my cheeks. We wouldn't be doing that for a while.

"Grab some food, Blue Eyes. Do you need another pill? You're looking flushed."

"I'm good." *Not.*

"Okay, but I want you taking one in an hour."

———•———

After dinner, he ordered me back to bed, saying he'd join me in a few minutes and we'd watch a movie. I was perusing the movies, my back against the headboard, when Neil walked in. With both hands, he grabbed at the bottom of his shirt and tugged. His shirttails popped out and he uncovered some flesh. Then he brought his hands to the buttons, undoing one, then another. He stopped and glanced at me. I probably appeared like one of those old-fashioned cartoon characters with big eyes and my tongue hanging out.

"Keep going."

His smile was gentle. "Pick anything out?" *Yes, yes, I had.* He undid the button-down and slipped it off with his T-shirt. He sat on the other side of the bed and pulled off his socks.

"I don't want to watch a movie." But for some reason, it didn't come out the way I thought it would.

"Babe, as much as I wanna get you naked, you need to rest. Not tonight."

I grinned and handed him the remote. "You're no fun."

"*I* get to pick?" he asked.

"Sure. Is that so hard to believe?"

He picked an old movie, and I cuddled into him on my good shoulder. At some point, I fell asleep and woke to the moon casting a softer glow over the room.

———·———

Neil was awake. He stroked my back. "How are you feeling?"

I had one leg and one arm draped over him. I reached out and pushed some hair off his face. "I'm not in pain, but I suppose I should take another pill."

"Sure." He jumped off the bed and went to get me a glass of water. He passed me the glass and handed me a pill.

"Thank you."

He held my gaze, his hand sliding slowly over my bruised

arm. "I've never been so worried in my life, and I've had some serious shit to be worried about."

"Neil…"

"I don't know if you should go out of town. I don't like the idea of you leaving."

I'd agreed to let my employees help more, but I'd stopped short of saying I wouldn't go. "The doctor said I should be able to travel."

He sat on the edge of the bed. "I've gotta find Billy." *He really does think it was Billy.*

His thumb glided across my mouth. I captured it with my teeth and licked the tip.

His eyes fired. "I think about your mouth all the time."

Oh, hell. He leaned down, and as he did, I caught him behind the neck, only then releasing his finger.

"Kiss me, then. I won't break."

We did more than kiss.

Then we fell asleep again.

———•———

Vivian, Reva, and Astrid babied me all day. "You need ibuprofen," was the first thing Vivian had to say.

Reva cut in with, "Nah, she needs a drink." Both girls hovered more than I liked, but they meant well. I knew that.

Astrid asked, "Whoa, boss, can I photograph those bruises?"

"No way in hell."

The main difference in the day was Leland. *Should I tell the girls I call him Dimples?* Neil's guy was hanging out with us and setting up a camera on my front and back doors. I then gathered up any of that info on Andrew Neil had asked about and gave it to him when he stopped by. He was kind enough to ignore the girls' chattering from the hall. I'd deal with them later.

Mid-afternoon, I called Lizzy and Donna. I wasn't made for hiding things from them, but I played down the accident only so they wouldn't worry.

Donna said, "We'll come over tomorrow and bring dinner." Then she handed the phone to Lizzy, who asked, "This neighbor, Neil. Can he come over for dessert while we're there?"

I told her I'd ask.

The rest of my day consisted of Astrid continuing to plead her case to take photos of my bruises.

"Please? The purple and blue look so on point with your skin tone."

"Oh my god, Astrid," I laughed. "No."

Passing my fingers over my arm, I flashed on Neil doing the same thing that morning. How could a touch feel so good? Then again, it was Neil. It always had. I swayed on my feet.

"You're tired, go take a nap," Vivian said.

Taking care of myself—that I could do. Then I did laundry, including Neil's forgotten boxers, which pleased me to no end. What would it be like to have a life with Neil? I shook my head. A week ago I hadn't wanted to put myself in a position to get hurt again. How could I have such a thought?

Not yet.

A text from Neil said he'd be over after work—with a pizza.

———•———

I heard him pull in and went to hold the door open. Watching him walk toward me, with the intimate knowledge of what he felt like, my body hummed to life. He stopped, bent, and put his lips on mine.

"You look delicious." He kicked the door closed. *Hey!* He

would need to stop doing that.

I asked against his lips, "Why do you keep kicking my door?"

"Neighbors." *Mmm, good point.* He put the pizza down. "You smell so good." He strung a necklace of soft kisses from one side of my shoulder to the other.

We made out like teenagers while eating, my earlier thoughts forgotten. After, he led me to my room.

I sighed and pointed at the prescription cream, and he grabbed it off my nightstand. Slowly, he unbuttoned my shirt, letting the back of his fingers linger from neck to waist. "I'll put some of this stuff on. Lay down."

I did as ordered, and he sat next to me. He smoothed his hand down the curve of my back and moved my hair out of his way. I was good with this, and that surprised me. Maybe I could change.

"I'm gonna kill whoever did this." He warmed the cream in his hands.

"Is it that bad?" I asked, but when his feather-light touch brushed over my bruises, I knew.

"Yeah. It's gotta hurt like hell." *Do it. You'd never hurt me on purpose.*

I wanted to only feel the tingle his touch created. "The drugs help," I joked and then groaned as he traveled on and got to my mid-back.

"Does that feel good?"

Lie. "So good."

He reached the dip of my lower back, one of the few not-sore places he'd found. "I've been thinking about your trip to New York. First I didn't want you going, but now I think it's best you get out of town." His fingers danced up the bumps of my spine.

"Will you keep going?"

CHAPTER 16

TOVA

He kissed my neck. "Mmhmm." His merciless fingers teased. He reached my butt, and what started out as Neil taking care of me turned erotic. He drew circles on my skin, his breathing changing from normal to excited as his big hands kneaded the skin of my bottom. Then he inched my yoga pants and panties down and off.

"Flip over, Blue Eyes."

I did and his eyes roamed. He ran his hand from between my breasts to between my legs. "The only thing that would make this better is if you were on my bed," he said. He took off his shirt, reached into his front pocket, and put a handful of condoms in my nightstand. I watched in avid fascination as he unzipped his jeans and stepped out of them. He wore white boxers that did nothing to hide his erection.

"Open your legs." He wet his lower lip and sunk his teeth into it.

If I hadn't been soaking wet before, I certainly was now. "I take it you don't think I'm too sore?"

He lay on his stomach and settled between my legs. The sight of his eyes on me, along with his wild hair rising from my thighs, burned itself into my brain. He winked at me. "You don't have to move, babe. I'll do all the work."

———•———

The next morning Reva asked, "What inspired you to buy all this chalcedony?"

"I love it. You know that."

She pushed her light brown hair out of her eyes. "You're really loving it."

I hoped she bought the load of crap I shoveled. The translucent light blue beads reminded me of Neil's eyes.

Astrid looked up from her desk. "I saw you made my favorite cake."

"Yeah, Lizzy and Donna are coming over for dinner. But you guys get to have a slice before they do."

"We should make bets on what Donna will wear," Vivian said, smiling.

I dropped a pile of packages. "Whoever's closest has to fill all of the orders tomorrow."

"I am in on that bet," Astrid stated.

Reva pushed her goggles down. "Me too."

Vivian scooted her chair toward me, dropping an invoice on my desk. "I've got the vibe she'll be in hot pink velour."

"Oh, no, she's going to wear something in leopard. I bet it will have a fur collar. You can never go wrong with fuzzy stuff," Reva said, placing her bet.

I gave my prediction. "I think she'll have on red. Lizzy wanted to meet Neil. She'll want to make an impression." The girls had to know something was going on with Neil, but they didn't ask and I didn't tell.

Vivian laughed. "That changes everything. I change my bet to a black-and-white big print. Velour will be too casual."

Astrid grinned. "I'll take velour, then. In beige or navy for evening wear."

"Maybe we should do a resort wear collection based on all of Donna's favorite prints," I said. The girls groaned and I laughed.

A few hours later, Donna honked her arrival. I opened the door as she pulled her boat-sized Cadillac into my driveway. Of course she swung wide and hit my ginormous, green garbage cans. They tumbled over like plastic bowling pins. Donna had the uncanny ability to run into things while going two miles an hour. She stepped out of the vehicle to see the damage. Astrid, Reva, and I each scored a point. Donna sported a dark red—to match her caddy—velour outfit with a leopard fur collar.

"Darn it," Vivian hissed.

———.———

"Tell us more about Neil," Lizzy said, looking at me with an inquisitive face. My grandmother wanted details on the man I'd been spending so much time with, which was my own fault. I had runaway of the mouth when it came to talking about him.

"I told you about his business, right? He's been helping my lawyer track down information on Andrew."

Lizzy glanced at Donna. "Is that when you met him?" Donna asked.

I cleared my throat. "Actually…"

"Are you keeping company with him?" Lizzy asked.

"Are you asking if we're dating? We're friends." I jumped up, ready to change the subject. "I'll get these dishes and start coffee."

Lizzy spoke to my retreating back. "Decaf, dear."

After I got that going, Neil knocked. He wore a gray polo, dark tailored jeans, and loafers. He'd dressed up.

"You look nice," I told him softly.

"Thanks." He ran a hand down my back. "How are you feeling?"

"I'm good." I smiled at him. "Come on, I want you to meet them."

Neil followed me and walked straight over to Lizzy. "It's nice to meet you," he said and held out his hand. "I'm Neil Hamilton."

My grandmother smiled and shook his hand. Nervously, I held my breath, waiting to see if she would approve. It was a tiny thing I suppose. No, that wasn't true—it was a big thing for me. I wanted Lizzy to like him.

"I'm Elizabeth Hudson, but you can call me Lizzy." All the pressure I felt dissolved when she said that.

Neil smiled. "Hi, Donna."

"Hi, Commissioner Gordon." I didn't know why, but Neil threw his head back and laughed.

With a wink, he said, "I see where Tova gets her sense of humor."

Donna and Lizzy chuckled. "I'm confused," I admitted.

"The man who played Commissioner Gordon in the old Batman show," Donna replied, "was an actor named Neil Hamilton."

"Oh." I turned to Neil. "I take it you've been called that before?"

"My brother, TJ, calls me Commissioner when he wants to get my attention."

"Does it work?" I asked.

"Usually."

I grinned. "I'll need to remember that."

Neil helped me pass out cake, and Lizzy started with questions. "Neil, Tova said the two of you go walking every morning?"

"Yes," Neil replied. "Tova needed to get out of the house. I knew it would help."

My grandmother focused on him. "Has Tova told you my ex-husband cheated on me and was verbally abusive, especially when he was drunk, which was often?"

Oh.

My.

God.

"Grandma!" I bugged my eyes at her, wanting to squash the conversation.

Neil looked at me, but when Lizzy spoke again, he turned back. "Did she tell you my son cheated on her mother for a decade before Ingrid kicked him out?"

Neil's eyes locked on mine, and I couldn't look away. "No, she never told me."

"This is crazy. Grandma, please stop. You're making Neil uncomfortable."

"This is not silly, Tova," Lizzy said.

"Mother," Donna pleaded. "Stop this."

"I think Neil should know."

"Why did you have to bring it up like that?"

"He needs to know."

My hands shook in my lap. "Enough."

Neil reached over and put his hand on both of mine. You'd be blind and dumb not to realize the intimacy of it. "Lizzy, I get what you're telling me."

Really?

Lizzy smiled. "Good."

I blinked. I'd entered an alternate universe. Lizzy's rant cleared, and the subject changed so fast I got whiplash.

Donna asked, "Are you excited to see your dad?"

Wonderful. Another topic I didn't want to come up. "I wouldn't say excited, but I want to see him."

Lizzy moved her cup aside. "Will the new one be there?"

She'd stopped learning my dad's wives' names a while ago—or so she claimed. "Yes, Claire will be there." I shifted to look at Neil. "Dad's fourth wife."

His eyebrows rose. "Oh."

"I'm having dinner with the two of them."

"Lord knows the list of your father's flaws is longer than a Tolstoy novel," Lizzy said, "but try and have a nice time with him. You only get one dad."

"Yeah, and you only get one mom and he made her miserable."

"*Tova*," Lizzy admonished.

"It's true. He may as well have killed her with his bare hands. I swear what he left behind killed her, not the cancer." I don't know what made me go off—maybe Lizzy's rant or all this bottled-up stuff—but I did. "She stood by him and look what it got her. I'll tolerate him, but we'll never have a normal relationship." I let out a long exhale. Lizzy's face held pure shock and sadness. My heart ached. "Grandma, I'm sorry. I don't know why I said all of that."

"It's okay, dear. I know he upsets you." She leaned in my direction. "You know it's not that you don't have a relationship with him. It's that you don't have the one you want. And like with Andrew, you need to learn how to accept that."

———•———

After Lizzy and Donna went home, Neil and I sat on my new, peacock-blue sofa. Drifting along, I felt like a deflated balloon. I'd been schooled by Grandma, and she was right.

Neil shifted toward me and gave my earrings a tinkling. "I like these. They're very pretty on you."

I tried to smile for him. "Thanks."

He sat back on the sofa, reached out, and lazily toyed with the long strands of my hair. "You ladies know how to make a night interesting."

"You assumed you were coming over for a little cake."

He laughed. "I gotta say, Blue Eyes, you make a mean cake."

"Thanks." I leaned into him. "I'm sorry Lizzy put you in an uncomfortable position—and I acted a little nuts." *More than a little.*

He put his arm around me. "Your grandmother loves you."

"She does, but I don't want you to think we're crazy. 'Cause we're not."

"It was very informative. Will you tell me more about your mom and dad?"

"First, I need a drink. You want anything?"

"I'll take a water."

I came back with two bottles, handed him one, and he pulled me down right next to him.

"Did you want me to sit on your lap instead?"

"You want to?"

"Silly," I scoffed.

"You wanna see silly?" He chucked his water, laid me across his lap, and started tickling my sides.

"Neil," I squealed and batted at him, trying to ward off the attack.

"If you don't put a smile on that beautiful face, I'll be forced to keep tickling you." I laughed uncontrollably. I don't think anyone had tickled me since I was a child. The kid in me loved it. "I'm feeling quite evil today." He waggled his fingers in front of me. "I wanna know where you're ticklish."

I giggled, defending myself, hoping to find a ticklish section on his hard body. But he thwarted that by flipping me onto my back beneath him—which, I must say, did not suck. He held my hands above my head and inched my shirt up a little, exposing some of my ribs to his view. His fingers teased my skin.

"Neil, stop," I begged.

He smirked. "Nope."

"You're gonna pay," I said with all the fierceness I could muster, but I cracked into a grin as his hand found a place on my side that weakened my sass.

The width of his hand swept over my stomach, making me squirm. He slid his hand up a little higher over my ribs and an inch from my breast, and what started out fun turned into foreplay. I swallowed and licked my lips watching him. He paid close attention to his hand, but I wanted him to kiss me. I started to lean up to catch his mouth when his phone rang. He didn't move to answer it, and eventually, it stopped. His fingers grazed my breast on a slow, leisurely journey.

His phone went off again. "Fuck," Neil said. "That's my partner Jack's ringtone. I need to get it."

He jumped up and shook his head as he sat on the end of the sofa. "I don't know what I was thinking. I'm sure you're still sore." He pulled out his phone and dialed.

"I'm not," I groused.

"You're not, huh?" He smiled, leaned in, and touched a finger to my bottom lip.

"Nope." I shifted closer and ran my hand down his chest.

His call connected. "What's up, Jack?"

I kept running my hand over his shirt, getting more and more turned on. I slipped my hand down over the bulge in his pants and wondered if...

"He what?" Neil stood. "Well, that's a bonehead mistake!" He paused and walked to the kitchen. I wondered what could get him so riled. A minute later, he was back. "I need to go down to the station." He frowned. "Sam's been arrested."

Even though I'd never met him, I decided to hate Sam at that moment. "For what?"

"Breaking and entering."

Holy cow. I'm pretty sure the one time I heard Neil mention Sam he did about the same job as Charlie. Either way, a month ago, I'd never had a talk like this. "Sam has a job similar to Charlie, working with your corporate clients?"

"Sort of. I just need to get everything cleared up so he doesn't spend the night in lockup. He doesn't look the part."

"What?"

"When someone messes with Sam, he really will be arrested."

"Oh."

"I'll be here to take you to the airport in the morning."

———·———

Neil did as he promised. "Where are you staying?" he asked as we made our way to the airport.

"We'll be at The Roger. It's at 31st and Madison."

"Text me when you get there?"

"Of course. Any word on the blood from the break-in?"

"No, but you know this state's problem with promptness. When I called yesterday, he said it'll be soon."

"You'll call me when you know something?"

"Right away." He pulled in front of the airport and got out. After he'd set my bags on the curb, he kissed my forehead. "Be safe, okay? You haven't had the best of luck this week. And don't overdo it. I don't want you getting a headache."

I drew back, looked at his serious face, and kissed him until we were honked at.

He caressed the back of my neck. "Call me tonight when you can, okay?"

The words *I love you* came to mind, but I didn't say them. I swallowed, "Okay." I walked backward and smiled at him, then turned and went into the Departures terminal.

———•———

I'd been in New York for three long days at a large show, getting plenty of orders for fall. Astrid, Reva, and I sat in the elegant lobby, with two-story high ceilings, natural wood walls, and sleek white furniture. We'd worked ourselves ragged, I was beat, and the evening still wasn't over.

Astrid took my phone and snapped a picture. When it buzzed with an incoming text, I stole it back.

You're beautiful.

I'd never get sick of him being sweet. Neil had called me every day, sometimes twice. I noticed Astrid had sent him the picture she'd took of me.

You're handsome.

A text came back. *No. You're BEAUTIFUL.*

I sent another. *AND YOU'RE HANDSOME.*

My phone buzzed again. *Stop shouting! I heard you the first time.*

I laughed out loud. "Hey, guys, I'm going upstairs," I told Reva and Astrid.

When I got up there, Neil texted. *Are you free?*

Yep, just got up to my room. A minute later, my phone rang. "Hi, beautiful."

I smiled. God, I loved him. "Hey, Handsome."

He laughed. "Who took the picture?"

"Astrid." In the image, I sat on a long sofa, my back against the white cushions. My legs were crossed. One black heel dangled from my toes, the other sat propped on the coffee table, and my head was thrown back as I laughed. I looked happy.

"I have a new screensaver."

"Really?"

"If I'm joking, I'm not breathing."

Funny. "Can I get one of you lounging for my screen saver? Preferably naked," I whispered.

He chuckled. "Anytime, sweetheart."

"What are you doing?"

"I got news today. The blood evidence on your break-in should be completed by tomorrow."

"Do you think anything will come of it?"

"Maybe."

"Any word on the tape?"

"TJ said he'll have a copy of your accident in a day. The investigators couldn't make out a license plate, and no other car with that description has been recorded stolen. You and your dad set up a time to meet?"

"We're going for a late dinner tonight."

"What's going on between you two? Will you tell me?"

CHAPTER 17

TOVA

"I don't want you to think it affects me the way Lizzy makes it sound." I tried hard not to let him get to me.

"Tova," Neil said, the serious note in his voice clear.

"It's water under the bridge. I just get a little wired when I'm going to see him."

"Okay," he said.

I took a drink of water and sat on the edge of my bed. "When I was thirteen, I found out my dad was cheating on my mom. I only knew about the secretaries, but I'm sure there were others. I'd get used to one voice, and when I called his office weeks later, it would be someone new. It's such a cliché that he banged his secretaries."

"And your mom knew?"

"Yep. That's how I found out."

"Christ."

"I woke up in the middle of the night to my mom screaming. She yelled something at him about keeping his dick in his pants and that she wasn't going to another office party where half of the secretary pool had slept with her husband." God, I was actually saying this all out loud. "I'd just figured out what sex was. I felt horrible for her, but it explained a lot."

Tears began to burn the corners of my eyes. "H-he always came home late, and my mother never seemed happy. The puzzle finally clicked. When I turned sixteen, my parents divorced after I told my mom she needed to wake up."

"I get why you don't like him so much."

"Yeah, and that's only half of it. My dad got a new job and moved to New York."

"Are you sure you even want to go tonight?"

It was the slightest of pauses. "Of course I'm going. I see him twice a year, maybe. I've put up with our contentious relationship this long. It's just one dinner."

"I wish I was there. I'd go with you."

Sweet, but at the same time, I thought, *I'm more than capable of handling my own father, Neil.* So of course I said just that. Aloud. If I'd been downstairs, the girls would have heard it.

There was a silence. Then came a snide, "*Of course.* You don't even need me. Well, I stand by that. I would go with you."

My heart skittered in my chest. I sighed.

"I would, Blue Eyes."

———•———

While waiting at a table in the middle of the packed restaurant, I admired the murals, painted almost a hundred years ago, of naked nymphs in the forest, their cherubic faces pink and glowing as though they held the secret to happiness. My father walked in. His gray hair appeared as impeccable as his navy suit, but he looked much older than he had six months ago. Something about that made my chest hurt.

"Hi, Dad." I stood and gave him a hug.

"You've lost weight," he said, matter of fact.

He always noticed. Last time I'd seen him, I'd been a size larger. "I have."

I hid my wince at his hug, and luckily the bruises were covered by my dress choice. Unluckily, this was summer in New York, and sleeves were out.

"You look like your mother."

I bit my lip. I'd picked a black silk dress that fell to my knees and reminded me of something she'd worn in a picture. I'd bought it for the same reason. Heat rose up my neck. My mother had been a gorgeous woman, but I'd watched something about her beauty die. I knew my dad meant I looked good, but I barely knew what to make of his comment.

We sat and ordered drinks and food. He took a sip of his whiskey. I guess we had that in common—the love of a good drink. I'd grasp at anything to give us some common ground.

"How's Lizzy?"

"Doing well. She's volunteering as a docent at the museum again." I smoothed my napkin down on my lap. How long would it take for him to start nitpicking?

"What's Donna doing? Still running her little hair place?" *Not long at all.*

"Yes. She's been thinking about retiring. Selling. Then she could work on her writing."

"Her writing." He laughed sardonically. It stuck out in the serene setting of fairyland nymphs, and heads popped up. He loved finding fault with her, just like he did with me.

"So what's this about you and Andrew getting a divorce?" At this, he bothered raising his eyes from his drink, his chin up, pointing it at me. "You're not going through with it, are you?"

Ice clashed in the glass as I bopped my own drink up and down on the white table cloth. "Yes, I'm going through with it.

He cheated on me."

"You're not getting any younger. Maybe you should give him another chance?"

I jerked back in my chair at the suggestion. "Are you nuts? He'd been cheating our entire marriage. And he was never home. There's no marriage to save, and I'd never, ever want to raise kids with him. I'd rather be alone."

"Well, you might be."

What a horrible thing to say. I should've walked right out of the restaurant. *Why didn't I? What makes me stay? Some bit of etiquette I learned from Lizzy and Mom?* Yes, I was just like my mother. And in her honor, I would be polite. But certainly not pushed around. This was a fine restaurant. We rarely came here together. And I was determined after the past few weeks not to let Dad ruin the experience. In spite of his next comment.

"You don't want to end up like Donna. No kids, living alone."

How dare he? I touched my silverware, lingering on the knife, but thought, *no.* "Let's not talk about this. You don't have a leg to stand on in the matter," I said, tasting every bitter word coming out of my mouth.

"Remember you're my daughter when you speak to me."

"You're joking, right? You cheated on Mom for years."

"You don't know what my marriage was like to your mother, and I'm not discussing it with you." That tone brought back so many memories, and my stomach clenched, remembering.

"Great. We won't talk about my marriage or the four of yours."

We finished our dinner in near silence. I couldn't wait to get out of there. He hugged me goodbye but didn't apologize.

I got back to the hotel, started packing up for my flight the next day, and found a note from Neil tucked in the small zippered compartment of my suitcase.

Blue Eyes,
Remember I'll be thinking of you. Stay safe.
Neil

I folded the paper, tucked the note into my wallet, and called him.

"Hi, sweetheart, how did it go?" He sounded tired.

"Not well." I really wished things were better with my dad. "You put a note in my suitcase. That…" Tears threatened again. I pinched the inner corners of my eyes to stop them. "…was awfully sweet."

"You're upset." He had that right. But it dawned on me then that I had Neil, this wonderful man who cared enough to write me a message and give a damn about me that he listened and talked.

"Hearing your voice helps a lot."

"Tell me what happened, Blue Eyes."

I did and he got upset on my behalf. But in the telling, I let go of my anger.

"How come Claire didn't come?" he asked.

"She had something come up." Or so my dad said, not that I believed that.

"What's she like?"

How do you tell someone your stepmom will come back as a blood-sucking leech because she's had so much practice? "Part-bitch, part-uninterested."

Neil laughed. "Wow, that good?"

Sadly, yes. "Last year, she decided my dad's heart issue should be treated with a month-long vacation to Monte Carlo. Oh, and she's eight years older than me." Okay, maybe I sounded a little angry, but I was trying. Something in the back of my mind sprung forward. "Neil, can I ask something?"

"What's that?"

"When you installed the security system in my house, I overheard something about your mom. You were fighting with Reid. What was that about?"

———•———

NEIL

My two conversations with Tova kept repeating in my mind, even as I held my phone to my ear. Her reaction to my wanting to be with her as she met with her dad had not gone as I expected and neither had the rest.

"Hey, Hamilton. Knew you'd call early," Joe, my contact from the crime lab, said.

"Did you end up with a hit?"

"We did, and I think you're going to like it."

"Who?" I asked.

"A Josie Lawson. Ring any bells?"

"Christ, you're sure?"

"Yep. The blood on the wall and the acrylic piece she cut herself on both clearly matched the sample on record." *I'd eat crow for this.*

"Anyone have an idea where she's at?"

"I'd start with your brother, TJ, or Reid if I were you," Joe said.

"Thanks, man. I owe you."

Why the hell had she broken into the house? Then I remembered the box. She'd wanted something from that box in the closet. I dialed Tova.

"Hi, Handsome." It still made me laugh when she called

me that.

I glanced toward her gray house and yellow door. She loved the place. Especially her yard. I didn't want to live in the same house her ex had, though. "Have you left the hotel?"

"No."

"Got a minute?"

She chuckled. "Only a minute?"

"Not for that." I laughed. "I just found out who broke into your house."

"Who?"

I had a feeling this would bug her. "Josie."

She didn't say a word for a second. Then she simply asked, "Really?"

"Yeah, it was her. They're positive."

"Oh my god, that creeps me out."

"Is it okay if I go look in that hall closet for the box she dumped?"

"Of course, but I put it with all of Andrew's stuff. It's gone." She sighed. "It's so creepy, Neil."

"You'll stay with me when you get home."

To my amazement, I heard no fighting for her independence. "Okay." I liked her willfulness, but I wanted her with me. After the trip and that scene with her dad, maybe it was just fatigue that made her pliable. Or maybe, when things settled, I could get her to move after all. Time would tell.

I headed over to her house and called Leland and put him on Josie's records. Maybe he could find a clue to her whereabouts. I unlocked the front door, turned off the alarm, and nabbed Tova's orange stepladder. It only took me two minutes to figure out how the damn contraption worked.

Nothing rested on the shelf. My phone rang. Tova. "Anything?" she asked.

"No. Just some dust bunnies."

"I don't have dust bunnies."

I spotted one. "Should I take a picture?"

"Yes."

"Hold on…" I leaned in, phone on camera, ready to take a shot. I started to fall and grabbed a shelf. It popped up, and I stumbled right off her atheistically pleasing ladder like a fucking klutz. "Fuck." I dropped my phone and hit the floor.

I looked up as the orange ladder teetered back and forth. The shelf I dislodged, slapped down, and sent papers raining to the floor.

"Neil!" Tova yelled. "Are you okay?"

I snagged the phone. "I'm fine. Good thing you've got dust bunnies."

"You fell!"

"I blame this ridiculous contraption you call a ladder."

"Sorry, honey." She'd never called me that before. "Are you okay?"

I stood and put my hand up on the wall. The papers had been jammed in a folder and stuck in an old shelf ledge on the back wall of the closet.

"Yes, sweetheart. One good thing about falling—a file folder just unwedged itself from the shelf and your wall." *I'd bet my truck this is why Josie broke in.* "Hold on one second."

I brought everything to the kitchen and sat down at her island. The first sheet was addressed to Mr. Svengaard and had results on a latex mold test. The next piece, another letter, dated after the first asked to have another mold tested, this one out of silicone.

"Who's Teddy Svengaard?"

"Andrew's best friend. Well, *was.*"

"Was?"

"Yeah, he died three years ago. A car accident. I never met

him."

"Why would one of his folders be in your closet?"

"They worked together at the same office. They grew up together. They even went to the same college."

For a man of few possessions, like Tova said, why would Andrew hold onto these papers? "I'm gonna track down Josie today. You can look at this once you get home, see if you can make anything from it. I'll be at the airport to get you."

Not long after getting off the phone with Tova, TJ called. He had a copy of the accident footage and said Reid would drop it off.

———•———

Reid waited. He wanted to watch it with me. "It's not Billy," he said, propping a leg on his knee and leaning back against my couch. "You sure are working your ass off for a married woman."

Not again. "It's not like that." I slipped the DVD in.

"You sure? 'Cause it looks like she's got you running in circles." He jumped to a conclusion based on his past, not mine.

I sat down and hit play. "She's divorcing him." I couldn't make out much, but the little I saw of the woman in the van made me realize I'd been worried about the wrong person all along. The slight features and the dark hair belonged to Josie.

———•———

TOVA

"I just turned on my phone," I said into the receiver. I'd already gotten my bags and made my way outside to the covered pick-up area. A blanket of heat and humidity hit me on step two.

"I'm here," Neil said. "Are you near baggage claim? I'm at door four."

"Okay." A police officer stood on my left, and when I glanced past him, the Yukon sat at the curb. Neil, grinning, sauntered toward me. His shirt clung to his shoulders and skimmed over planes of muscle. Not having seen him for days did nothing to soften my memory of how spectacular he appeared in motion, but more than that, the adoration shining from his eyes made me melt into him when he put his arms around me.

"I missed you."

"Missed you too." He rubbed my arms. "Your skin's cold." He moved his hands to my sides, his eyes sweeping down my body.

"Air conditioning." I wore a black pencil skirt, probably the sexiest piece of clothing I owned.

One of his hands slid to my hip, the other around and up my back, and he kissed me. Long and deep. "Fuck, I missed you." He held me against him, then patted my ass. "Get inside."

He loaded my bags, got in, and moved into my space. "Love the skirt, Blue Eyes."

"I wore it for you."

He put a hand on my knee. "Will you un-wear it for me later?"

"If you're good." Out of the corner of my eye, I saw the edge of a file folder. "Is this it?" I snatched it from between my seat and the center console.

"Yep. Take a look."

I could see that the first few pages held information on latex molds and then correspondence about changing the quality to silicone. Not really interesting, but all of them were addressed to Teddy or from Teddy.

"I've been calling the company that did the testing, but I've gotten nowhere. Bigger news, though. I got to see the tape today. It was Josie in the van."

"What? How did she know where we were?"

"She did break into your house. Maybe she grabbed a calendar or a schedule."

I thought about it for a minute. I hadn't thought anything was missing.

His phone rang through the truck. Neil answered it on speakerphone. "What do you have, Wade?"

"Lawson is staying in North Minneapolis."

"Good, I've got Tova."

"Hey, Tova. You sure have me busy in some low places."

"Hi, Wade, how low?"

"Really low, and I know low. Neil, I've got an in on watching her from an apartment nearby. Should I wait? You gonna drop Tova off?"

"Yeah, I'll do that first. Wait for me."

"I want to come with," I cut in. "Don't you dare take me home."

Wade laughed though the phone.

Neil shook his head. "Call you back, Wade."

"I want to come with. She broke into my house," I reasoned. "I'll stay in the truck."

"That's half the problem. Where we're going is just as dangerous if you're with me or sitting alone in the Yukon."

I pleaded. "Please let me."

His jaw clenched. When he glanced at me, his eyes looked resigned. "This isn't good."

"How long will it take to get me home and double-back, Neil? Wade could be in danger. What's not good about me coming with you?"

He pulled into a gas station. "Me, caving. You have jeans in one of those suitcases, right? I really can't believe you're talking me into this."

"Jeans? Sure."

"Good 'cause you need to change."

I kissed him and grabbed my bag.

———·———

Twenty minutes later, we sat in front of a cluster of small, two-story brick buildings set around a court. Every one looked exactly the same except for the odd screen door hanging on by two hinges instead of three. The old tan roofs changed to near black at their gutters. Three boys on bikes watched us as we parked. The sun cast their shadows long and lean into the road. Heat coming off the pavement made a hazy fog that radiated skyward.

Neil texted Wade, and seconds later, he called. Some button Neil hit made the call come through the truck's speakers.

"She's alone in 327," he reported. "I can see where you parked. It's the third building on your left in the center unit. There is a back door. Obviously, anyone can see us coming. The guy she's been staying with is a dealer. While he's gone, we need to grab her."

"You called for backup?"

"No one's available. They're working the runway case. I'm in the fourth building next to hers, looking at the front door. You see those boys? I paid them to watch the back. I'm texting them now to get out of here. I'll take the front. You take the back."

This is like watching a movie.

"What about the neighbors?" Neil asked.

"They'll stay put. Move on my whistle. Tova with you?"

"Yep."

"Keep her in the truck."

A streetlight flickered and switched on. One of the boys drew out his phone, looked at it, glanced at us, said something, and he and his friends took off.

"I'll be there in one," Neil said, ending the call. He turned. "Keep the doors locked. Do not move. Only unlock them for Wade or me."

I nodded. "I know."

He leaned over and kissed me. "I mean it, Tova. No matter what happens, don't leave the truck."

"Right."

CHAPTER 18

TOVA

Neil got out, beeped the locks, and slipped his gun out from behind his back. I watched him stride across that court, and I froze as he kicked once, busting in the door before disappearing inside. Two gunshots startled me. My heart hammered. Should I call the police? Fixated on Neil, I missed the man walking up to the Yukon.

He knocked on the glass behind me. I jumped and stared into Billy's dark eyes. He pointed his gun.

"Out," Billy bellowed. Could I dial Neil fast enough? Had he left the keys? But I couldn't abandon him either.

As I thought about my options, he tapped the glass again. "Don't make me."

I waited too long, and he gave me a look of pure smug hatred, aimed the gun, and shot out a tire.

I got out.

"Funny seeing you here, Mrs. Hudson."

A chill ran down my spine. He knew my last name.

"Yeah, funny," I said, knowing I'd done the one thing Neil warned against. My pulse shook, as did my hands. This was bad. Billy was bad.

"Come on." He grabbed my arm. "Your boyfriend seems

determined to make a mess of things." *What did that mean?*

With his gun tucked against my head, Billy marched me toward the door Neil had gone through moments before. "Don't do anything stupid."

Through the kicked-in door, shouting poured out. I heard Wade yell, "Crocker!" He could see me. I looked around for him, and Neil came into view, his eyes lasered onto the gun at my head. I mouthed, *I'm sorry.*

"I want Josie," Billy said, loud over the shell of my ear. A stiff resolve marked Neil's body as he looked me over. "You let her walk out of here and I'll leave Tova behind." Billy knew Josie?

Neil nodded, and his eyes cut away. I presumed to Wade.

"Josie!" Billy yelled. "We're going."

How were they connected? And why was he trading me for her?

"Billy?"

He kept moving me closer to the ruined door. "Yeah, Josie. I came." Billy's tone turned sweet as he shoved me up the steps.

"Can't you see I'm busy?" she cackled. Was she high or did having two guns on her do that?

Billy pushed the cold steel of his weapon to the back of my head. "Drop it," he said to Neil. "Your friend, too."

Hard-faced, both Neil and Wade lowered their weapons.

"Kick them over here."

They did, the metal sounding heavy as it pinwheeled toward us. Billy picked up the guns, tucked them in his pants. "Now come on, Josie. We gotta leave. The police'll be coming."

Her hair limp and eyes crazed, she peeked out around the corner. She glared at Billy. "You brought her here!"

"Come down now."

She looked like an ad for getting off meth. Josie obviously

had a problem, but I couldn't feel too sorry for her. She'd broken into my house and tried to kill me. She took a wobbly step in her high-heeled boots, pouring every bit of concentration into the maneuver. As her foot lowered, the gun she held swung to me. Why were these two together? Not good.

"Now it's me holding the gun," Josie stated and grinned. "Not so fun, huh?" She looked from me to Neil. Going very, very slow, she took a step, then another. "I loved him more than you ever could," she stated, eyes lifting. She was talking about Andrew.

Frankly, I hadn't thought about it. I hadn't let my mind wander to the reality that Andrew loved her. How could she love a man who married me? Who would treat someone they loved with no regard for their feelings? But maybe I had been the other woman.

"Why'd you break into my house?" I asked.

She stopped. "What?" she asked, shocked.

"I know you broke into my house. Why?"

Her cheeks got pink. Feigning innocence, she said, "I have no idea what you're talking about."

"Don't, Tova," Neil warned.

"Did you break into her house?" Billy asked.

Avoiding my eyes, she tilted up her chin and took another step. "I don't know what she's talking about."

"Yes, you do," I said adamantly. Police sirens whirred from far away.

Billy bent slightly to the side to glance at my face. I knew he believed me. Even Josie caught sight of it.

"I didn't!" she yelled. Her face scrunched in determination, begging to be believed.

Josie jerked the gun at me, her focus like a laser pointed between my eyes. She took another step. Her pointy heel caught. Fear slackened her face. Time slowed, all movement slowed, even my heart slowed. Things I shouldn't notice—I did. Like how the streetlight slanted through the open door and particles of dust sparkled in the air around us.

Her free hand lunged at the railing, but she slid and stuttered, not connecting. Her body fell. Neil leapt in front of me. The gun went off.

As slow as time felt, it hadn't slowed enough for me to reach out and stop what happened as Neil dropped. He hit the floor with a grunt. I followed as panic gripped my vitals organs and made them flip. Blood seeped from his hip. I reached out, put my palm over the wound, and began to pray.

I barely noticed Billy grabbing Josie off the floor and hauling her away. Wade called 911 and cut in front of me, shoving me away and placing his hand where mine had once been, holding the blood in Neil's body. But what I remembered most were Neil's eyes closing before I told him I loved him.

The police and an ambulance arrived, and Wade and I were pushed aside. They loaded Neil inside, taking him away in a flurry of flashing lights.

"He's gonna be okay," Wade reassured me over the blare of sirens as we followed the ambulance. Neil had lost so much blood, I didn't know how he would. I wore it on my hands and knees. So did Wade.

So many mistakes layered on top of each other. What had I done? How much blood could one person lose before…? I couldn't think about it.

Why hadn't I told him I loved him?

Neil had lost consciousness, and I hadn't told him. Inside, my heart screamed at me.

More scared than I'd ever remembered being, I rocked back and forth in the passenger's seat. Wade set his hand on my leg.

"He is."

I bit my lip. "He is," I repeated. Tears ran down my cheeks.

We arrived covered in blood, but the staff we encountered didn't look at us funny. I was just handed a pair of blue scrubs and ushered into a sterile-looking room to clean up.

"Put your clothes in the grey bag in the corner," a nurse told me. "You can wash up at the sink." She gestured at the empty stainless steel basin and then left. The astringent smell of disinfectant hit my nostrils, and it dawned on me how real this all was. Did the police want my clothes? I set the scrubs on a cold metal table. I unfastened my jeans and started lowering them.

The paramedics had plunged scissors between Neil's skin and jeans to cut them off. Sheers had torn through the fabric as they were shifting him into the ambulance. I whimpered. What if I lost him?

Tears ran in rivulets down my cheeks. *How was he doing? Did they have him in surgery yet?* Too many thoughts. No answers.

After I cleaned up, my efficient nurse took me to the waiting area. "Sit down, dear," she said sweetly. I figured she'd heard me crying. Why couldn't I stop? But then more of the event rushed into my mind.

"What if..." I whispered. *No.* I brought up my hand, but before covering my mouth, I saw his blood the paramedics hadn't been able to wipe from my fingers. What had I done?

I knew without looking that my eyes were red. More tears ready to spill. The nurse was speaking to Wade now. "We'll let you know how he is soon."

Wade paced, but his shoes made no sound on the patterned carpet. He talked quickly on his phone.

If it hadn't been for me, Neil would be fine right now.

Charlie showed up, his easygoing attitude gone. Then TJ, Neil's brother, came rushing in. What could I say? I wanted to hide. Cry. Give him a hug. Even though I'd only met him the day Neil moved in, I felt I knew him.

"TJ, I'm so sorry." *How inadequate.* I needed him to know how bad I felt. The words came tumbling out. "I'm the reason he was shot."

"No." He squeezed my hand. I lowered my head, and the freckles on his wrist blurred into more tears.

A hot flush swallowed me. "I am. None of this would've hap—"

He drew me into a hug. "Don't do that." I nearly fell into his chest as his arms wrapped around me. He felt like Neil for a second.

Wade moved back to us. "None of what happened is your fault. I've known Neil a long time. He doesn't regret what he did."

I took a shaky breath, brought my arm up, and wiped my cheeks again with my bicep. I wanted to believe, but I didn't know how I could.

Reid showed up next and started in with questions "What happened?" he asked Wade. He looked like a thundercloud. The navy blue of his uniform showed no silver lining at all.

Half of us sat along a single row of waiting room chairs, as if for a class or a movie. Wade on one side of me, TJ on the other. Reid and Charlie sat across from us. It dawned on me that Charlie had been silent all this time. A few nods at the others showing up, but nothing more.

They murmured to each other in low tones. Half-listening, I stared out at the dark sky. Wade started in. "Clearly, Josie didn't want Billy to know she'd been in Tova's house."

My stomach roiled. It hit me then—*Billy and Josie knew*

each other. I blurted, "How did those two get paired up?"

Charlie glanced at Wade, then me. He spoke finally. "We don't know yet."

I turned and bumped Wade's knee. "Is Billy gonna hurt her?" Something about the way Josie had reacted made me think yes. She'd lied to him.

"No idea, Crocker."

TJ got up. Although he wasn't in uniform, the cop vibe was still strong in his manner of pacing. "Anything from your end?" he asked Reid.

"Nothing. Not one sign of them." All four men pointed their attention to me. Reid put on his cop voice. "Tova, tell us everything from the beginning."

"What do you mean?"

"We need to know every detail. Don't leave anything out. Josie's involved in this, so I just want to know first. How'd you meet your husband?"

Shouldn't they be worried about Billy and Josie? What was he implying?

Coaxing me to start, Charlie tried, "It helps us put the puzzle together."

Fine. I'd bore them with the details. I didn't know how this would help. "He had an idea and wanted to know more about a process so he could make design decisions. So he signed up for a class I was in on pouring metals and making molds."

"How long did you know him before he asked you on a date?" Reid asked.

I didn't like his tone, but I answered. Anything to help Neil. "Six weeks."

Reid stretched out in his seat, his long legs eating up the floor space. "Why do you think he asked you out?"

Really? I frowned. "No idea. Just suddenly seemed

interested." That nurse came back in, and I held my breath. We all turned to her. But she'd come to talk to another group, waiting on the other side of the beige room.

"What'd you talk about?" Reid pressed, crossing his ankles, angling his body in the chair to try to get comfortable.

You prick! I ran things though my mind. "We talked about my jewelry business. He asked to see my studio."

Wade leaned forward, his bare elbows meeting my blue scrubs. "So you invited him over?"

What were these guys on about? "He seemed nice enough. It wasn't a date." I spread my hands, showing them how empty this all was. *Who cares about some dates? Billy and Josie were together!*

"And you didn't know about Josie?" Wade asked for the second time since the break-in.

Had I known? Had I had a clue? "Uh…"

I caught the glance Reid tossed Charlie, a brow going up. Was that Reid's way of saying *I told you so*? "When did he ask you to marry him? How long had you been dating?"

At the time the decision had seemed impetuous; we were so in love, we couldn't wait. Now, I knew better. And saying it out loud made me feel foolish. "This has nothing to do with Josie and Billy."

"How long?" When had sweet Charlie become a pit bull like Reid?

"Two months," I snapped.

Reid smiled. "How soon did you get married?" *That absolute prick!*

It had just been a few of us at the courthouse. We'd done it on a Thursday. "A month later. His best friend had just died in a car accident, and my dad and I weren't getting along, so we decided on simple." I got pissed for explaining and sat straighter. So what if I'd gotten married quick? I knew it was stupid now, but I shouldn't be embarrassed.

"And fast," Reid commented. *How dare he?* This was all making me die to stretch my legs, so I got up, throwing a few looks of my own around at them.

It didn't help. "Neil told us your mother died and your parents were divorced. You're an only child. You got her estate."

Where was Reid going with this? My gaze travelled counterclockwise, taking in all four men. "I did."

Reid went on. "And your dad's a lawyer. You come from money." Something sour ran up my throat. Reid leaned back, getting comfortable. "Not just anyone can buy a big house and start a business without having some serious cash." My eyes narrowed, but he kept on. "Your doctor was smart enough to know that, too." He tilted his head, dropping it to a shoulder. "Think back. When did he start asking you about anything having to do with money?"

I gestured to the way he sat in the chair. "Why don't you get more comfortable while you make me feel like a fool?" He frowned. *Good.* "To answer your question: right away."

"Okay, that's enough, Reid," TJ intervened.

I straightened even more. "Do you feel better now?"

I'd known in some way that it'd been terribly convenient that I could easily cover the loans with my inheritance as collateral, but at the time, what Andrew had asked for benefitted both of us. Plus, he worked hard. I thought he'd succeed.

I met their eyes. "When did you figure out I was a sucker?" But no one answered. *Pussies.* "I'm sure you knew as soon as you met him." I moved toward those wide windows, then faced them all again. "I'm getting a water. When I get back, you can embarrass me some more."

I called Cassie and Grace. I needed my friends. They said they were on their way, so there was nothing to do but head back to the viper pit. The guys kept their mouths shut for a while and let me drink in peace.

Finally, Wade spoke. "Who are his friends?"

Ah, not again. Why not just haul me into the station for Christ's sake?

Friends? Had Andrew really had any true friends? "He has one friend in Minneapolis. They play racquetball together. I can get you his info." Taking out my cell, I texted Wade.

"What about family?" Wade asked.

"What does this matter? You need to find Josie and Billy."

"We need to figure out why she broke into your house and tried to run you down, let alone kill you. Josie either took something or not," Wade went on. "I suppose she could've left something behind. But, Crocker, she's got it out for you. Doesn't help you keep saying nothing was missing."

"Did your husband ever claim anything was missing from his stuff?" TJ wondered next. He was the only one who'd never met Andrew.

"No."

"Like I was saying—" Wade looked around me to TJ, "—Josie wouldn't admit it. But she wanted Billy to believe her." *That's why they don't know if she's in danger.*

"So what do you think Andrew's hiding?" Reid asked Wade.

Were they moving on to figuring this out instead of focusing on me? I jumped in with, "What about the file Neil found in my closet? The one with Teddy's name?"

All four heads cut to me. They had no idea.

"This afternoon, Neil went to my house. He found a file

that belonged to Andrew's best friend, the one who died." All eyes stayed on me. "Neil wanted me to look at it. He brought it to the airport. I glanced at the papers in his truck before we made it to Josie's. Information and correspondence," I shrugged. "On silicone and latex molds."

Charlie edged forward and rubbed his jaw. At least his expression had softened. "Were the two of them in business together?"

"They were dentists at the same office before Andrew started his business."

TJ's phone rang, and he got up. "Scarlet, sit down," he said. He paced around the waiting room in front of us. "Neil's been shot."

My heart beat a path to tear out of my chest. Déjà vu swept over me as I relived the news of my mother's death and getting the phone call from one of her friends. She'd told me to sit down, too. What if TJ had to call his sister and tell her Neil died? My hand flew to my mouth, a ripple of nausea hitting my gut.

"He's at Hennepin County Medical Center having surgery."

Wade hooked his arm around my shoulder. "Gonna be okay?"

I nodded. I was done with holding things in. Look where it'd gotten me—sitting in a hospital wishing for a minute back.

All we could do now was watch the secondhand move on the big clock. I wondered when we'd know something. TJ's phone kept ringing. Neil's parents were getting on a plane and flying in from Florida.

Cassie and Grace came roaring into the sedate waiting room.

"Any word?" Grace asked, glancing at me, then Wade.

"No."

"Let's go to the bathroom and get you into your own clothes," Cassie said, pulling me out of the chair and giving me a hug.

Grace looked at Wade. "I didn't bring you clothes."

"I've got some in my truck," Charlie said, and Grace nodded.

Cassie dragged me to the bathroom ladies' room, and I yanked down my scrubs.

"Holy shit…" Grace took a step from me. Looking like she might faint, she grabbed at the counter. Maybe I hadn't done a bang-up job cleaning myself up.

Cassie put her arm on Grace's shoulder. "Can you keep your dinner?"

She closed her eyes and nodded. The short breaths she took echoed off the tiles. "Yes."

"I had blood…all over my legs," I apologized, reaching for the taps to get more soap into my palms.

Cassie surveyed me from all sides. "I think we need to clean you up some more. You missed the back." She grabbed paper towels and wet them.

Eyes still shut, Grace asked, "None of that's yours, is it?"

I turned on tip-toe. Red-brown streaks marked the backs of my thighs. A physical ache knocked in my chest. "No. Just Neil's."

Cassie cleaned my legs and washed her hands, and then it was my turn. Grace kept her eyes squeezed shut until I'd put my new jeans on.

"I'm so nervous and scared for him."

"We know," Cassie said.

"I didn't tell him I love him."

Grace gave me a hug. "He knows."

"How?"

Cassie patted my back. "Chickee, we've known since we saw the two of you together."

Really?

We walked in a huddle back to the waiting room. I whispered, "You'd better keep Reid away from me. He's being an asshole."

"What did he do?" Grace whispered back.

"Asked enough pointed personal questions to make me see how Andrew only married me for my money. As if I hadn't figured that out."

Both of my friends wanted to hear everything from the beginning, so we stopped there in the hallway and I told them before going back.

We were in the waiting room, my eyes locked on the door, when a surgeon came through the doors. "Are you all friends and family of Neil Hamilton?" she asked.

TJ came over and sat next to me, dropping a hand on my knee.

"Yes," we answered.

CHAPTER 19

TOVA

"Good news." We all exhaled.

"The bullet grazed Neil's hipbone. We repaired the damage. He'll need to spend a few days in the hospital." I leaned forward, stared at the carpet and felt tears coming again. She gave us more details, then reminded us, "He got lucky. An inch to the left and this would be a different discussion."

"He's gonna be fine, Tova. Stop crying, okay? Neil wouldn't want you crying," TJ whispered. "He's gonna be fine."

"They're happy tears. Grateful ones."

———•———

An hour later, an older, well-dressed woman raced into the waiting area with Charlie in tow. *Neil's mom?*

"TJ!" she called. Her son stood and wrapped her in a hug. "Is that right? Charlie promises, but are we sure?" A man followed, blinking in the harsh waiting room lights—Neil's dad. He looked just like him.

"Yes, Mom, he's gonna be okay." Tears pooled in her eyes. She reached behind and grabbed her husband's hand. "Mom, Dad, this is Tova. Neil's friend."

"Hi, Martha." I gave her a hug. I figured she needed one.

"Oh, Tova." She squeezed back. "It's nice to meet you." Her short hair seemed immaculate, like she hadn't been on a plane. "Neil's told me all about you."

He had?

Neil's dad, Tom, held his hand out. "Tova, Tom Senior."

I shook his hand. "It's nice to meet you." I don't why I said that.

He smiled. "The circumstances could be better."

I winced. "I know. I'm sorry." If it hadn't been for me, Neil wouldn't be in a hospital and I wouldn't have been meeting them this way.

A nurse came back, a new one this time, and said family could see Neil. She led his parents back to see him, and then TJ got a chance.

When TJ came back, I was waiting, but he told me, "No visitors for a while." I about cried.

Martha sat next to me. "He was out of it when we went in," she explained. "I told him you were all here."

I soaked up her words. Like she was speaking just to me. Knowing it could be a long while, I sent Grace and Cassie home. And I was glad they went. It was another five hours before the first nurse came to say Neil wanted to see me. Had a whole shift passed since this started?

I peeked into Neil's room first to make sure he was awake. He was propped up, IVs and machines hooked into him. His skin had no color and his sunken eyes were on me. Considering he'd been shot hours ago, he looked like a damn miracle.

All my fault. How could I possibly go back to that waiting room with all his family, his friends? I'd done this.

His voice, pure sandpaper, cut into my numbness. "Come here. Let me kiss you, Blue Eyes."

I stepped closer. "I'm so sorry, Neil."

Neil patted his raised bed. "No crying. Come here." I looked at the bed, wondering how I'd sit and not hurt him. "I was shot on the other side," he joked.

Tentatively, without thinking, I reached out and moved his curls off his forehead. "I'm sorry." I felt lost, like he should hate me.

"Nothing to be sorry about."

"You jumped in front of a bullet for me."

He brushed my hair back. "Don't do that."

"Don't *you* ever do that," I stressed.

"I'd do it again in a heartbeat." His hand slipped behind my neck. "Give me a kiss."

"It's all my fault," I said against his lips. His mouth was rough, and he tasted of mint. It hit me then, what I had to say, what I had to tell him.

"I love you," I said through tears. I'd been waiting to say that, but still, I drew back. Neil's eyes sparkled, all fathomless ocean and moonlight. Something passed between us; it resonated before the words left my mouth. He knew how I felt.

His entire face warmed. "Love you, too." He pulled me forward and kissed the corner of my mouth.

I think I even believed him. We sat soaking in the moment until I blew it. "You brushed your teeth."

His eyebrow did a little dance-y wiggle. "I knew you were coming."

I took a deep breath. *Back to normal.* It finally felt like I could really breathe. "How much pain are you in?"

He smiled. "I'm doped up, sweetheart. I need you to do something for me, and I need you to not give me a hard time."

I'd do anything. "Sure."

"I need you to stay at my house."

I ran my hand down his arm, needing to touch him. "Housesitting?"

"You'll be safer, I already have cameras on my doors, and my parents will be more comfortable."

Everyone would talk—everyone being our neighbors. "They're gonna think we're sleeping together."

"We are."

"Neil, they'll think we were having an affair." I got up and paced the small room.

"We're not. Why is this such a big deal?"

"I remember how everyone gossiped about my parents." I rubbed my forehead with my fingertips. "I don't want that for us."

"We haven't done anything wrong." It was nice he didn't think so, but we weren't complete innocents either. "I'm trying to keep you safe," Neil said, taking the wind out of my sails. How could I say no, now? "Josie wants you dead and who the hell knows what Billy wants."

I nodded. "You're right."

"Charlie is going to stay with you and my parents. I'm gonna make sure you're never alone. Call Eve. Tell her what's going on. She'll spread the right rumors."

I sat back down. "Charlie is staying with us?"

"No, with you. You'll have my men with you until those two are caught."

"Reid?" *Please don't say Reid.*

"Yeah, sweetheart. I need to know you're safe."

Neil wore the same worried expression I remembered after my car accident. When he put it like that, paired with that face, I couldn't fight him. "Sure, Handsome."

Neil's shoulders relaxed. He took a deep breath. "Charlie here?"

"You want me to go get him?"

"Yeah, but first I want another kiss."

———·———

NEIL

Charlie came into my hospital room, talking before the door even closed. "Jesus, man, you scared the shit out of us." He sat next to my measly table and IV. "I always thought Wade would be the one to get shot next, not you."

If it had been Tova, I don't know what I would've done. "I lucked out."

"Sure. Real lucky."

"I need you to take care of a few things. You need to stay with Tova and my parents until Jack gets back and can help me." My business partner, Jack—his life kept getting in the way of work. He had as many problems plaguing him as I did. "That means staying with them at my house."

"Not a problem."

"And I need you to arrange for Leland and Gabe to get cameras installed on Tova's doors." Charlie took out his phone and started taking notes. "Go over the panic button with her again and make sure the women who work for her know about it. The first one there in the morning is Vivian, the redhead."

"She has a redhead working for her?"

TJ poked his head into the room. "Neil, I gotta go. I got a call about a lead, but first—what's this about some papers you found?"

"There was a file in Tova's closet, hidden. It's in my truck. Sam needs them."

"Sam's the new guy who has a job like yours?" TJ asked Charlie. How could my brother not know who Sam was?

Pins and needles ran down my leg. My entire right side seemed to be waking up. Shifting on my bed, I got caught between some wires. "Let me know as soon as you know anything." TJ's eyebrow lifted. My hands didn't seem to work, and I had the urge to just rip the equipment off when everything started beeping. Fuck! I took a deep breath and got untangled. "I know I'm stuck here." My voice rose as the beeping intensified. "I wanna know what's going on."

TJ unfolded a cable I sat on.

"I'm blind now, too."

"All right, bro. I'll see you tomorrow. Get some sleep."

He disappeared out the door. How was I supposed to take care of Tova stuck in this bed?

I looked Charlie in the eyes. "You're like glue with her until Jack gets back."

"Got it. We've all left messages for him. It all hands on deck."

"Which reminds me—I want Sam delving into any records he can find on Josie and Billy, anything, even in places we're not supposed to be looking. And I want Gabe to check all of Tova's computers." I blinked and found it hard to reopen my eyes. Damn drugs, I couldn't stay awake. "Hold on, there's more. How do Josie and Billy know each other? And why the hell did he risk his ass to get her out of there?" My eyes closed again.

"You need your rest. I'll take care of Tova and getting your parents settled."

"And find out what Billy wants…"

If Charlie said anything after that, I didn't know. I fell asleep.

—·—

TOVA

Charlie escorted Tom, Martha, and myself back to Neil's house.

"You take the master. I've got the couch." He came over, yawning, and gave me a one-armed hug. "Try and get some sleep, okay?"

I answered with a matching yawn. "That's not gonna be a problem. I've been awake for two days."

We slept for a few hours, then Charlie drove us all back to the hospital. Neil had a little color in his cheeks. A twinkle shined bright in his eyes, and when I saw it, I couldn't help but smile.

His mom sat next to him, pouring water and straightening the tray before he took his first sip through a bendy straw. She re-fluffed his pillows, refolded blankets, and reminded him three times she'd brought a bag of clothes and toiletries. She also had Tom gather up magazines. They were stacked neatly on the only side table.

"We're going to get coffee," Martha said, patting Neil's hand.

I almost wanted to tell her no. I feared her coffee intake would have her dusting when she returned.

"Come here, Blue Eyes." Neil patted his bed.

I sat on the edge, still aware of possibly hurting him. "You look so much better today." I moved his hair off his forehead. Making my heart expand, he leaned into my hand.

"I'd been counting down the days till you were home from New York," he sat up straighter. "And now I'm laid up."

"Are you whining, Hamilton?"

He grinned. "Maybe you can spend the night with me. That's all I want."

I kissed him.

"You'd be safer," he mumbled against my lips. Then he shook his head. "No. You need a good sleep."

The kiss turned into a makeout session. I could think of nothing, not one thing, more life-affirming than his mouth on mine and his warm hands on my face.

One of his hands swept into my hair near the base of my neck and held me, and I reached out and placed my hands on his chest, careful how I touched him. His teeth drew my bottom lip into his mouth. I repeated the move on him and closed my mouth over his plump bottom lip and let it slide out between my teeth.

He growled before pulling away. "How come I can't stop kissing you?"

"Knock, knock," came a voice.

Neil's focus darted to the door. "Hi, Jack. Your timing, as always, sucks."

I twisted around. Infamous Jack Waters, Neil's business partner, smirked. My details on the man were limited. I knew he'd been a professional football player, and like Neil's parents, he loved to golf.

"You look better than I thought," Jack said, sauntering over.

Neil huffed. "Thanks."

Jack's salt-and-pepper hair and tan skin put my guesstimate for age at mid to late forties. He smiled at me and held his hand out. "You must be Tova?"

"I am. Nice to meet you, Jack."

"You got yourself into some trouble yesterday."

"Yeah, I did." More like I got Neil and Wade in some trouble.

Jack turned his attention back to Neil. "Has your mom been in here cleaning?"

The corner of Neil's mouth tilted up. "Some."

"Sit down," I said, pointing to the free chair.

"Nah. I just wanted to check on the big guy, let him know everything's under control. See how he's doing."

"I'm alive," Neil said.

I frowned. "Neil!" I didn't like that joke.

"I see that. I'm gonna go say hello to your folks. Bye, Tova. I'll be seeing you soon, I'm sure."

Neil leaned forward. "Before you go, Jack, I need you to follow up with a company that Andrew dealt with. Sam has the info."

"Not a problem," Jack said as he left.

I decided Jack Waters could be a bit of a whirlwind.

Neil grabbed my hand. "Come here." I sat on his bed again and he kissed me. His stubble scratched my face, but his soft tongue played with my mouth. "This sucks," he whispered.

"What?" I nibbled on his neck. "My kissing?"

He leaned away, a gleam in his baby blues. "That I'm stuck in this hospital."

I kissed his earlobe and, speaking of sucking, pulled it into my mouth. "That does suck."

Gently, he pushed me away from him. He closed his eyes for a flash and shook his head. "Okay, that's it, Blue Eyes. You gotta sit in the chair."

"Why?"

One of his cheeky eyebrows came up. "Because that thing you did to my ear was not a good idea."

"You didn't like it?"

He growled at me. "Tova, Tova, Tova. You…" He drew me forward. "Christ, I missed you." He kissed me once, fast but delicious. "Now go sit over there," he ordered.

I drank my latte and glanced at him over the rim. "Tell me what the doctor said."

Neil informed me they would be getting him up with the aid of a walker and some big, strong guys.

He held his wrist up. "I need you to make another bracelet. They cut the other one off."

———•———

I went and got a snack, and when I came back, Neil had fallen asleep. I sat down, and not long after, Tom came in and stole the spot next to me. He said he and Martha were leaving later in the day but coming back when Neil went home. They'd stay with him for a week or whatever was needed.

"You'll keep an eye on him while we're gone?" he asked.

"Of course."

"You know he thinks you're quite exceptional."

If possible, I think my heart sighed. "I think the same." We were interrupted when Neil started talking in his sleep.

"Stop, Mom," he said. "Stop." Tom roused him from his sleep.

———•———

I left Neil's room and was halfway down the corridor when I heard Tom. "Tova, I'd like to talk to you about something."

"Sure." I took a step and sat down on a bench next to a water fountain, and Tom joined me.

"Has Neil told you about his birth mom?"

I blinked. We'd never gotten to that. Neil managed to avoid telling me when I asked. "No."

"I had a feeling he hadn't. He doesn't talk about her." He rubbed the back of his neck. Neil did that when he was uncomfortable. "That's who he was dreaming about. He has nightmares." Tom got up and paced around in front of me. "He'll tell you about her when he's ready."

My heart closed into a fist. Neil had nightmares?

———•———

Charlie left mid-afternoon, and Reid came to cart Martha, Tom, and myself to the airport. I wanted to make sure his parents got off okay, and then I planned to come back to visit Neil. Reid agreed. Reluctantly.

When I got back to Neil's room, he was asleep. I crept in and sat in one of the stiff, upright chairs and replayed what Tom said. I shouldn't feel sorry for myself. My mother had been depressed and slightly delusional, but she'd been there. Neil's had disappeared.

Neil groaned and opened his eyes and looked around the room in a panic.

"You okay?" I asked.

His eyes settled on me. He nodded. "Glad you're here."

"Do you need something for the pain? I'll go get your nurse."

He looked groggy and almost childlike. "Just dreaming. I'm okay."

"You sure?"

"Yeah, come here." He propped himself higher with the controller at his hip.

I handed him his water. "Your mom and dad got off okay." I ran my hand through his hair. "I like them."

"I like them, too." His fingers curled around my neck. "As soon as I see you, all I can think about is kissing you. I'm starting to think I have a problem."

Someone knocked on the door and came in. I did a half-turn, and Reid stood there with his perpetual scowl.

"Visiting hours are over in five."

"Can you give us a minute?" Neil asked me.

"Of course." I got up and grabbed his water jug. "I'll go fill this up."

When I got back, Reid looked like steam was about to come out of his ears.

I said my goodbyes to Neil and followed Reid out to his truck. "Are you upset about something?"

"Yes." His focus was fixed out the window.

"Do you want to talk about it?"

"Not with you I don't."

That stung. "Are you always this cranky?"

"No. You bring out the best in me."

What did I ever do to him? "Now you're just being mean."

"Get used to it. I'm your new bodyguard."

CHAPTER 20

TOVA

I heard Reid come out of the guest room and down the hall.

I hip-bumped the dishwasher closed. "Coffee's fresh." Today my house was getting scrutinized and I didn't even care. I was over all that on day one. I swiveled around as Reid reached past me to grab a mug. He wore nothing but a towel.

Okay, then.

I took a step away as he poured. His toned torso and thick arms were quite nice. Not that I looked too hard.

Like a bird of prey, his head turned, but not his body. He glared. "Stop staring."

Flustered, I grabbed a paper towel and wiped down the island. "What's the plan for the day? I need to know if my employees are okay at my house."

"Gabe and Leland will be there. I suppose you need to see Neil this morning." Disdain thickened his voice. Reid seriously needed to get laid.

"Yes, I want to see him."

"Fine. After I check in with TJ, we can go, but you need to tell your employees what's going on. They need to stay out of the way."

Sure, I'll argue with you in your damn towel. I took a step toward him. "Don't you dare be rude to them. It's one thing for you to act like you have a wicked case of PMS around me, but this has nothing to do with them."

Over the rim of his cup, he blinked, then strode off down the hall, calling back, "Good coffee, Crocker."

The ass.

———•———

I spent two days working, going back and forth to the hospital, and watching my house get torn apart by Leland and Gabe, looking for any clues. All the while, Reid stuck to me like a grumpy parasite. I started to wonder if he liked anything.

Guys were coming and going out of my house and Neil's at all hours. They were also doing everything they could to find Josie and Billy. With everyone working around the clock, the whole Hamilton & Waters lot was nearly as cranky as Reid. Myself included.

Neil was supposed to be coming home tomorrow, so I sat at his island making a list.

"I need to go shopping," I said to Reid. "Tom and Martha are flying in, and with everything else going on, I need food to feed everyone."

Reid's jaw got tight and his dark eyes bore into mine as though I were the devil. "Fine."

My phone rang with Neil's ringtone. "I'm going to the store by myself," I said without even saying a hello to him. I didn't even care about guns or my own personal safety. I'd show Reid.

Neil cursed. "Tova, you can't. You're being irrational."

Try me. I scowled at Reid. "Then tell Mr. Grumpy Pants to stop giving me the stink-eye."

Reid marched over and held out his hand. "Give me the

phone."

"No." I got up and went to the bedroom.

"What are you two arguing about?" Neil asked.

"He thinks I'm a total pain in the ass. I'm not a pain in the ass. *He's* the ass."

Neil released a loud breath into the phone, and Reid had the gall to laugh as he followed me down the hall. I slammed the door in his face.

"The two of you are acting like children," Neil said.

"What!" I grabbed my hairbrush and tore through my long, tangled strands. "I am so not the child in this equation. I'm going to the store by myself. I need a minute alone!"

"No. You're. Not," Reid said, coming into the bathroom.

"Get out of here." I pointed my brush at him but thought better then to swing it.

"Not on your life." He snatched my phone and took Neil off speaker. "She won't be going anywhere." He smiled at me. "Got the car keys. Even hers."

I walked past the ogre. "You realize you need to get laid." I spun around to emphasize my point. "But I'm starting to think not even getting a good blowjob would help you." Neil laughed through the phone. Both of them were insufferable.

Reid hung up and stalked me with intent in his eyes.

"What?" I asked. "Did I hurt your feelings?" He didn't say a word but kept coming. I found myself backing into Neil's dresser.

"Get your list and let's go." He stared at me, the lines on his forehead creasing before he walked away. *Seriously, what is his problem?*

I grabbed my things and followed Reid to his truck. *Maybe the situation is getting to me.* "Why do you hate me?"

Instead of putting the key in the ignition, he turned to me.

"First, you're driving Neil crazy because you're married and not acting like it. Then you brush off the dentist so you can cause my buddy a bunch of grief."

"Are you crazy?"

He started the vehicle and peeled down the driveway. "Oh, I've got your number."

I stewed on this as he drove. Is that really how he saw me? We pulled into a parking space. Not waiting, I got out before he even had the key out. I marched into the store and called Neil.

When I got his voicemail, I cursed and started throwing produce into my cart. Halfway through my angry shopping expedition to feed Neil, his family, his friends, and his employees, my cell rang with his ringtone.

"I don't want him anymore. Get me someone else, Neil."

"You two are worse than teenagers."

"I can't believe he's your best friend." Neil tried hiding a laugh, but I heard it. "And now you're laughing?" I hung up on him. Why couldn't I let this go? I just didn't know, but I couldn't.

To think, I'd made them brownies that morning.

———•———

Two hours later, after the groceries were put away, Reid fell asleep on the sofa. He left the keys on the coffee table, so I procured the ones to the Yukon and decided to drop off some mail. I'd get a latte, too. I told myself, *you deserve one*. Those two could jump in the lake. What could possibly go wrong?

I turned up the music, opened the windows, and lowered my sunglass. Neil and Reid could bite me. I knew I was frustrated being followed around every minute of the day, let alone by Reid, who hated me. I just needed a moment to myself. A minute to breathe. For god's sake, I was used to being alone. I went through the drive-thru and got my latte. One of the best things in life was Starbucks on a sunny day, and not waiting at the counter. Mail in my hand, I walked into the post office.

All I had to do was get a roll of stamps.

My phone rang as I wandered out, and I nearly ignored it, figuring it was either Reid or Neil. I didn't need that right now. But then I changed my mind—they might be worried. I picked it up on the third ring.

A smoker's voice asking, "…get your coffee and your stamps?" Then a click. Who was that? My eyes darted around.

My phone rang again, the name *Reid* on the screen. As my fingers slid across the screen, they shook.

"Where the hell are you?" he growled.

"I'm just walking out of the post office." I had the urge to run back inside.

"I'm coming to get you. Are you at the one off of Louisiana?"

I could hear his door close, the key in the ignition, and the start of the radio. Should I tell him? My eyes jumped to a car pulling in.

"Do you have a death wish? Or is your goal to get sliced and diced by Billy?"

I winced at his on-the-nose comment. Did he have someone call me? Scare me? Of course he had. I strode to the Yukon. As I unlocked the vehicle and grabbed for the handle, my shoulder was yanked back. The door flung open. I spun around.

Billy.

Instinct took over. He let go of my arm, and in a move I'd not thought possible, I pulled back and put my fist in his face. Specifically, his nose. Pain radiated up my arm.

Howling and swearing, Billy staggered back. "Gonna make an example of you!"

I jumped into the Yukon. For a second, my hand shook, I couldn't get the key in. I did lock the doors. Reid yelled from the phone as I moved the truck into gear. He was so going to kill me if Billy didn't.

The Yukon slipped into drive, and I aimed it over the curb and grass. In the rearview mirror, Billy cupped the middle of his face. He stumbled to a black van. The menacing vehicle reminded me of an armored truck, but not as lethal.

I held the phone to my ear. "Did you hear any of that?"

"Yes!" Reid bellowed.

"I got away." Coming to a light, I stopped and looked in my mirror again. The van lurched out of the parking lot, gaining speed. "He's coming after me."

"No shit he's coming after you." The light turned green, and I turned, hitting the accelerator. "Where are you?" Reid yelled.

"I'm on Cedar. I just turned left off Louisiana." He swore, and behind me, the van picked up speed. "Should I drive to the police station?"

"Yes."

"Where are you now?"

"I'm turning onto Virginia." I lifted my foot off the pedal, flattened the brake, and turned left. I lay on the gas, the thick, toxic scent of burning rubber clawed at my throat. Billy's van rushed forward, ready to take a bite out of me. I passed three cars. With how fast I was driving, it didn't look like they were moving at all.

"Hold on. I'm using my other phone to make a call. Don't hang up on me," Reid said.

Homes studded the street in a blur of beige as I flew under

the old concrete railroad bridge. My tires screamed, and I managed the wicked curve. How had he found me? I hit the gas and catapulted forward.

"Where are you now?" Reid asked.

I hit the brake and aimed right. "I'm on Texas." Ahead, cars zoomed by in the busy intersection. "The lights are red ahead of me. What the hell am I going to do?"

"Slow down near the intersection, honk your horn, and run through it. If you can, turn left. You can do this," Reid assured me. "We're all on our way."

As I approached, all I focused on was the swath of vehicles crossing the street. I glanced back. He'd told me to slow down, but the van was a few lengths away. I started honking and cussing a blue streak, but just in time, my light changed. *Thank the Lord.* I slammed on the brakes and aimed left. My entire body railed to the right. With no oncoming traffic, I roared away. Billy pursued.

"Are you okay?" Reid yelled. I'd forgotten I still held the phone.

"Yes," I said, bringing it to my ear. "I'm almost to Louisiana again."

"I'm not far behind you."

Oblivious to my speed, two cars were in front of me were dallying along. The whap whap of police got closer. I hit sixty and dodged both cars. The van easily swung around them, too, and was on me again. The light ahead glared red. I pounded the steering wheel in frustration and honked the horn but had to slow down; cars were crossing. As I did, Billy clipped my back bumper. The Yukon fishtailed and slid off the road, gravel kicking up and shooting behind me. It was all I could do to hang on. Blood pounded in my ears, and I watched as Billy gunned it and rammed into me.

I'd never naysay Neil or Reid again.

My head jerked back and to the side. This time, I did a one-eighty and lost control in a clearing just past an ominous railroad bridge. The sound of tires breaking ripped through my ears. I blinked and looked in front of me. The bridge loomed and Billy was coming at me.

Something solidified. Some sort of super-strength. I jumped out of the Yukon, wobbled for a moment, and got steady on my feet. Rage emanating from him, Billy held a red, livid rag to his nose. He staggered. Rainbow-colored lights swirled over his torso, painting his white T-shirt in something other than blood.

He wanted to kill me, I was sure of it.

I figured I'd get one chance. Neil said Billy was carrying. Without dwelling, I lowered my head and ran at him. I hit him in the chest. With a grunt, he tumbled down. All of the frustration building inside me found a release.

Billy wanted to scare me, threaten me. He'd killed Lena, and he knew Josie. He'd had a hand in Neil getting shot. Deafening noises bleated in my ears. I'd had all I could take. I sat on his chest and wailed on him.

If Billy hit me back, I don't remember feeling anything. The last thing I recalled was yelling, "Stay the hell away from me!" and punching him once again. Then an officer pulled me away.

———·———

"You and Hamilton are going to the morgue, Billy yelled.

I tried to get up as the paramedics examined me. Reid put a hand on my shoulder. "You need to sit!"

"I'm really tired of people poking at me." I looked up at

the kind paramedic. "Sorry, I'm in a bad mood." She nodded.

"I should spank you," Reid said.

Like hell. "Make an attempt and you'll be eating your teeth for dinner."

He laughed. He effing laughed. Did he not see what a mess I'd made of Billy? Or him carted away in cuffs?

Someone should be coming by and giving me my badass badge.

"You've got no fucking clue how dangerous that stunt was." Reid shook his head. "What if he'd had a gun? Neil's gonna have a coronary."

In all seriousness, I suggested, "Maybe we shouldn't tell him?"

Reid smiled so big I almost forgot I'd pissed him off. The wide grin transformed his face from severe grumpiness to pure joy. *Oh my god, he's human.* "What are we gonna tell him then?" He kept smiling; teeth even joined the happy party on his face. "You ran into a fist a few times?"

"He's been through enough. Let's not."

"Not gonna happen. You don't know my best friend like you think you do."

With that, Reid left me there, wondering how I could get out of telling Neil.

————◆————

We spent the afternoon at the police station, then Reid informed me we were going to the hospital.

I thought about running away. I probably would have, if I had known what I was about to walk into.

"You're really nervous about this, aren't you?" Reid asked as he drove. He put his hand on my fidgeting knee, stopping it.

"I don't like the idea of disappointing him." He was probably getting used to it, though. I stared out the window. "I've been a real bitch, lately." I laughed. "Just like you keep telling me. I can see why you hate me. I'm sick of myself."

"I don't hate you."

I turned to face him. "Then why are you so mean to me?"

"I owe you an apology," Reid said. "I had the wrong idea and made some presumptions. I didn't think you had the best of intentions." He looked around and sighed. "The last woman I dated was married and I didn't know."

"Ah. You thought I was trying to seduce Neil. Have a little sugar on the side."

"You weren't just yanking his chain." It was a twisted form of an apology, but I'd gratefully accept it.

"Thank you, Reid." We were only a block from the hospital. I gave it one last try. "I still don't think we should tell Neil what happened."

Reid parked his truck, and we got out. He didn't say anything until we got to the elevator. "You break Billy's nose, get away from him, drive through the city like a goddamn race car driver." He stopped his rant to smile and usher me inside. "You tackle him, knock him out, and now you're acting like a pussy because you need to tell Neil? He doesn't like the Yukon that much."

"I'm not worried about the truck. I let him down." He'd done so much, and here I was being foolish.

"Get over it," he said as we came to Neil's floor.

He was right. I walked to his door. Time to buck up. I opened the door and marched in there.

"You should have seen her. She beat the crap out of him. The cops who scooped him up were laughing…"

My eyes widened. Charlie was regaling everyone—and I

mean, everyone. Jack, Leland, Gabe, and Wade. *How could he?*

They all turned. Charlie stopped talking. The low hum of machines didn't fill the silence.

Jack got up. "Let's go get a drink, gentlemen."

I got a few *good jobs*, a pat on the shoulder, and a wink as they filed out.

Neil worked his jaw back and forth.

I sat in a chair. "I'm sorry. I've been a stubborn pain in the ass. A complete idiot."

"Maybe I forgive you, Blue Eyes, but I'm mad as hell you didn't call me. You let me hear it from Charlie?"

"Well, technically, *Reid* was the one who told Charlie." But I nodded and bit my lip. Neil was right. I could see it, then. I sucked at communication.

"I want you to listen. I'm stuck in this bed, and all I want to do is take care of you. I need you to shelve your pride. I get it and I forgive you, but please don't do that again."

"I won't." Neil was right—I needed to let some stuff go.

"You broke his nose, huh?"

"I think so."

He grinned. "Remind me not to ever truly tick you off."

Jack pulled the door open. "Turn the news on."

We cut in as the local news anchor told us, "…he wouldn't go without a fight."

I smiled. I'd finally done something for Lena. I turned to Neil. "I hope Lena saw me break his nose."

Neil pulled me in for a kiss. "You did good."

"…A handcuffed man arrested on attempted murder charges attacked an officer guarding him and escaped police custody in Minneapolis today, according to the MPD. The circumstances surrounding the charges against him weren't immediately clear. The man, identified as thirty-one-year-old

Billy Culver, escaped around 3:30 p.m. at Fifth Street and Fourth Avenue in Minneapolis and remains unaccounted for..."

"Not happening!" Neil's fist jolted his tray, dousing my hand in cold water.

"How?" I asked aloud. Billy had been led a way in cuffs. I saw them load him into the back of vehicle.

They played a video of Billy running. His hands were behind his back as he zipped down the street.

"...Culver was being taken to central booking when he pushed the accompanying officer to the ground and took off, fleeing the area..."

What a bunch of idiots. The surveillance video showed Billy flying by the camera, only slightly hindered, as two officers lumbered behind.

"...Culver has an extensive record..."

I turned to Neil. "How is that possible? How could they let him get away?"

———•———

I was busy in the studio with a torch in my hand when Vivian waved my cell phone in my peripheral vision. *Neil,* she mouthed.

I flicked off the torch. "Thanks. Can you tell him I'll call right back?"

I left the studio, washed my hands, and dialed him. I passed by Leland, who'd set up a mini-office in my kitchen. After the craziest thing I'd ever done, I never got one minute without a bodyguard.

"Hey, Blue Eyes."

"Hi, how are you?" Darting into the guest room, I peeked

through my curtains to look at his house.

"Good, we just got home." Neil's garage door sat open, his Yukon inside.

"I see that."

"Stalking me?"

"What else do I have to do?" He chuckled. "Do you or your parents need help with anything?"

"No, we're good. I want to kiss you for my brownies."

I let the curtains close and leaned against the wall. "You know you have to share those."

"We'll see. You know you could've saved me the hassle and hid them in my shower or something."

I laughed. "How are you feeling?"

"I'm gonna crash for a bit. I slept for shit last night. Every door in the place kept banging. What time will you be home?"

He didn't realize I was home? Or was it the pain meds asking?

"About five."

CHAPTER 21

NEIL

Charlie took me to the office, which was good because I needed to get out of the house. Everyone clustered around our conference table, eyes on me, then Wade.

"We have nothing on where Billy or Josie are," Wade finally said. "And Andrew's off the grid."

Charlie leaned back in his chair. "Just because Andrew is MIA doesn't mean he's with Josie."

Wade seesawed and leaned forward. "I had a source tell me last night that Billy and Josie were in foster care together. Now the source isn't the most reliable, so I'm looking for someone else to corroborate. My gut tells me it's true."

It would make sense. "TJ said the police are going to ping Josie's phone again. Of course, if it isn't on, they won't get anything." I doubted it would work, but it was something.

Sam came in wearing a suit. He sat across from me, looking at his phone. He'd been busy with the runaway case, staying on top of Andrew, and a corporate security job. "I've finally found the mold maker," he said. "He moved to Hawaii. I have a call in to him."

"I should've followed up on who bailed Josie out after she was arrested." I put my elbows on the table. "TJ told me it was

Billy and not Andrew."

We discussed other jobs and finished the meeting. After, I hobbled into Jack's office. The guys were damn busy, and with my hip, I was almost useless. Jack sat at his desk, feet propped on its monstrous top. He dropped them to the floor with a thud. "You need a ride?"

"Yeah."

We made our way to his truck. "Have you forgiven Tova yet, or are you going to stew on it some more?"

"I've let it go." She'd been through a lot. I knew it was getting to her. The question was why did I have to keep forgiving her? It didn't matter that she was proud, stubborn, and smart-mouthed. I wanted her—all of her—the parts she hid and the parts so bright she couldn't.

Jack smiled. "Good. If my ex ever tackled a man, we'd still be together."

———•———

TOVA

We sat outside on Neil's deck having dinner. "You're stealing my fries," he complained.

"No, not really. I'm helping you finish them." I tilted my head and smiled. "And they're not fries. They're pommes frites."

Tom and Martha had picked up dinner, and we were finishing our meal while they went inside to watch the news. I think Neil had told them to skedaddle.

His hand traveled the inside of my thigh, but he kept his eyes on mine as his fingers ducked under the hem. *Game on.* Neil watched, waiting to see what I'd do. I steadied his hand and bit down, nibbling off the end of the fry.

He wet his lips and slowly made his way closer to my

underwear.

Trying not to be derailed, I stole another bite—a big one—close to his fingers. Neil swallowed, his Adam's apple bobbing. I had his undivided attention.

Would his fingers be salty? My teeth grazed the calloused flesh of his index finger and thumb. I sucked and stole my prize.

He leaned in. "You're playing with fire, Tova."

"I am?" I asked, knowing exactly what image I'd placed in his head. This was what we did. Push and play.

He narrowed his gaze and smirked, then let it drop as he started organizing our plates. I carried them in and did the dishes while he checked his emails on his phone. Constantly distracted, he couldn't let things go and kept hoping for word on Josie or Billy.

"Any news?" My hands twisted in a dishtowel.

"Billy and Josie were in foster care together. Wade just sent me a text confirming it." Neil rubbed his forehead. "TJ brought up something today." Neil looked at me, regret in the set of his mouth. "Said I should've checked on who bailed Josie out after she was arrested at your house. It was Billy."

"Nothing about any of this is your fault." I went over and put a hand on his neck. My thumb started massaging.

He dropped his head, encouraging me. I kneaded the cords. He whispered, "Have you forgiven yourself for me getting shot?"

He had me there. "Not really."

"Let's go watch a movie."

I followed him down the hall. "Where am I sleeping tonight?"

"With me."

"Neil, your parents are here."

His mouth lifted at the corner, like he found me amusing. "So?"

"I'm not sleeping in the same bed as you. Your parents will think I'm a floozy."

His amusement turned into an outright grin. "They won't."

"Not happening." He'd opened his door, and we'd slipped in. I paced in front of his bed. I really liked his bed. "I'll sleep on the sofa."

"The hell you will."

"I'm not sleeping with you." I changed topics. "What movie have you got for us?"

At some point, we both fell asleep. I woke up, grabbed a blanket from the closet, and went to the sofa. I hadn't fallen asleep when I heard his bedroom door open, along with the distinct *clump-step-step* of his crutches and feet.

He nodded to the sofa and my blanket. "Now you're the one trying to be clever." He reached for my hand. "Blue Eyes, I want to wake up with you," he tugged me from the cushions. "It's all I've thought of since you went to New York."

NEIL

Stretched out like a sleepy lion, I woke for a moment and slipped off the bed into the bathroom, quiet as I could, to take a shower. I needed to get the stink of frustration off me. I opened the bathroom door to the thrill of seeing all of Tova's things in my space, still fresh and exhilarating. It made me too happy to see her stuff on my counter.

That was what she'd reduced me to. The scent of her body wash and shampoo—scented with mango and coconut, I now knew—still lingered. Her perfume, something called Cleopatra, sat on my granite countertop. The liquid skimmed the bottom of the bottle. I'd order her another one; I didn't want her to run out. That, also, was what she'd reduced me to.

If she did something else stupid or risky, I knew I'd forgive her all over again because how could I not?

I loved her.

When I got back to bed, she was awake. "That was nice," she said, smiling like mad.

I smiled back. "It was, wasn't it?"

We stayed in bed longer than we should have. I decided I didn't care that my parents knew we were sleeping together.

—·—

TOVA

I grabbed Neil's hand. "Can we talk?"

"Sure."

I led him outside onto the deck so his parents wouldn't interrupt us.

"What's going on?"

"I wanted to talk about the get-together." We were going to Tate and Gillian's for a baseball party later in the day.

That dividing line popped up between his eyebrows. "Okay."

I didn't want to harp, but it came blurting out, "I don't want everyone to know we're together."

He stiffened at my side. "How long are we gonna be friends?"

I hated upsetting him. "I don't know. A month? Maybe two?"

"A month or two," he repeated. His annoyed tone matched the set of his mouth.

The thought we could easily become neighborhood fodder made me cringe. Not that my friends would jump to those conclusions, but what reasonable adult wouldn't? When my parents were married, I could tell when my dad's coworkers, their wives, even people from our church were whispering. I knew what they were saying. "*Robert has a new secretary again. It must not bother Ingrid.*" I always wondered if my dad took his flings out on dates. If his peers caught him with other women.

"What does it matter?" Neil snapped.

"Please, I'm just not ready yet. I don't want that for us."

"You better get ready." He turned on his crutches and went back inside. "My patience is wearing thin. I'm not a dirty secret."

"I know." He didn't storm off, but I knew he wasn't happy.

Later, TJ and Neil drove their parents to the airport. Charlie drove me to a meeting, then he dropped me off at the party.

CHAPTER 22

TOVA

Tate, my neighbor around the corner, greeted me at the door. "Great jersey. Is it the real deal?"

"It is." I wore a cream-colored Twins jersey with navy pinstripes. "Sorry, I'm late. I had a work thing." I followed him inside.

"No big deal. Gillian wants to introduce you to her friends from the office."

After introductions, I grabbed an ice-cold beer and went in search of Neil.

Max sidled up next to me. "Hey, kiddo."

I stole a glance at the television. "Hey, who's winning?"

"We are."

Neil came through the patio door. As gracefully as he could, he walked toward us with one crutch. He'd decided earlier in the day that he'd try just one. I wanted to kiss him when he smiled at me, but then I remembered our conversation.

"How did it go today?" he asked. His arm reached out to touch me but stopped. I guess he had the same problem.

"I got a nice order. Thanks for asking." Considering Andrew, Billy, and Lena, if it weren't for my business going so smoothly, I might be a basket case. My eyes slid down his form. "How are you doing with one?"

"Just fine."

We made awkward small talk with Max until a gust of hot, humid air came through the living room. I looked over. Brooke walked toward us wearing a white top that appeared to be made from plastic wrap. I could clearly see her nipples straining against the fabric. She walked right to Neil and hugged him.

The hussy.

"Can I talk to you?" her voice took on a saccharine quality. "Privately."

Neil moved them to a secluded corner. I settled on the couch and tried to watch the game, between bouts of watching Ms. Saran Wrap. She touched Neil's hip and the Yankees scored.

"Damn!" I shouted at the screen.

"Tova, I didn't realize you cared," Tate said.

"I was hoping we'd win today and the Yankees wouldn't hand us our balls." The guys around me laughed. "Don't you think it's infuriating they always take the American League?"

Tate turned toward me. "Yeah, I do, but I'm more impressed you know what the American League *is*."

"Well, I do, and I hate the Yankees."

Neil listened to Brooke. His eyes stayed on her face, but if I caught him glancing at her tits, I decided I'd go over there and beat him with the beer bottle in my hand.

"You want another?" Tate asked.

"Sure." If Neil hadn't slept with her the night Lena died, I would've been able to keep my cool, but it made me so mad to see him talking to her *privately.* My mind skittered to the one place I tried keeping it from. History repeating itself. *Damn him.*

"Have you always been a baseball fan?" a male voice asked from behind me.

I glanced over my shoulder. I didn't know him. "It's one of the few things I could do with my dad."

Mystery Man handed me a beer. He wore glasses and perfect combed hair. "Tate asked me to bring this in for you." He took the spot Tate had vacated next to me on the sofa.

"Thanks," I said. I still didn't take a sip.

"You're Tova, right?"

"You found me."

His whole face smiled. Adorable. "I'm Graham."

Glasses equal Graham. That I could remember. "Thanks for the delivery." I took a sip and glanced at Neil. His icy blue eyes cut to me for a second, then returned to Brooke. "How do you know Tate and Gillian?" I stumbled on my words as Brooke touched Neil's arm.

"Tate and I work in the same department." Graham shifted on the sofa. "You live in the neighborhood, right?"

Brooke had touched Neil so he wouldn't look at me. I was sure of it. "Yeah, I live around the corner."

"I heard a rumor you own your own business." Graham's glasses magnified his friendly brown eyes.

"I do. A jewelry line."

His eyes slid over my ears to my neck and wrists. "How come you're not wearing any?"

The only sparkly thing I had on were a pair of metallic wedge sandals. I laughed. "It's hot." I stroked my neck. "I took it off."

Graham's eyes went to my hand, chest, and quickly back up. "That's bad advertising."

Not touching that one. "Hmm."

My blood pressure ramped up as time ticked by. Everyone watched the game except Brooke. She kept whispering to Neil, dead-set on something.

Graham's hand gripped my knee. I looked at his hand, then up at him, startled. "Want another?" he asked.

"Sure." I glanced at his hand and he removed it.

He brought me another beer, and I started flirting with intoxication. When Brooke rested a hand on his thigh, Neil did nothing to remove it. I wanted to drag her away and tell her to go get her own Neil. Instead, I excused myself and went to the bathroom. While I was in there, I told the mirror nothing was going on.

When I came back, the two were gone. I went to the kitchen. Neil sat at the island, his butt on a bar stool, his back to me. *Why had they moved?* In slow motion, Brooke's palm landed in the center of his chest. I wondered if what I saw was actually happening. Unable to move or say anything, I watched her head lower. She kissed him. My heart constricted. Jealousy suffused my body.

Neil's hand came up to her shoulder. He pushed her away and said something in a voice too quiet for me to hear. Brooke nodded, straightened, then glanced over Neil to me.

I fled out the front door. I would've been able to go in the kitchen and let Brooke have it if I hadn't made a big deal about Neil and I not being a couple. I hated myself almost as much as Neil at that moment.

"Tova, you okay?" Graham followed me.

Humidity slapped me in the face. "Yeah, I'm fine." Damn, I was sick of saying that! Repeating the same bullshit, I sounded like a scratched record. "Just need some fresh air."

I leaned into the railing and set my sight on the street. A wall of angry heat lifted off the asphalt. Graham neared my side.

The front door opened, and the unmistakable clunk of Neil's crutch came closer. "I need to talk to Tova," he said. I turned. Neil sized up Graham. "Alone."

Graham stepped away from me and left without a second glance.

"What you saw inside isn't what it looked like."

I braced against the railing. "What do you think it looked like?"

"It looked like I was kissing her." *Damn straight that's what it looked like.*

"You're a mind reader."

"She kissed me. I didn't kiss her." Neil step-clumped closer. "There's a difference."

"Isn't that convenient?"

"It's true."

"Okay, it's true." I sounded like a petulant child, but I didn't care. Forget Billy. Forget Josie. Neil was the man I was most worried about.

"Don't patronize me."

"It looked like you were enjoying it. Since. You. Didn't. Move. Away."

"You don't believe me?" Hurt, his face slackened. "It looked like you and the suit-guy were getting cozy."

Suit-guy? "Don't be ridiculous."

"You need them coming and going?"

He couldn't be serious. "You're joking, right?"

"You think I'd let some guy ply you with alcohol and put his hands on you in front of me?"

"What?"

"He brought you two beers, checked out your rack, and put his hand on your knee," he growled in my ear.

"That was nothing."

Neil grabbed my ass. "You flirted with him. In. Front. Of. Me."

"Your kissing escapade is *my* fault? I wouldn't have let him kiss me." My hand went to the center of his chest. "You, on the other hand, did nothing to prevent her from kissing you. Pushing her away after the fact is too little too late." My voice grew louder with my anger. I tore away from him.

"Where are you going?"

"Home, okay? Stop being an ass!" I yelled, surprised at my atomic reaction.

A side window was cracked open. Everyone knew we were together now.

———•———

NEIL

I told myself I should go after her. But I needed to calm down. Mostly because I wanted to ring her pretty little neck. I faced the street. Tova *should* be mad at me. I was an ass.

My phone rang. Reid. "What's up?"

"An informant gave me a juicy bit of info. He saw Josie with a guy that matches Andrew's description, down to the make of car. The guy said her face had some serious bruises." Scenarios ran through my head. If Billy had her, I didn't think she'd show up alive.

"Did the informant say anything else?"

"No. I figure either Billy or Andrew gave them to her."

"Her drug problem could've gotten her in trouble. The

261

thing that's been bugging me—Josie didn't want Billy to know she was in Tova's house. She seemed petrified, wasn't gonna give on it either. And it was plain as day on her face she lied. Tova had her completely flustered when she said the police report came back with Josie's name on it."

"Then Josie lied about something and knows she's liable to end up in front of Billy's knife."

"So why'd Billy bail her out? She didn't even try to get Andrew on the phone." *Lover's spat?* Josie seemed dead set on Tova not taking Dickhead back, but at the same time, she thought he was still living in her house.

"The informant is still here," Reid said, cutting into my thoughts. "I'll try to get some more out of him."

———·———

TOVA

I answered the door, assuming Neil had come to apologize. Instead, Andrew stood there in a wrinkled, untucked shirt. *What would make him go out like that?*

He charged past me and into the house. "What are you doing messing with my business?"

What was he talking about? The loan?

"I'm not *messing* with your business." He could shove his precious business where the sun doesn't shine. "Your girlfriend shot my boyfriend."

He laughed. "Yeah, I heard about that. Hope he's okay." He glanced around. "I knew you were screwing him."

"I never cheated on you." I thought about it, but… "Your lawyer can talk to mine." I pointed out the door. "Now get out, Andrew."

He came toward me, moved my hand, and slammed the

door. "We're going to talk this out. Your *boyfriend* has been making calls. People are canceling orders. I've worked too hard for him to come along and wreck everything. If he keeps at it, you'll never get your money back."

Something in me snapped. "You and my fucking money. You only married me so you could get your hands on it." I took a step closer and put my hand over his on the door handle, to kick him out. Fury rolled over his features, but I kept pushing. "It would be fun to watch your whole business implode. After all, I can afford to watch it crumble. It would serve you right." My anger reached epic proportions as I thought about all the time he'd stolen from me, used me, made me his patsy. "Get the fuck out of my house, or I'll watch your business fall to pieces. Better yet, I'll have my lawyer go after and take it."

He put a shoe to the door to stop me from getting it open. Then he reached out and grabbed me by the neck. "You're not getting my business."

I pushed at him, but his grasp on my neck tightened. Fear thrust up my throat. I tried backing into the foyer. "Let me go!"

I couldn't get loose as he jerked me back and shoved. My head hit the full-length mirror across from us. Was he going to strangle me? Had I pushed him that far? He held me with one hand, pinning me against the mirror. Needing to get to the panic button, I slapped and punched at him, pushing with everything I had. He let my neck go and grabbed a hold of my wrists, clasping them above my head, restraining me with his body. I squirmed, trying to get out of the manacle-like hold.

"You just need to push, don't you?" He shoved his hips harder against me. How was I going to get out of this? Why hadn't I looked before I opened the door? He held me as though it was no struggle. "You've been fucking that private eye." His head reared back a fraction, and he scanned me. "You look good. Almost as good as when we first met. I could probably stomach fucking you."

I tried to pull my hands free. "You bastard."

"You don't like hearing that, huh?" He laughed. "Trust me, it was a hardship. I'd come home and you'd have gained another five pounds."

On the verge of tears, I started fearing what he planned. All this security for what?

"Don't worry. I don't want to fuck you," he said, reading my mind. "I still remember how fat you were."

I pushed against him, but still couldn't unglue myself. "You're gonna end up in jail for this."

I braced for retaliation. Andrew's eyes darkened, then narrowed. His free hand moved, his thumb pressing wickedly hard into my trachea. My eyes went wide. I pushed with my hips. His grip held strong, his hand a vise.

Andrew pumped my throat. The pulse lifted me up on my toes. "You see the fatal mistake? Think you could threaten *me*?" His voice was the same old grating Andrew. He squeezed my neck, making me light-headed and dizzy. With a jolt, he shoved me into the wall with such force the mirror came off and started to slide, but with me wedged tightly against the glass, the massive object couldn't fall.

My thoughts skittered to Neil. Would he find me dead?

Andrew loosened his hold. With a rush of adrenaline, I kicked him in the groin and broke away. Rushing toward the door, my balance off, I careened into him as I tried to bolt. I swung the door open. It banged against the wall.

Neil's panic button! I pulled back and slammed my fist onto the system panel.

But that let Andrew wrench me back with a hand on my jersey. The fabric ripped. He backhanded me hard enough for me to sway, but not lose my feet. I yelped in pain. *He wanted to kill me.* Desperate, I reached out and raked my nails down his face and kicked again. He hissed in pain. I could feel skin under my nails. He staggered, and I ran out the door. I got to the end of the driveway and locked eyes on Neil.

"Andrew," I said, pointing to the house. I held my throat, barely able to get the word out.

Neil dropped his crutch on the road, drew the gun from his jeans, and ran toward me.

I glanced back. "He's in the house," I panted. He wrapped an arm around me and pulled me off the street. His gaze slid down my body, focusing on the ripped fabric at my shoulder, then my neck and face. "I'm okay."

"Call 911." He gave me his phone. A dog barked. Both our heads swiveled in the direction and caught sight of Andrew sprinting along the creek.

Neil took off. "Lock yourself in the house. Call 911, then Wade."

———•———

NEIL

I took the road for my leg's sake, but I'd stopped feeling pain a moment ago. *Dickhead would have to be a runner.* He saw me, saw my gun, and turned slightly, moving his right hand to his back. I knew that motion. The fucker was carrying. I cut over closer to the house as I ran. Unless he came up between two ramblers, he'd have to shoot at an odd angle. He was way ahead of me. He got to his car. I'd passed by it, mixed among all the others for Tate and Gillian's party. A mini van slid by him. I thought about taking a shot but another car was coming. He roared off down the street, catching his bumper on a blue

Honda.

Letting Tova down hurt more than my hip. A fuck of a lot more. She was going to be so damn disappointed in me.

She ripped open the door as I got close. "Are you okay?" Frantic, she eyed me up and down. Dickhead could've killed her.

I nodded. "He hurt you." I took her in my arms and put my forehead to hers. "Fuck, Tova, I'm sorry."

"I'm okay," she said. "Are you all right?"

I drew back, my eyes dropping to her red throat. Marks like that meant one thing—he'd wanted to kill her.

"I'm sorry, Neil." Tears tracked down her cheeks. "I trust you," she said emphatically.

Christ, I could take anything, but not her apologizing to me. *For that.* "Don't." My head shook, willing her to stop. Words failed me. I made an oath at that moment to stop being such an ass. Gently, I ran my fingers down her neck. "He's dead when I catch him. Where else are you hurt?"

"Just what you see," she said, holding up her chin.

I doubted that. The sound of the sirens whirred in the background.

She started walking toward her room. "I want to change."

"You can't."

She turned around. "What? Why?"

"They'll need to take pictures."

She bit her lip, shoulder slumping in defeat.

I followed her and noticed the door. "Did you leave your closet open? Or was that Dickhead?"

She swallowed hard and righted the torn material on her shoulder. Her face grimaced when her arm came up. I was gonna kill that motherfucker.

"Dickhead." That's what I thought.

The sirens stopped. I took her hand.

She looked at me and smiled just a little. She wanted to assure me she was okay. "Let's get this over with."

———.———

TOVA

I took Neil's hand and led him down the hall. Andrew had wanted that folder. I wondered if that's why he came back.

A paramedic looked me over, and the police asked a million questions before they captured picture after picture. A few hours later, they left, along with more than enough curious neighbors and a few folks from Tate and Gillian's party.

The sky, gray and littered with thick clouds, loomed overhead as we walked toward Neil's.

"You don't have your crutch."

He squeezed my hand. "Don't need it anymore." He led me into his bathroom and I got a look in the mirror.

A fresh bruise covered my cheekbone and my throat was an angry red. How many times was someone going to beat me up?

"You've got to be kidding me," I said to the pale version of myself and righted my torn jersey. It fell off my shoulder, showing my black bra strap. *If it wasn't my underwear, it was my bra.*

Neil touched my arm. "I'll take care of you."

"I can't believe he did that." I sat on his big counter. "He was going to hurt me."

"He did hurt you, sweetheart. He wanted to kill you. But he isn't gonna touch you again."

"How can you be so sure?" Not the best thing to tell Neil, but it popped out.

He unbuttoned my jersey. His fingers skimmed up my

stomach, between the valley of my breasts, and caressed my chin. "Because I'm gonna find him."

And just like that, my doubt disappeared. He handed me two ibuprofen. I cupped some water in my hand and swallowed. His fingers grazed over my neck.

"I'm sorry, Blue Eyes. I let you down."

The pure anguish on his face broke my heart. "No, you didn't. My security system doesn't work if I answer the door."

His brow furrowed. "It won't happen again. Do you want to shower?"

"No. I just want us to lie down."

He led me to his bed, unbuttoned my shorts, and let them drop. "Climb in. I've got some calls to make. I'll be back in a bit." He covered me up and closed the door.

CHAPTER 23

TOVA

I woke to Neil along my back. "I didn't kiss Brooke," he whispered.

I'd forgotten all about the kiss. I tried to turn, but his heavy arm locked me against him. "Neil…"

"She kissed me. I was distracted." He held me tighter. "Didn't see it coming."

I knew when he'd pulled back from Brooke he hadn't wanted to kiss her. "I believe you." He exhaled. His breath skated against my neck. "But it shredded me."

"I know." *Did he?*

"Don't put yourself in that position again."

"I won't."

How would he react to me being kissed by a man I'd slept with? "Especially since you've slept with her." He'd never even seen Andrew kiss me.

"Turn around, sweetheart." He lifted his arm, and I shifted to face him. "I haven't slept with her."

Really? "That night at Crave, you took her home and didn't come back. I know. I listened."

"I got a call about a case. I didn't spend the night with her." Relief eased through me. "No?"

"No."

We were chest-to-chest. I ran my hand through his hair. Part of me, the evil part, wanted to tug and make him understand what that felt like. Then I remembered the ring twirling and realized maybe he knew.

"You gotta know there was no way I could take you home that night." He washed his hand down his face. "It kept getting harder and harder to be around you." He gathered my hair and moved it over my shoulder. "When you brought over beers and stretched your long legs out and told me Dickhead was gone for a month at a time, I vowed to stay away. But when you flirted with Wade, poison hit my blood."

I had tortured him. "Neil…"

"And when Dickhead came home and didn't kiss you, I thought maybe, just maybe, I had a chance. He had something I wanted. I'd had a firsthand account of him suffocating what you gave him. When you confirmed you were divorcing, for the first time in weeks I felt I could breathe."

I raised my hand to his chest. "Neil…" I couldn't string words together.

"I worried, but I knew…I fucking knew you were going to be mine. So, yeah, I saw that poison eating you up, outside on Tate's porch, but if you don't understand right now that I've been with you for months, then I need to get you some goddamn glasses." He skimmed my heart with a fingertip, light. His words might've been hard but not his touch. "This is mine, and I've been working to make it mine and I will stop at nothing to make sure that it stays mine."

The things he said.

Needing him to shut up, and make my own grand gesture, I kissed him.

And I kept kissing him until I felt him relax. We lay there

for a minute until the need to question him became too much. "Did you really think I was flirting with Graham?"

He reached for my hip. "You were."

"I wasn't."

"I watched. You slid your hand down your throat, almost invited him to look you over." *Had I?* "Your flirting comes natural, I get that, but you can't do that to me, Blue Eyes. When I saw him lay his hand on your—my chest was on fire. I wanted to deck him. Still do."

"She touched you."

He blinked. "So that's why you flirted? 'Cause she touched me." *Was it?* "You heard what I said. My chest was on fire. I don't want anyone but you, and I'm not gonna fuck around like Dickhead or your dad. Okay?"

I knew he wouldn't.

He kissed me and touched my raw cheek. "On a scale of one to ten, how sore are you?"

"Seven, maybe six. You know what I'm most upset about?"

"What?"

"Dickhead ruined my jersey."

Neil shook his head, a grin tilting his mouth. "You're gonna give me a coronary."

"Me? What about you? You're limping, I'm worried."

"Don't worry about me." He slipped my bra strap off my shoulder and caressed my neck. "I'd do anything for you."

I nuzzled into him. "I know." And I did.

With no forethought, I asked. "Will you tell me about your birth mom?" We never had delved in. I put my hand on his chest. "You mumble in your sleep."

"I do?" He gave me a look that held surprise and enlightenment.

"Yes, at the hospital you did, and your dad filled me in a

little. And you've been doing it again, especially last night."

"That would make sense," he said with a sigh. "I got into this business looking for my mom." He smoothed a hand down my arm. "I'll tell you all about her." Part of me didn't want to hear what he was going to say. I figured it couldn't be good. "Are you mad I didn't tell you?"

"No. Of course not."

Neil nodded. "Good. I wasn't hiding anything."

"I understand."

"My mom was an alcoholic. Dad said the only time she was sober was when she was pregnant. She left when I was three months. I was too young to remember, and Dad met Martha when I was one. She's the only mom I've ever known. She *is* my mom." Neil shifted toward me. "But I reached the age where I wanted to get to know her. I wanted to know how she could abandon me." Hearing him say *abandon me* made tears well in my eyes. "Every year or two, I'd get a card on my birthday. Sometimes at Christmas, a present would show up. Once she knocked on our door drunk. I was about ten when that happened." I took his hand in mine and squeezed. "What I didn't count on was that I wouldn't be dealing with a whole person."

Neil ran his free hand through his hair. "I had a god complex." His light laugh sounded jaded. "She was living out of a grocery cart in an upscale town in California, and I thought I could save her from her demons. When customers left the stores, she'd beg them for money. There was a restaurant on every corner, and the patrons would leave their doggie bags next to the public garbage cans for all the homeless people." Neil closed his eyes for a second. "I thought I could take her away from that life. Set her up in an apartment. Help her get a job. Help her get on her feet. I thought she needed someone to give a shit." He took a deep breath. "I was wrong. What she needed was mental health help, but I couldn't get her to a facility. I couldn't even get her to come back to Minnesota with me. One day I about hauled her off, and tried kidnapping her. She slapped me and got away. Told me to stay the fuck away from her." Neil stared at the wall for a beat before meeting my eyes. "And I did. I went home knowing I couldn't get her to swallow the only thing she thought she still possessed. Her pride."

"Neil," I whispered.

"She was found a week later, dead from alcohol poisoning."

I held onto him. "I'm sorry."

"Didn't know I was dreaming about her, but it makes sense I would. I worried about her like I worry about you."

What did that mean? Did he view me as a pet project that needed doing?

"Your wheels are turning, Blue Eyes, it's not like that. The reason I love you isn't because I can help you. I love you for everything you are. You'll stick your neck out to help anyone. You make people brownies, pick up dead squirrels, and get sappy about an old man helping his wife get in the house." He ran his thumb over my lips. "You lit up when I gave you a nickname, you work your ass off at everything you try." He smiled. "And you're stubborn as all hell, and I love your eyes on me, just about as much as your mouth." He winked. "And your rack isn't half-bad." I laughed. "I love you. Plain, but not simple. So don't start thinking I'm in this to rescue you. Okay? I'm not."

Relief swept through me.

"But," he said, emphasizing the word, "your pride is so strong, sometimes I think I'm dealing with my dead mom. You don't want to be seen as weak or incapable. You'd rather hold on to something, sit on it, and let yourself suffer than ask for help." *Damn, he had my number.* "The truth with my mother was there was no saving her. She wouldn't ask for help, and if offered, she was too proud to accept. I wanted a different outcome. I wanted to have a relationship with her so bad, I thought I could make it so by sheer will, but that's not how it works. Just like Lizzy—your grandma—said, about you and your dad. It wasn't that I didn't have a relationship with her. I just didn't have the one I wanted."

That I understood. Hadn't I been expecting the same thing for years?

Neil smiled. "You're getting better with your iron will, but you gotta know, babe, I'm gonna keep on you. For instance, I know you want a better relationship with your dad, but you aren't solely responsible. He needs to meet you halfway. You need to stop being so proud and let it go. It's a two-way street. He'll either come around and treat you right or not."

"You're right." I kissed him. We stayed next to each other until my hand slid down his stomach, and I tucked my fingertips into his pants. "What is going to happen?"

"We'll find him. We'll find them all." With the back of his hand, he swept down my shoulder to my breast and I froze.

Andrew's words came back and I closed my eyes. "He said the worst things to me. Horrible, horrible things." I leaned my head against his and let it out. "He said—"

"Tova…" He gathered me close. "He hurt you—" Neil cursed. "He's dead."

———•———

Neil poured his coffee. One arm on the counter, he asked, "Tell me more about Andrew's mom."

Neil hadn't called my soon-to-be was-band by his real name in weeks. "I'm pretty sure she's his only redeemable quality. He loves her almost as much as he loves himself." I cupped my mug. How could I put this? "It borders on obsessive. He'd talk to her multiple times a day." It bothered me at me first, and then I'd realized I was jealous of how close he was with her. "When Andrew and I met, she was recovering from a double mastectomy. She's cancer-free, but now he worries over her rheumatoid arthritis."

"What about his dad?"

"His father's dead. Cathy remarried years ago." Andrew and I had that in common, the loss of a parent. I longed for mine; he did not. "He never talked much about him, other than to say he was glad the man was dead. I don't think he's close to his stepdad. They came to visit us once. Otherwise I've only ever talked to them on the phone."

"You've never been to their farm?" Neil asked.

"Every time I brought up going to visit them, Andrew had an excuse saying he couldn't go. I stopped asking after a while."

Neil moved on with a knowing nod. "Something's been bothering me about those molds. Were Dickhead and his friend going into business together? Is that why he had that folder?"

We'd all gone over and over various reasoning paths, but nothing felt like the answer we were looking for.

"Andrew never said anything."

Neil tapped the island counter with his knuckles. "I'm sure Josie was in your house looking for that folder. I also think that's why she didn't want Billy to know she'd been there."

That made sense. "But why would she want information on some old molds? Let's say that Andrew—I mean, Dickhead—" I smiled at Neil. "—and Teddy were planning on going into business together and that's why the folder was at my house.

Why would Josie want it?"

Neil tipped his head to the side. "She thought it was important."

"But why?" I sounded like a broken record. "Andrew doesn't use that type of mold anymore. That's why he was in my class. That's why we met. He needed a material that would hold up better."

"That's what we need to figure out. Does the good doctor have any other friends in Stanley?"

"He never mentioned anyone. He always said he couldn't get out of there fast enough."

"I'm gonna have Charlie find Teddy's parents." Neil pushed his chair back, and it scraped on the floor. "We're gonna pay them a visit." He got on the phone and planned our trip.

———·———

"I'll be replaying that all day," Neil whispered in my ear as I leaned in to grab the coffee pot. I was sure he would. I'd gotten a little worked up in the shower. "You can do that every morning if you want." He wore a cheeky grin along with wet, curling hair.

I smiled at him. "I'll keep that in mind."

He tapped me on the ass. "You do that."

I poured two travel mugs, grabbed bananas and granola bars, and slipped on some shoes.

"You ready?"

I took a deep breath. "Yep."

I pictured our first road trip entirely different. It certainly hadn't included driving to a farm in Stanley, North Dakota, yet that's what where we were going. Technically, we weren't alone. I looked in the side mirror; Charlie and Wade followed behind us. The highway dragged on, nothing but the occasional gas station and fields of corn. The reedy stalks along the highway barely moved as we sped by. Then my dad called.

"You didn't call me. Now I had to hear from Lizzy you were beaten up?"

"Hi, Dad." I didn't want a nasty conversation. "I was going to call."

"When? After he kills you?"

"He's not gonna kill me." Neil glanced over. *Dad*, I mouthed.

"Lizzy said you're staying with your boyfriend."

"We're on our way to North Dakota."

"I'd come if I could, but a case I've been working on for over a year is going to trial next week."

His saying that came as a complete shock. "You don't need to come. I'm fine, Dad."

"The man you're dating—I looked into him. He's good at what he does."

I listened, horrified. It was one thing to say he would come to see me, but this? "How is that even possible?"

"Lizzy told me about him after you visited." I sat, dumbfounded. "I'm coming in two weeks. The case should be over then, and I want to meet him. Can I talk to him now? Is he available?"

I placed the phone against my chest. "He wants to talk to you."

Neil reached out and grabbed my cell. "Hello, Mr. Hudson."

They talked, first some pleasantries, and then about my security system. Neil provided my dad with a synopsis of everything, including what was going on with the investigation—which was a lot. "Yes, I'll keep you updated," Neil said.

He handed my phone back. "Your dad's worried about you."

———·———

After lunch, lulled by the moving vehicle, I fell asleep.

"Blue Eyes," Neil said, patting my leg.

I sat up straight. Nausea and nerves kicked in. I blinked and focused out the window. A dirt field, with brittle, yellow grass and a pair of large beige machines, came into view. Lifeless clumps of brush spotted the muddy ground. One part of the beige equipment, a hammer-looking piece with a cable attached, fell to the earth, then lifted again. Over and over, it pumped. Along with that, one of the strangest sights I'd ever seen forced my back against the leather seat.

Rising straight from the earth and into the air, a narrow metal pipe shot fire into the sky. A trail of black smoke lingered against a pretty blue sky. "What the hell is that?"

"Oil drilling," Neil answered. "Amazing, isn't it?"

"Wow." Further in the background, a tall white skeleton, similar to the structure of a crane, stood like a skyscraper against the flat landscape.

"This is part of the Bakken shale oil fields. It's been called the Saudi Arabia of the U.S."

"I've heard of it."

"Dickhead never talked about growing up on some of the most valuable land in America?"

Absolutely not. "No. Andrew didn't come from money. His mom worked her tail off to keep a roof over their heads."

"Take a look at that folder," Neil said, handing me papers from his center console.

What I read blew me away. A few years ago, this section

of North Dakota produced more oil than all of Saudi Arabia. Most of the farms held multi-millionaires. "Andrew's parents live on one of these farms?"

"According to that they do, but they don't own the mineral rights."

"Who does?"

"I have no idea. But Charlie and Wade just turned off. They're paying the county a visit to see if they can find out. All we see online is a shell company. The thing is, with the price of oil dropping, they think all this will come to an end. I read an article online that they're already taking down equipment. The oil rush is over."

"Andrew grew up on land making someone else rich? That must've been fun for him, seeing as how he's a greedy bastard."

CHAPTER 24

TOVA

"There—it's to our left," Neil said.

I gazed out his window, to get a better view of the farm. The gravel road kicked up dust all around us and Neil slowed down. The flat, dirt expanse held small outcroppings of drilling equipment, not much green. Nothing screamed life except trees in the foreground. I wouldn't call it a farm. Pebbles hit the car's undercarriage and pelted against metal.

I could see why Andrew couldn't get out of here fast enough; he hated anything dirty and unkempt.

"We're not gonna stop right now," Neil said as he gained speed. "Charlie texted. He got a hold of Teddy's parents—Ted and Gail—and they're home. They live closer to town. We're going there first."

If Andrew's mom had owned the mineral rights, she would've been a wealthy woman. When I read more in Neil's folder, I learned that farmers who sold their rights now lived on land that barely functioned as farms. The drilling had taken a toll on the soil.

"It must be horrible to look out your window and see that," I said.

"Yep, especially if you know someone else is getting rich

and you aren't."

"That would've been like waving a red flag in Andrew's face."

We headed toward town and pulled in front of a stately two-story brick home on the outskirts. It appeared out of place. My eyebrows rose, and I glanced at Neil, surprised by the grand facade. "Teddy's dad runs the bank," he said in explanation.

"What do you hope they can help us with?"

"I want to know more about Dickhead's family and if Teddy and Andrew were going into business. They also might know who owns the mineral rights to the farm."

We got out of the Yukon, and as we each shut our door, a tall, lithe man opened an oversized, front door. "You must be Neil," he said in a joyful greeting.

We introduced ourselves.

"Tova… That sure is an unusual name." He smiled at me. "Let's go in. Do you want coffee?"

"Sure," Neil and I both replied. Ted led us into a foyer, then to a large, open kitchen with a true farmhouse table. Even though the outside of the house was stately, the inside was simple and homey.

"So you came from Minneapolis?"

"Yes," Neil said, sitting down "Thanks for talking to us."

"That sure is a long way to come to discuss Andrew," he said.

"I know Charlie told you a little about why we were coming, but I'm trying to help Tova," Neil stated.

Ted gestured to my throat. "Is that boy the reason why you have that bruise on your neck?"

I raised my hand to cover it, even though he'd seen it. "It is."

"And you're his wife?" Ted asked. His eyes went from me to

Neil and back again.

"Yes, but we're separated."

"I guess the apple didn't fall too far from the tree," Ted stated. I glanced at Neil. Did that mean what I thought? "I don't know how I'm going to help. I saw Andrew in passing about a year ago. That's the only time since our son's funeral, three years this fall."

A woman walked into the kitchen. "Sorry for not greeting you right away. I was on the phone." She smoothed her pants at her hips, then held her hand out. "I'm Gail." She wore a warm smile and pearls.

"I'm Tova. Thanks for letting us barge in on you."

"We love visitors." She grabbed a cup of coffee and sat. "So the two of you are looking for Andrew?"

"Yes."

"Gail," Ted cut in, "I was just telling them I haven't seen Andrew since last year. You haven't seen him, have you?"

"No." Gail turned to me. "You'd think he'd come over and see us when he visits his mom, but he never has."

"How often does he visit her?" I asked.

Ted looked perplexed. "Don't you know?"

I set down my coffee cup. "Andrew didn't exactly tell me everything."

"We always did catch that boy in lies—" Ted rubbed his throat. "—but that was when he and Teddy were young."

"He usually comes home to see Cathy every two or three months," Gail answered. "He only visits for a day, but everyone in town knows when he's here because of that fancy car of his."

Every few months! Seething mad, I looked at Neil. It shouldn't have been a surprise, but it was.

"How long have you and Andrew been married?" Gail asked.

"A little over two years."

"Did you ever meet our Teddy?" she asked.

"No, I never did. I'm so sorry about your son. No one should ever lose a child."

"Thank you, dear." She reached out and put a hand over mine. "He was the light of our life." My heart ached for them.

"Andrew and Teddy went to college and dental school together?" Neil asked.

"Yes. They did everything together. They even worked at the same practice," Gail replied.

Neil's phone rang, and he glanced at the screen. "I need to take this. I'll be right back." He got up and went outside.

Ted spoke up. "Andrew should've known what Teddy was working on when he died, but he couldn't tell us anything."

The coffee in my stomach bubbled and turned acidic. I shifted in my chair. "What?"

"Those two were inseparable, and Teddy was working on something that he said was big," Ted glanced out the window. "But he wanted to surprise us. He didn't want to tell us more until it was further along."

Gail cut in, "Teddy was always tinkering, always making plans."

Puzzle pieces locked into place. I wrapped my brain around what they were telling me and tried not to appear as though I was sick and crawling out of my skin. That was why Josie wanted the folder. Andrew had taken what belonged to Teddy—or, at least, hadn't shared what the two had been working on together.

"After the funeral, we tried to find out more, but Andrew didn't know what we were talking about," Ted said.

That folder held his lie.

That folder held the secret.

I didn't want to ask my next questions, but I knew I had

to. "Andrew never told me. How did Teddy die?" He had, but I wanted to make sure he hadn't lied about the car accident.

"He came home for the weekend," Gail said, her voice turning jagged.

Ted continued, "Teddy had too much to drink, so he left his car at the bar and walked home. Someone hit him with their car and left him for dead."

That acid climbed up my throat, burning its way to my mouth. I could barely get words to come out. "That's horrible. I'm so sorry." With my recent events, I wouldn't call getting run down by a car an accident. My hands shook. The mug in my hand rattled on the wood table. I let go and placed my shaking fingers in my lap.

"Thank you, Tova," Gail said.

"Did they ever find who hit him?" *Of course not. Because Andrew did it.*

"No, dear." Gail answered. "We've never had any answers."

Ted cut in. "Last minute, we went home to see Gail's family. Maybe we'd have found him in time."

"Ted, stop saying that," Gail said.

"Teddy was found in the corn field. He tried getting home," Ted said proudly.

"I'm so, so sorry." I wanted to tell them what I knew. For peace of mind, I wanted to give them the answers they needed. I wanted to tell them Andrew *did* know what their son had been working on. His papers had been in my closet. But at that moment, I didn't have proof. They'd find out soon enough that their only son was murdered by his best friend. And it would break their hearts all over again.

Neil walked in. "Sorry about that." He tilted his head to the side. "You okay?" he asked me.

"I'm just tired," I said, trying to smile. "We should get

going. I know we need to head over to the county offices." I implored him with my eyes. Neil's eyebrow shot up. I turned to Ted. "Before we go, you wouldn't happen to know who owns the mineral rights to Cathy Cain's farm, do you?"

Ted got up from his chair, the legs skittering on the floor. "We own the rights. We have, ever since Andrew turned fourteen and Cathy was about to lose the place."

———•———

TOVA

"You're white as a ghost," Neil whispered as he led me to the Yukon. "What's wrong?"

"Andrew killed their son."

He stopped me. "What?"

"I'll tell you while we drive. I need to get out of here before I go running back in there to tell them." I was gonna be sick. Andrew married me so I could finance a business he'd killed for.

Neil got us to the end of their driveway. "Why do you think Dickhead killed Teddy?"

"I married a murderer." I rocked in my seat. "I financed his business. Oh my god, Neil."

He pulled over to the side of the ditch. "Slow down. Tell me what I missed."

I shifted toward him, talking a mile a minute. "They said Teddy was working on something big and he hadn't shared what. After he died, they were surprised Andrew didn't know what it was. They said the two were inseparable. Gail said Teddy was always tinkering with something." I rubbed my temple. "Also, Andrew told me Teddy died in a car accident, but someone ran him down here in Stanley as he was walking home from a bar." My voice wavered. "Why would Andrew lie about that? Ted said he tried crawling back home through a cornfield." I waved my hand in front of us. "He was found in one of these fields."

"Christ, Tova."

"Andrew killed him for what he'd been working on; he didn't want to share. I'm sure of it. That's why Josie wanted the file. The proof is the molds and the correspondence. It was all addressed to Teddy. I never saw one piece in there with Andrew's name."

"I'll have the guys start looking into Teddy's death."

"Can we get out of here? And please tell me we don't need to talk to Cathy."

"We're not. We're getting a room and some dinner."

Neil got hold of a detective at the police station. He placed us on speaker so we could both talk. Teddy's death was infamous. The wealthiest man in town's only son died and they never had a lead on a suspect.

I knew in my gut that Andrew had killed Teddy.

Neil took a call before we checked into the hotel. Sam had tracked down the guy who made the molds. The gentleman had gotten rid of all his files, but he did remember Teddy Svengaard. Confirming my suspicion, the mold maker said the last time he did any work for Mr. Svengaard was a year ago, which would've been impossible. Teddy was already dead and buried.

———•———

We stood on the small patio of our hotel room, glancing at a field and beyond. The wind rolled over us, blowing my hair around. Neil stood behind me, his arms holding me to him. The events of the last hour sank in as light broke across the horizon. Andrew had killed a man, and I felt like his accomplice.

"What was the phone call you took at the Svengaards' about?"

"Reid said they're gonna ping Josie's phone again. He also has an informant who he's meeting. The guy told Reid that Josie got away from Billy. He's also obsessed with finding her."

"That doesn't bode well."

I turned. Neil's shirt collar was open and exposed his neck. I kissed him there. He gathered my hair and held it. He held all sorts of things—my heart mainly, but also my trust. "Tell me we're gonna find him?"

"We're gonna find them all."

"I'm getting a headache. I think I need to skip dinner. Will you tell the guys I need to take a nap?"

He kissed my forehead. "You sure?"

"Yeah."

After he left, I took my pills and laid down in my jeans and T-shirt. There were too many things to think about. My brain raced, yet I could feel myself drifting off.

Once sleep hit, I felt my mother's presence in the hotel room. As if paralyzed, I couldn't speak or move. I was rendered useless, and she—her ghostly self—was mute.

More impossible, she spun around me like vapor and wrapped me in a cocoon. I tried to grab hold of her. Chasing was better than not having at all, and all I wanted, all I craved in that dark place was to have her again and recapture what I'd lost.

She became clearer and I tried to pull her forward, but she floated away, out of reach. I couldn't grab her. Like an ominous premonition, she attempted to tell me something with her eyes, and then her blond hair—set in curls, like she always wore—

bounced as her hands moved.

She finally spoke, clear as the last time I'd heard her voice over the phone. "*You know what to do, Tova.*"

The morning before she died, she'd told me to get my car serviced. *You want to be prepared*, she'd told me. Even with that warning, I hadn't been.

All too fast, she floated away through a window. A gauzy white curtain fluttered in her wake. I tried to chase her. I wanted to believe the moment was real and not a figment of my overactive imagination.

I sat up straight and woke to my door being kicked in.

My mom wanted to make sure I lived.

———•———

NEIL

I sat down at the roadhouse as my phone rang. "Hey, Reid."

He started right in. "Just got word they pinged Josie's phone. She's in Stanley."

Panic roiled in my gut. "Christ, and I left Tova alone at the hotel. I gotta go."

I ran out of there, dialing Charlie as I went. "We need to get back to the hotel. Josie's in Stanley. Most likely so is Andrew."

"Shit," Charlie said. "We'll meet you there."

I hit the accelerator, peeling out of the parking lot. "I'm on the other end of town. Keep an eye open."

My phone rang. It was Tova. My anxiety eased. "Hey, sweetheart."

What I heard in response made my stomach sick— Dickhead's voice muffled in the background.

———•———

TOVA

I scrambled up the bed and grabbed for my phone. My hands shook so fiercely I dropped it in the sheets and covers. Andrew stood with a gun pointed at me.

"Get up," he said with a flick of his wrist. He yanked at my arm, ripping me out of bed. *There it was!*

Andrew let go of me momentarily. I fell on the bed face-first and slid my phone down the front of my pants. None too gentle, he yanked me up by my hair. I yelped, my chin snapping back in pain. "Stop!" I yelled, getting up on all fours.

"I'll hand it to you, princess. You're determined."

Neil called it stubborn and proud. "I'm smart, too. That helps."

He huffed and pushed on my back hard enough that I collapsed like a pancake. He got on top, straddling my thighs. Rope burned across my wrists as he held them against my back and tied them together.

In my dream, Mom had told me I knew what to do. How long had I been asleep?

"I figured out you killed Teddy."

He cinched my bindings until they burned. "Teddy, you, and Billy, if all goes right." My smart-ass comment only made him handle me rougher, risk telling me more about the plan he was so sure of completing.

He got off and flipped me around. His eyes narrowed. "How'd you come to that conclusion? About Teddy?"

The only thing I could think was to keep Andrew talking and keep us in the room as long as possible. I sat up, even though my hands were bound.

"We found a folder, one you were trying to hide. I suspect it's the one Josie'd been searching for in my closet. Did you know she cut herself and left some DNA behind? That's how we found out she'd been in my house."

He didn't say anything. Had he even known? Andrew was calm and cool, but his tongue passed over his upper teeth. He only did that when pissed.

"The guy who made those molds said he made some a year ago." I followed my gut and went for it. "Which is odd seeing as Teddy was dead. He'd also never heard of you."

"A folder proves nothing."

"Billy bailed Josie out of jail. He convinced her you were never coming back."

Andrew sat down in the chair across from the bed. As he did, I wiggled, trying to shimmy my hands loose. I got nowhere.

He placed the gun on his lap, then gestured with it. "Go on, this is quite amusing." Unfortunately, the tilt of his chin and the darkness of his eyes said he wanted to shoot me.

"The break-in made no sense. Why raid my panty drawer? Did you know she did that?" Andrew's jaw worked back and forth. "She sure is classy. You need to get her some help."

"I have before and I will again." *This was news.*

"If she hadn't left a box of yours overturned, Neil never would've gone looking in that closet." My heart pounded in my throat. "Why'd you kill Teddy?"

Andrew face flared red. "I helped him, and he wouldn't give me a cut. I decided to take it."

"'Cause that's what his dad did? He took your family farm?"

"Serves the old man right. I almost wish I could tell him his son was alive after I ran him down. Always a lucky fucker." I didn't want to hear this. He smiled at me. "Had to strangle him." *Andrew* was *going to kill me the other day.* "Oh, yeah, you got me all worked up. That's wasn't planned. You got lucky, princess."

———•———

NEIL

I could hear only snippets of what Tova said. My phone beeped. Charlie. I made the split decision to put her on hold and answered.

"Charlie, Andrew has Tova. I think they're still at the hotel."

He swore. "Good thing Wade just walked out of the gas station with Josie then."

"You're fucking kidding me?"

"No." Then I heard Charlie ask her, "Where were you going?"

"To pick up Drew," Josie replied.

"Where at?" Wade asked.

"None of your goddamn business."

Charlie got back on. "You hear that? They've got to be at the hotel." *Christ, I hoped so.* "We'll meet you there. Wade, cuff her and drive their car to the hotel," Charlie yelled. "I'll call the locals."

Wade yelled back, "On it! We'll see you there."

Then his line went dead.

———◆———

TOVA

Keep talking, the voice in my head said. "Did you know the guy who made those molds went out of business and moved to Hawaii?" Andrew knew this, but I didn't know how else to stall. Was Neil on his way back after dinner yet?

"A guy who works for Neil finally found the mold maker. He remembered Teddy, not you. He said he would testify to it." I made that part up. Andrew's back went straight against the chair. "But I knew you killed him after I talked to his parents.

Did you know I spoke to Teddy's mom and dad?"

Andrew crossed his legs. "As a matter of fact, I saw a black Yukon pull out of their driveway today."

"I figured." *Keep talking.* "How did you meet Josie?"

"The cancer treatments were doing my mom in. I needed marijuana. Josie's boyfriend at the time was my supplier." That I could believe.

"You know she's got a serious problem."

"She'd been doing great," he stopped and looked down, "What the hell do you know about anything?"

What I was about to say might put him over the edge. "Well I know the local police are now aware of Teddy and his plans. They were going to talk to your mom."

CHAPTER 25

TOVA

Andrew's chin jutted out. "I'll say this, princess, I think I may have underestimated you a bit." He tilted his head to the side. "Your boyfriend sure keeps you wrapped up tight. Shame you aren't being followed around by one of his lackeys. That's not gonna be good for you."

I wasn't going to let him see me scared. But I did wonder yet again if Neil would find me dead. And if he did, if anyone would see the pattern Andrew intended on repeating. If I kept Andrew talking, maybe he wouldn't. It was my only hope. "Where's Josie?"

"She's coming to pick us up. None of this would be happening if you hadn't provoked me when I came to see you."

Of course, this was my fault. I got it then.

"Andrew, are you going to make it look like Billy got me? What about Josie? Did you send her or was she trying to steal your papers? I bet she was gonna give them to Billy."

Eyes narrowing, his brow slammed down. "You don't know shit." His phone chirped.

"You love her, don't you?" He didn't answer. "I know you married me for my money."

"Ding-ding-ding," he said. "I'm gonna be rich enough to

take care of my mom and get our mineral rights back, thanks to you." Even though I'd already known, it still killed to hear. He put the gun in his waistband, hooked me around the neck, and pulled until I stood.

"What about Josie? She must really love you to stay with you after you married me."

His fingers dig into the muscle of my nape. I winced. I still hadn't healed from him trying to strangle me. "She loves me more than you could ever imagine. Unlike you, she worships me."

He would like that. We stood by the door. "Then how come she's always second best? Is that why she's an addict?"

Something like understanding slackened his sharp features. A car honked. "Time to go." With a manacle hold on my wrists, he led me to the door.

Andrew pushed me forward and let me slide on my heels. *Why the hell did I bring heels with me?* When he opened the door, dusk had settled in, orange rays bleeding across the horizon. He pushed the gun to my back. "Walk." Heat caused my clothes to cling. Where could he be taking me?

I marched slow, tottering on the heels. The only thing I could think about was ending up like Teddy, dead in a cornfield.

A few doors closer to the parking lot, I heard Neil. "Hey, Dickhead."

Andrew grabbed me and held me up against him, using me as a human shield.

"We've got your girlfriend!" Neil yelled. "And two guns on you. Let's make a trade."

Andrew cursed a string of jumbled words.

"You're going to do it, aren't you?" I asked. "Look what she's given up for you." Crickets created an insistent hum.

He clutched me tighter. "Shut your mouth." He glanced to

the side. I followed his eyes and saw Charlie's gun aimed at us. In the other direction, Neil had stepped out from the building. His eyes trained on me.

"Drew!" Josie yelled. "You better fucking trade for me or I'm gonna hate you till the day I die!" Wade moved so Andrew could see her clearly.

That seemed to do the trick. "Where's our car?" Andrew yelled over the shell of my ear.

Wade took a step closer. "Right here!"

I saw a flash of red enter the parking lot. Dread stopped my breath. I went for it.

"You said she loves you more than I could ever imagine," I badgered him. "Prove to her she should."

Had he heard? Would it sink in? Andrew's focus seemed set on Charlie. I motioned with my head to the pickup truck, hoping Neil would notice.

"Tova, remember how Wade and I became friends?" Neil asked.

How could I forget? The visual of a little Neil breaking a kid's nose to protect someone he didn't know cemented his unusual character.

I didn't even think about the possibilities. I whipped my head back and stomped down, slamming the point of my heel into Andrew's instep and pulling forward with all my might. A bullet screamed as it cut through the air and hit. I could feel warm blood spray my skin. What I didn't do was turn to look as I ran.

Josie screamed. My ridiculous shoes caught on the cracked pavement. I tripped and careened into the bumper of a car, landing face first on a white trunk. My legs shook. With my hands tied behind my back, I couldn't move for a moment. The air rushed out of my lungs.

"I got you," Neil said, tagging me around the waist. He lowered me, my knees digging into gravel. Bullets broke the glass above us, raining sharp icy pellets over our heads.

Josie screamed again.

Already knowing the answer, I asked, "Is he dead?"

"He is." He cut the rope at my wrists. "You okay?" I was silent. "Charlie had to do it, sweetheart." He glided a finger softly over the marks on my arms.

"I know." Another bullet broke a window near us. My knees ached with the hard road below. "Is that Billy shooting?"

Silence, pure silence, sliced the air. "Yep. You did good warning me and getting away from Andrew."

Josie still wailed.

"Stay where you are!" Wade yelled.

My legs still not obeying, I struggled to get closer to the car we crouched behind. Neil rose to peek out yet again. "Fuck," he whispered.

"What?"

"Josie must've gotten away after Charlie sh— Wade's trying to get to her, but she's working her way over here."

I shifted to get a look. Josie came on her hands and knees, moving around cars. She was coming toward us. I knew her intentions, but Neil didn't see she was frantically set on getting to Andrew.

"I'm coming, Drew!" she rasped.

Billy's head darted out, that damned hat back on it. My stomach roiled, and for a moment, I couldn't feel my fingertips. They'd gone cold.

Neil put a hand on my shoulder, shoving me down. "Stay put."

I could hear Wade yelling again. "Josie, stay where you are!"

Charlie reached us, gun out. His eyes on the scene, he

didn't look at us when he spoke. "You guys okay?" Easygoing Charlie was gone, and in his place I saw the marksman who'd taken Andrew down.

Another bullet whizzed by. The impact it made on metal sounded like a sharp slap. When a barrage of bullets sprayed next, my eyes slammed shut, the noise a reckoning.

The loudest sound now was Josie. She kept begging and pleading after the gunfire died away. Nothing could protect us from the acrid smell of cordite floating in wispy clouds toward where we crouched.

"I've got her!" Billy yelled.

As he spoke, the earth below us rattled. A car exploded, catapulting Neil and me to the ground. Everything near us moved with the blast. A protective shell, Neil crawled over me. Heat swallowed and swirled around us, then debris rained down. After a moment, Neil lifted off me and looked around.

"Everyone okay?" Charlie yelled. An engine switched on.

"Yes," we all answered, including Wade.

"He's getting away!" I yelled. I couldn't see Billy leaving, but I knew.

"I'm out of ammo," Charlie said. The whir of police got louder. Through the noise, the texture of wheels coming closer met my ears.

Gun in hand, Neil stood. I scrambled to my feet. Wade fired off a shot but hit nothing. And we all watched as the red pickup sped away.

Charlie and Wade ran to their vehicle—Wade at the wheel, Charlie in the backseat.

Neil took my hand. "You okay to come with me?"

He didn't need to ask; we were already moving.

We scrambled into the Yukon. Wade pulled onto the highway ahead of us, and we followed. Police went flying past—some down the road, others to the hotel.

After a minute, the caravan of cars and trucks peeled off the paved road onto gravel. Dust filled the air, so thick I could hardly see. Oil-drilling equipment dotted the barren fields. Where would Billy go? Would he harm Josie? In the haze, taillights spread in red tendrils. We'd finally managed to catch up to everyone. Then, a deafening boom jerked me back against the seat. A pillar of fire and black smoke rose into the sky. *Oh my god.*

Neil slowed. Police cars skidded into the ditch, along with Wade and Charlie. We got out and stood among the officers. The curl of heat and the caustic stench of crude oil permeated the air. No one dared help, even if help was possible. We stood, watching the unapproachable flames shooting up from the oil-drilling rig.

Fire trucks sounded behind us, shrill and closing in, but it was all too late. Plunged into the rig, the charred frame of the once-red pickup ignited. With that new bang, I saw then that Billy and Josie were gone, ghosts drifting off with the rising smoke.

———•———

We still didn't know if Billy had purposely drove them into the drilling station or if Josie had gotten involved and somehow he'd lost control. Either way, it was a horrible way to go and I couldn't believe it had happened as we all watched.

We spent half the night at the police station answering questions. The humidity settled as the four of us walked out; it must have been two a.m. by then. All that buzzed were streetlights and fireflies. The police, thankfully, let Charlie go. He wouldn't be charged. Neil kept an arm around me all night.

—— · ——

The next morning, we all sat around a table drinking coffee in a cafe across the street from the hotel. I stared into my black liquid, hoping for answers.

Charlie spoke first. "Reid's informant gave everything up. The whole deal. He said Billy started asking Josie questions about Andrew after he saw the car. He must have been following her, saw Josie being dropped off somewhere. With that fancy car, he knew Andrew had money."

"He didn't buy Andrew the suit with the drug addict, Josie," Neil added, cutting in.

"That's right," Charlie went on. "Billy must have started obsessing. He knew the guy was shady so he got Josie good and wasted, asking her questions until he figured out Andrew had stolen something from someone. Josie also let it spill that the guy, Teddy, was also dead. Originally, Billy was just gonna try blackmailing Andrew."

Wade turned to me. "After he bailed her out, Billy figured out who you were. Josie saw your picture in *Twin Cities Magazine*."

"When were you in that magazine?" Neil asked.

"Over a year ago. Because of my business." I shrugged. "Lucky me."

Neil ran a hand through his unruly hair. "But things got messy,"

Charlie leaned in. "Billy figured he could trade his old friend Josie for money. After all, the police were on him for Lena's murder and he needed to get out of town."

"How convenient," I sassed.

"As we know, Billy figured out Josie was hiding something. Whatever it was, he thought he could use it against Andrew.

Ironically, the file she was after was now tucked inside Neil's Yukon. Billy could've grabbed it when he dragged you out." Wade shook his head like it was serendipitous.

"All for greed and jealousy." I looked out the window. "Andrew didn't know Josie had tried stealing that file, but at the same time, he forgave her. It didn't matter." His love for her trumped the rest.

"She loved him, too," Wade said. "Even with Billy coming after her, all she wanted was to get to Andrew."

———·———

We finished our breakfast, and I filled them in on what had happened in the hotel room. Then we got on the road. Crossing the state line and entering crops of hearty wheat, we were about halfway home when Lizzy called. Neil had just programmed my phone to his Bluetooth device, so I had her on speaker.

"Tova, your dad flew in this morning. When will you be home?"

"Dad's in Minnesota?"

"Yes, dear, that's what I said." Lizzie tone sounded far too haughty. Neil laughed. "Is that you, Neil?"

"Hi, Lizzy."

"Are you taking care of my girl?"

"Always. We'll be back in three hours."

"Perfect. I'll send your father over in four." *Just great.*

"I didn't think he was coming for a few weeks."

Lizzy chuckled. "His case got settled out of court."

Of course it was. "Thanks, Grandma."

"He wants to stay with you. Make him something good for dinner." And with that, she hung up. My dad never stayed with me.

"I can feel your blood pressure rising from over here," Neil stated.

"I'm sure you can."

"Everything will be all right."

"Easy for you to say." Neil patted my knee, it didn't help. "He's gonna say things, embarrass me—or worse, insult me in front of you."

"No, he won't. We'll have words if he thinks he can." Neil wove our fingers together. We drove like that the rest of the way.

———•———

We stood on the deck, watching Rocco run free in the backyard. "I'm gonna miss sleeping with you tonight," I said into Neil's chest.

He laughed. I felt it though his chest.

"Well, you can't spend the night if my dad's here."

"Your dad knows a man like me doesn't get involved with a woman without sex being involved." Neil palmed my butt. "So keep your hair on, dear. He already knows."

"We'll see about that."

Cheeky. Two could play at that. I tapped his behind. "We will."

My dad hugged me when he arrived. A big hug. The kind you give when you know someone could be gone from your life and you've finally realized it.

My dad's a formidable man, a strong character, and a foreboding presence. Yet Neil handled him well, never backing down when Dad asked about Andrew, Billy, and Josie, and how everything was handled after the shooting. I couldn't tell what he thought about North Dakota, but he did look at Neil with a curious eye.

Later, when my father and Neil stood next to each other in my kitchen, leaning against the counter, having a beer and laughing, I stopped dead in my tracks. One was the man I'd grown up trying to please, but never could. But now he was happy, not surly like always. The other, I was hopelessly in love with and knew we'd just started making a life together. Seeing them at ease with each other would be stamped in my mind until the day I died, the rightness of the moment cementing itself.

The two continued their conversation, my dad asking Neil tons of questions, wanting to know about business and Neil's family. He also asked about his education and what sports he followed. Neil, in turn, asked his own series of questions. What type of law he practiced, how he and Claire met, and what he did to let off steam.

Boxing, I found out. I'd had no idea.

"Dinner won't be ready for a while. Do you want to see my studio?"

"Sure." Dad followed me, grasping his beer.

"I've been working on pieces for spring. You should pick one out for Claire." I didn't adore her, but I tried being nice. Neil followed us and came up behind me, putting his arm around me.

My dad studied us, then the desks in my office. "How many girls you have working for you now?"

I really hoped he wouldn't start giving me a hard time about my "little business." "Three. You met two of them last time you were here. Reva and Vivian."

He glanced at my workbench. "Hmm, that's right."

"There's also contract help when I get large orders. Business is good. I'm actually thinking about hiring a fourth person."

He looked over the central table, piled high in samples. "It's such a shame." *Here we go.* I frowned. "You could have done something lucrative with your brain."

I glanced at Neil and read his expression: *Such an ass.*

Knowing I was better than Dad's opinion, I'd often hold my tongue. But even last time I saw him, I couldn't. Neil clutched my hip and the energy in the room changed, but I got there first.

"Dad, I'll forgive your comment because you never asked what I make." It was time to exorcise that demon. "I net over six figures a year. I'm by no means hurting for money."

This felt like a key moment, but then Dad's proud chin rose. "What about health care for your *employees?*"

"They get health care. They even get raises." I took a deep breath; he wasn't going to get to me. I wouldn't let him. "I'm happy. Please don't turn my success into something beneath me."

He rubbed his chin and smiled tightly. "You'll be hurting for money what with those loans you signed for Andrew."

"Robert," Neil warned. "You need to let it go. We'll see to it Tova gets her money back."

"I knew he was slimy."

That ticked me off. "Then why did you try to tell me I should call off the divorce?" If he said it was because I was getting so old, I'd laugh.

"I made a mistake." Just like that my dad had me taken aback. His stubbornness was another trait we had in common. I doubted my dad had ever admitted to any wrongdoing. He came over and patted my shoulder. "I've made a lot of mistakes."

———•———

My dad stayed for two days—we had a nice visit—and other than the first evening, he never got out of hand.

When he left, I hoped we'd keep taking steps forward to mend our relationship, but only time would tell. I was okay with that.

TOVA

"Penny for your thoughts?"

Daydreaming, I braced against the roughed-in doorframes and looked into one of the bedrooms. Neil slipped his arm around me. My back against his front, I smiled and leaned into him. "I was just thinking about how amazing this is."

"Yeah?" I could hear the smile in his tone. He spun me in his arms.

"Because I didn't think life could be this good."

"Tova." Neil drew me closer and held me to his chest.

"I didn't think I could ever be this happy." Sighing, I hugged and grasped him tighter. "Thank you."

"Now I'm gonna have to tickle you."

I laughed. "Please don't." He could say the word *tickle* and I'd break out laughing. "I forgot to tell you. You were right."

"I usually am," he said. His chin rested on my shoulder as he admired the room, too.

I chuckled. "This was the right decision."

"I know."

We'd bought Stan and Eve's house before they put it on the market. During the remodel, we'd decided to stay at Neil's. The contractor had sheered the roof right off the top, and we'd gone up a story. At first, when Neil had brought up buying their place, I didn't think I could give up my house. I loved it so much. But the idea of making a home together without history mucking it up held an irresistible appeal. And, Lizzy reminded me, we'd make new memories together.

I thought I'd miss my yard, but Eve was an amazing gardener and I could add my stamp on the place as time went on. Besides, their yard had an outrageous oak that could hold a tree swing, and I decided that was better than my mountain ash.

"You need to get moving. We have a wedding to get to," Neil said, pulling me toward the stairs. "Its not everyday you're in a wedding for your friends." I was bridesmaid. I'd never been a bridesmaid. And Neil was a groomsman. "But first I need you to help me with something. A surprise."

I was a sucker for those. I stopped on the steps. Neil had surprised me handful of times in the last year. "You do?"

"I hired a landscaping company to plant a few of those trees you like. They're going to be here in five minutes." A lump formed in my throat. He knew.

"No bawling, Blue Eyes."

"You got me trees?"

He grinned, that goofy kid's grin that made my heart melt. "They're huge, too. Cost so much you'll need to give up Starbucks."

"That's the sweetest thing. You know, you make it hard for me to get you anything. You keep blowing anything I can think of out of the water."

He tugged on my hand. "Come on. Let's go and decide where some trees should grow."

AUTHOR'S NOTE

Thank you for reading Greed & Jealousy. Please consider supporting an indie author and leaving a review.

To find out about Grace and Wade's book, please sign up for information on my new releases (I will never share your information). www.tinaellery.com

Sincerely yours,
Tina

ACKNOWLEDGEMENTS

I jumped off a cliff this year. Here's a BIG thank you to those of you who gave me wings.

My writer girls, Tamara Lush, Dylann Crush, Alice Duthwaite, and all my fellow MFW members, thank you for your support.

I'm a firm believer that writing is easy, learning to craft a story is not. For anyone that's read my work, given me a critique, or advice, I'm grateful.

Thank you for making this book it's best EJ Runyon, Bethany Robinson, R.A. Weston, Sherri Hildebrandt, Judy Brown, Jade Eby and Hang Le.

RWA (Romance Writers of America) is a fantastic organization for both learning and meeting the most generous of wordsmiths. Thank you, Stephanie Taylor and Margo Karolyi.

To Lizbeth Selvig, Barbara Longley, Cat Shield, Nan Dixon, Tamara Hughes, Brighton Walsh, Courtney Milan, Penny Reid, Tiffany A. Snow, and Alessandra Torre, you ladies rock! Thanks for answering my countless questions.

To the best beta readers: Lorrie Lilja, Carole Lilja, Tanis Agar, Suzy Manning, Erika Bruno, Tracy Nelson, Reba Martin, Melissa Rodriguez, Flavia Davids, Kathy White, Natalie Saxton,

Jessica Broatman, Teri Gaston, Nicole Brighton, Gretchen Hodges, Shaunna Wiseman, Whitney Martin, Carmen Damian, Sivy King, Cassie Fite, Keri Lierman, Michelle Larson, Rosie Morris and Wendy Pariseau, thank you.

Last but not...oh you know. Thanks to my family and for putting up with me. I'm sorry for writing when I should be making cookies, playing and cleaning.

I almost forgot. Thanks, Starbucks, you're my fuel.

ABOUT THE AUTHOR

After a successful twenty-four-year career as a business owner, Tina Ellery, is now an Indie author. She's writing the type of romantic fiction she wants to read. A little mysterious and a lot sexy.

Ellery lives in Minneapolis, MN with her husband and two children. She'll tell you her writing started because of her son, Salty, and her daughter, Sweetie, and one too many cartoons.

When she's not clicking on the keys, she's holding some caffeinated beverage. She's a freelancer with her hoard of recipes, and in her free time, a jewelry designer.

Writing became her obsession in 2013 when she filled six yellow legal and decided to "type the darn thing up." Be careful when talking to her, though, she's bound to find you interesting, and you could end up as material, or one of the characters in her next book.

Twitter: @TinaEllery
Facebook: @TinaElleryWrites

www.ingramcontent.com/pod-product-compliance
Lightning Source LLC
Chambersburg PA
CBHW021205250626
47155CB00008B/2685